CONSORT OF FIRE

THE WITCH'S CONSORTS #4

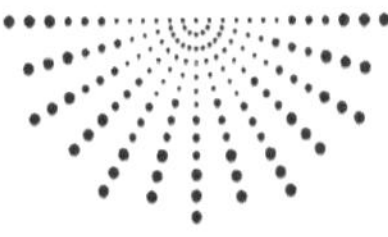

EVA CHASE

INK SPARK PRESS

Consort of Fire

Book 4 in the Witch's Consorts series

This is a work of fiction. Any resemblance to actual persons, living or dead, or actual events is purely coincidental.

First Digital Edition, 2018

Cover design: Cover Reveal Designs

Ebook ISBN: 978-1-989096-14-7

Paperback ISBN: 978-1-989096-17-8

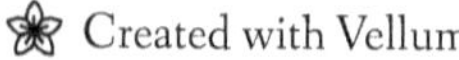 Created with Vellum

CHAPTER ONE

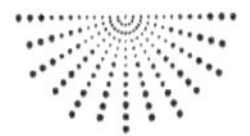

Rose

Naomi had thought of everything. My stomach was full of seafood linguine that had included crab she'd ordered straight from the coast. The cherry-and-chocolate sweetness of the cake she'd arranged lingered in my mouth. Some of the best wine I'd ever drunk had been flowing from the bottles still at the ready on one of the side tables in the Hallowell manor's huge great room, and the playlist carrying through the speakers set up with her phone was the perfect mix of peppy and groovy. She'd even put up streamers, gold and silver twinkling where they crisscrossed overhead.

And all that didn't even include the fact that she'd come all the way from New York just to throw this party. Taking it all in from where I'd ended up standing next to her as I took a few minutes' breather, I couldn't help saying, "You know you really didn't need to do this."

My cousin shrugged with a smile and a bob of her chestnut ponytail. "A witch's twenty-fifth birthday is supposed to be the biggest deal in your whole life. I couldn't let you spend it like any other day. Besides, you deserve the chance to make some more good memories after everything you've been through."

I couldn't really argue with that. The last few months since I'd moved back to my family's country estate, the one where I'd spent my childhood, had been a roller coaster. The kind where you spend most of it clinging to the safety bar for dear life afraid that the next jolt will toss you right out of the car.

Naomi nodded to the two young women on our temporary dance floor. "Also I figured I really should check in after I started sending witches in need your way. How are they doing?"

I considered the estate's newest residents. Lesley—twenty-six and recently widowed, prone to hiding behind her fawn-brown hair and rectangular glasses—had turned up at the gate first, about three weeks ago. Imogen—twenty-two and unconsorted, with an almost hyper energy that matched her bright red curls—had shown up a couple weeks later.

"I think it's going okay," I said. "It's awkward, not being able to ask all the questions I'd like to or tell them everything I know, but they were both scared when they got here and they've relaxed a lot since then."

"Have they told you much about why they came running?"

"Some. Lesley's family started putting a lot of weirdly insistent pressure on her to marry some new guy just a few months after her first consort was in that accident. Which makes me wonder if the accident was even accidental. Imogen lost her parents when she was a kid and ended up with an aunt and uncle. They've put a bunch of suitors in front of her in the last year, and she's gotten a really bad vibe about all of them. I think they just needed some space, somewhere no one would try to force a consorting on them, for them to start to figure things out."

I rubbed my mouth against the itch to tell her more and the knowledge that if I tried, the oath I'd been forced to take would stop me. Last month, I'd discovered that Charles and Helen Frankford, high ranking witching folk with positions in the Witching Assembly that governed all our society, were the leads of a faction that had been essentially enslaving young witches for their own dark purposes. Dark purposes that had something to do with immense, terrifying creatures they called demons, living in a world the Frankfords had accessed through a portal in a seaside cave.

My own father and stepmother had tried to arrange a consorting for me within that circle—one that would have left me unable to deny their chosen consort's requests or to use my magic in any way he didn't approve of. I'd escaped that trap only through luck, a lot of struggle, and the love of the men who'd been my beloved childhood friends. But so many more witches might be caught up in their schemes or about to be.

We'd found plenty of proof. We'd stolen a hard drive from the Frankfords' estate. Unfortunately they and their allies had caught us before we'd been able to leave with it.

I'd been forced to make a deal to save my consorts' lives. They'd sworn an oath not to do or order harm to our lives, freedom, or happiness—and I'd sworn that none of us would speak of the files we'd discovered or the crimes we'd recently uncovered. The fact that we'd managed to copy over those files before they'd destroyed that hard drive didn't help with that. I couldn't mention their contents even to my own cousin.

Lesley's father and Imogen's aunt and uncle were named in those files. Only a few times, as minor supporters, but that was damning enough. It was a good thing they'd come to me.

"Do you know if their families were involved with the Frankfords?" Naomi asked. She knew the basics of what had gone on—she'd been with me when I'd gotten the lead that brought us to the Frankfords—but nowhere near the full picture.

"I can't talk about that," I said, my stomach tightening.

"Ah." She grimaced. "Sorry. I shouldn't have asked about that tonight. This isn't the time for thinking about that stuff. I know how hard you've been working from all the time you've spent holed up with your computer since I got here yesterday. Between you and those guys, I'm sure you'll figure something out. And at least you're keeping some of the potential victims safe until then."

"That's what I keep telling myself," I said. The pressure in my gut didn't totally lift.

A mischievous glint came into Naomi's eyes. "So how *has* consorted life been treating you now that you can finally settle in without worrying about getting arrested or worse?"

A smile crossed my face automatically as I looked at my five consorts. None of them were witching men, which was bad enough in the Assembly's eyes, but it was also unheard of these days for any witch to take more than one. I hadn't been sure it was even possible until I'd managed it. For most of our relationship so far, I'd had to keep our love and our consorting secret.

"It's nice," I said. "Just being able to *be* with them, like normal consorts can."

"Just 'nice'?" Naomi said, arching her eyebrows. She'd been alternately amused and fascinated by my expanded consorting since I'd first revealed that secret to her and the rest of my long-dead mother's family, even though she seemed very happy with her own consort, Gregg.

My smile twitched wider. "Okay, amazing."

At that moment, my gaze met Gabriel's across the room. My newest consort grinned back at me from where he was dancing with Imogen. The redheaded girl was boogying down with abandon, but I suspected from the avid glances she kept shooting Gabriel's way that she might be developing a bit of a crush. He kept a friendly distance between them, his smiles for her warm but mild.

I couldn't really blame anyone for crushing on him. Gabriel had always been the leader of our little group when we were kids, and he still exuded that confident charisma. The striking combo of dark red hair and bright blue eyes with his handsome face didn't hurt either.

Kyler, my tech-fanatic, had managed to get reserved

Lesley dancing too. The slim guy laughed as he tried to pull off an ambitious spin, his tawny curls swaying as he had to catch himself. His playfulness had gotten Lesley smiling, so I figured that was a win.

Not far from them, Jin, my artist, had managed to drag Kyler's more stoic and more brawny twin Seth away from where he'd been watching the festivities from the sidelines. Jin obviously knew his moves. He whipped around in time with the beat, so gracefully it was difficult not to watch. The blue streaks in his smooth black hair glinted under the chandelier's light.

Seth stepped and dipped with the music, his movements a lot more awkward, but the expression in his gray-green eyes was amused. As long as my consorts were all having a good time, I was happy.

It was hard to tell with one of them. Damon was skulking near the wine table, nursing a beer he'd grabbed from the fridge rather than bother with fancy glasses and vintages. His jagged dark brown hair shaded his eyes, and the set of his shoulders suggested he was missing the protective shield of his leather jacket.

He caught me looking at him, and one side of his mouth curled up. Setting down his beer, he sauntered over to us. "Doesn't seem right that the birthday girl is stuck playing wallflower," he said.

"I was just catching my breath," I said. "Are you asking me to dance?"

"It's not really my scene, but I can't let you go ignored, angel."

He held out his hand, and I took it. Naomi raised her wine glass to us as he pulled me into the middle of the floor. Damon leaned close, his bitter chocolate smell drifting over me as we started to move together. His hand was hot on my waist, his dark blue eyes even hotter with the promise of all the things he'd like to do when we had more privacy.

I gave myself over to that heat, to the music, letting the buzz of the wine I'd drunk take the edge off my nerves. We had a long way to go before we could hope to cut the toxic elements out of the witching community. Our progress so far had been slow. But at least I had my guys here with me, free in a way we'd never been before to love each other with every bit of our hearts.

It was getting late. After a few more songs, I noticed Lesley yawning. Naomi moved to the table to start clearing the wine. I stopped the music and said my goodnights to the two witches I was sheltering. As they headed to the guest bedrooms I'd offered them, all five of my consorts gathered around me.

They were ready to say their good-byes too. There was room for all of them to live on the estate with me, but small-town gossip traveled fast, and the unsparked employees on the estate would have noticed their constant presence pretty quick. While we figured out the best way to navigate the minefields of their regular lives, where our relationship wasn't all that usual either, Gabriel had still been acting as the garage manager, living in the apartment overtop that building. Seth had moved into the house he'd renovated just beyond the Hallowell property, where we all sometimes met up and spent the night. And the other three guys had kept their apartments in the town that was a fifteen-minute walk down the highway from here.

But tonight was special. Tonight marked the birthday when every young witch came of age, when I would have taken control over this estate if I hadn't displaced my father from it to the Hallowell home in Portland as part of my deal with the Frankfords.

I was Lady Hallowell in every way now. And I wanted to keep celebrating that with my consorts.

"Stay the night?" I said.

Kyler's face brightened eagerly.

"Of course," Gabriel said, taking my hand and squeezing it.

"Whatever the lady desires," Jin murmured with a wink and a little bow.

We'd gotten up to an awful lot of fun of various sorts in the master bedroom's king-sized bed. This night, I found when we reached the room that I really just wanted to cuddle. To soak up all the affection between us in one peaceful heap.

My resolve was tested momentarily as Damon helped me peel off my dress. The brush of his fingers down my sides sent a warm shiver through me. He pressed a kiss to my back.

"In the morning," I said, touching his cheek.

He tucked his chin over my shoulder with a wordless grumble. But his voice was pleased when he said, "I'm looking forward to it."

It was a tight fit, all of us piling together on the bed, but we'd had a fair bit of practice now. Lots of different blankets—that was the key. I ended up partly sandwiched between Gabriel and Seth, with Jin's hand on my hip and Damon's on my calf, and Kyler sprawled at the end of the over-long mattress in the vicinity of my feet.

With all of them there with me, all that love around me, I'd thought I might get to skip the dreams I'd been having lately. No such luck. Somewhere in the middle of my sleep, images rose up from our confrontation with the creatures in the Frankfords' cave. That huge demonic face loomed through the portal, leering at me with a flick of its forked tongue. Then a massive arm reached out, and another. The monster pulled its torso through, its burning gaze fixed on me.

Heart thudding, I spun to run for it, and found myself surrounded by a crowd of witches in pale consorting dresses, their eyes wide with fear. "Stop it from taking us!" one cried, and another clutched desperately at my arm. A sharply hot breath gushed over me from behind.

I couldn't save them. I couldn't save any of them. I wasn't even sure I could save myself.

The demon swiped its clawed fingers right at me— and I jerked awake in my bed. The room was dark, everything still and quiet except for the murmur of the summer breeze through the trees outside. A clammy sweat had broken over my skin. My pulse was still thumping.

"Hey," Seth mumbled, sounding still half asleep. He hugged me tighter where his arm was looped around my waist. "S'okay. We've got you."

I relaxed back into the warmth of my consorts, letting

my eyes drift back shut. But the horror of the dream didn't quite leave me.

It wasn't okay. That nightmare might not have been real for me, but it was real enough out there on Frankford's seaside property. Real enough for the other young witches his faction might be dragging out there to do whatever it was they'd wanted me to do before I'd wriggled free from their clutches.

We had to save them. The question was how.

CHAPTER TWO

Kyler

"Everything looks good," I said, pushing myself away from the computer in Marvin Heard's office. The landlord used his databases to keep track of properties he owned here and in a few of the larger towns nearby, and they'd been a mess when I'd first taken him on as an IT client. But that'd been three years ago. Everything was clean as a whistle now. "Unless you purposely go throwing spanners into the works, you should be good to go for a long time."

"Where is it *you're* going, anyway, Mr. Lennox?" the older man asked, leaning against the wall by a county map he had pinned there. "Suddenly you're such a hot shot you don't have time for us little guys anymore?" A grin stretched across his grizzled face to show he was teasing.

"I'll still be available in case of emergency," I said,

although I was planning on being *very* selective in what I accepted as an emergency. The truth was, Rose needed me tracking down all the leads the Frankfords' files had provided. Protecting her from whatever else that faction might throw at her was a hell of a lot more important than helping Mr. Heard file overdue payment notices a few minutes faster.

I didn't think telling him that would go over all that well, though, if I'd even wanted to—or if the oath Rose had taken on my and the other guys' behalf would have let me.

"I'm shifting my focus over to the programming side of things," I added. That was the standard line I'd given to my handful of local clients. It was sort of true. I was paying my rent with a couple of online gigs I could pull up to clear my head in between reconnaissance sessions. Gigs where I didn't have to worry about someone calling me up at any hour to demand to know why they'd gotten this error screen or how to connect the printer they'd accidentally unplugged.

"Hmm," Heard said. "Just more work then, huh?"

There was something prodding about his tone. I smiled at him, but a prickle ran down my back. Gossip traveled fast around here. People were always a little wary of the Hallowells and their estate, and I had been there an awful lot in the last few weeks.

The landlord wasn't insinuating anything all that specifically, though, so I shrugged the comment off with a laugh. "What can I say? I like keeping busy."

"I'm sure you do," he said as he saw me out, with a narrow look that set off another prickle.

It didn't matter. He and anyone else could think whatever they wanted. Most of the people in this town had thought I was pretty weird all along—for my interest in computers and all the things I could find out about on those computers, for going away for college and then inexplicably coming back, for not hanging around much with anyone outside my family—in person where they could see, at least. Not that I figured mentioning my online social life would have impressed my neighbors any.

In some ways I'd been coasting, those few years after college. I'd enjoyed myself, sure, but there'd never been much sense of direction to my meanderings. Now I had a purpose. A mission that had somehow spiraled into a quest to rival the ones taken up by the heroes in my video game collection.

I pulled out my phone as I headed down the street, checking a couple of my non-recreational online accounts. No returns yet on the latest feelers I'd put out. That didn't mean they were total dead-ends, but the longer those queries sat unanswered, the less chance I'd hear anything useful back in the end.

Ah well. I still had plenty more avenues to pursue. I wasn't sure I was quite a video game-level hero yet, but Charles and Helen Frankford sure as hell could have qualified as final-boss villains. Their files had given us all sorts of data—names of witches who'd come to their meetings and contributed financially to their efforts, schedules of visits to the Cliff that held the demons' cave, business and political schemes they'd undertaken that must have been tied into the whole conspiracy somehow

—but we needed outside proof if we were going to expose any of that, since we couldn't show anyone the files themselves.

I didn't only have my computer skills to rely on. My little foray into spy territory, sneaking into the Frankfords' home and stealing his hard drive, had reminded me of that. Tomorrow I planned to drive out to the area near his coastal property with its demon-portal cave to see if I could find anything useful in the local archives. You never knew what might have been committed to paper that had never made it onto any digital platform. Especially since the Frankfords had been using that property since the '6os.

Thinking about getting that close to his base of illicit operations sent a quiver through me that was both nervous and excited. I didn't exactly relish the idea of stepping into the line of fire again... but maybe I had gotten a taste for more concrete adventure.

First, though, I had the much more mundane mission of restocking my fridge. I ambled into the grocery store and started grabbing my usual go-tos off the shelves, with a nod to the other shoppers. One guy, whose name I couldn't remember but I knew worked for the post office, let his gaze trail after me as I walked by, as if he were waiting to see what else I'd do.

Okay, *some* kind of gossip had definitely been going around. Maybe I was better off not knowing what it was.

I turned the corner from one aisle to the next and almost walked straight into my mother.

"Oh, hey, Mom," I said, managing to jerk my basket to the side at the last second. "Sorry."

Mom laughed. The faint sprinkling of flour on the side of her purple skirt told me she'd come straight from a baking session. "Out of everywhere in town, this isn't where I'd have thought I'd run into you," she said, and patted her own basket. "It's the mid-afternoon slow period at the café. We were running low on sugar, so I figured I'd put my break to good use."

"Reasonable," I said, and groped for something else to add. I wouldn't say I was especially close with my parents, but we'd always gotten along. There was just so much from the last couple months that I couldn't talk to them about. The weight of all those omissions made it hard to think of what I *could* say.

"You know, I'm glad I did run into you," Mom said. "You've been on the go so much, sudden road trips and all, we've hardly seen you recently. Why don't you come back to the café? You can have the first slice of the strawberry pie that just came out of the oven."

I didn't actually have any definite plans for the rest of the afternoon. It might be a good idea to take a little time just to chat, both to show her everything was good and to help me relax around her again.

Also, my mother made the best pie in the state, with the fair ribbons to prove it.

"Sure," I said with a grin. "Can't say no to pie."

I did relax into the conversation as we meandered over to the café where Mom worked. She commented on the weather and Dad's recent renovation projects, totally non-stress subjects. I found myself telling her about some articles I'd read the other day about mini houses, and she shook her head and said, "Oh, I doubt that'll last very long. If I've learned anything from hearing about your dad's work, it's that almost everyone always wants bigger rooms, more space when they have the chance."

So, my guard was down. I sat down at one of the quaint wooden tables in the otherwise empty café, breathing in that fresh baking scent that filled the place. Mom set a plate with a slice of strawberry pie and a scoop of vanilla ice cream on the table in front of me. I'd just taken my first bite of sweet fruit and buttery pastry when things took a turn in the wrong direction.

"I hear you're letting go of your clients around town," she said.

My fork hesitated for a second in mid-air before I took another bite. Of course word would be going around about that. "I am," I said. "Just making sure they're good to go, no computer emergencies on the horizon, before I move on."

Mom set her hands on the back of the chair across from me, her face with its framing of gray-blond hair suddenly looking wearier than usual. "It just worries a mother a little, you know, when she sees her son putting himself out of work."

"You don't have to worry," I said quickly, waving my fork. "I'm not out of work. I'm just changing focus. I've got online clients and enough work there to cover the bills that need covering."

"It seems like relying on people you've never even met face-to-face would be a lot less secure."

"Not at all. We sign contracts; it's all above board. Really, Mom, I get paid more by the hour that way." We wouldn't get into how overqualified I was at this point to troubleshoot printer problems or remind people how to run a reboot. "And it gives me more flexibility, in case I feel like setting off on any other impromptu road trips."

I gave her another grin, hoping she'd take her cue from my tone, but her brow stayed furrowed. She looked away for a second, and something in her stance made me tense up with the suspicion I wasn't going to like whatever she said next.

She pulled her gaze back to me. "I've also heard you've been going out to the Hallowell estate."

No point in denying that. "Why wouldn't I? Rose is back, and she's a friend." I wasn't allowed to say how much more than that she was to me. "Maybe people need to find some new hobbies if that's the most exciting news they're finding to pass on."

Mom still didn't return my smile. "We might have been distracted by our own concerns after the family picked up and left all those years ago"—and fired Mom and Dad from the jobs they'd had on the estate, she didn't add—"but I know it shook you up pretty hard too. You cared a lot about that girl. I'm glad you've been able to reconnect, I just... I don't think you should extend yourself too much."

I raised my eyebrows. "What do you mean?" She'd seemed perfectly happy to have Rose over for lunch a couple months ago.

"You know what they're like," she said. "The Hallowells. They don't really mix with us here in town. She might enjoy having your attention, but I wouldn't want to see you get your hopes up for more than that and then—"

"Mom," I interrupted. It was almost ridiculous, how little idea she had of how much Rose had already committed. And even more ridiculous that she thought she needed to lecture me like this. "I'm not a lovesick teenager. I'll be twenty-six in a month. So far I haven't gotten myself into any catastrophes I couldn't find my way back out of. Come on." Was this the whole reason she'd invited me over?

Mom shifted her weight uneasily. "I just wanted to say my piece. Her coming back, this strange trip you went on, leaving all your clients—I don't know what to think. I just want to know you're okay."

"I am," I said. "Nothing's wrong at all." Well, other than the malevolent demons lurking less than a day's drive from here, but she didn't have a clue about that. She was just, what, trying to protect me from a broken heart?

She'd always fussed a little more over me, as if she wasn't sure I really could handle the real world after all the time I spent staring at screens, but I'd thought she'd gotten over that. I *had* survived on my own just fine since I'd left for college eight years ago. How much more proof did she need?

"Ky," she said, "if you'd just think what I'm saying through, make sure you really know what you're doing here..."

I got up. I didn't know whether I felt more hurt or angry, but neither of those emotions was going to take this conversation anywhere good. "I always know what I'm doing, Mom. I thought you'd trust my judgment more than this by now. Are you hassling *Seth* about how he's been spending his time lately?"

Mom blinked at me at the mention of my twin. "Why?" she said slowly. "What has your brother been doing that I'd be worried about?"

Crap. She didn't realize how much time he'd been spending with Rose too. I guessed with him out in his new house out of town where he could hop the stone wall into the estate without anyone noticing, the gossip mill hadn't started going about him too. He'd slipped under the mom-concern radar... until now.

"I don't know," I said, hoping my face didn't show how flustered I felt. "I was just making a point. You definitely don't need to worry about him either. And I, ah, do actually have a job to get back to at home, so I'd better get going. Thank you for the pie!"

"Kyler," Mom said, but I was already heading out the door with a little wave.

CHAPTER THREE

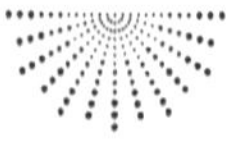

Rose

When I stepped close to the stone wall that surrounded the estate, the magic I'd already cast into and over those worn blocks tingled over my skin alongside the cool early morning breeze. Still there, still holding, but not with enough power that I felt completely secure.

The sun was only just peeking over the horizon, streaking the sky with a hazy glow, but I had to do this outside work now before the estate's few remaining employees from town showed up. I could only imagine what people would be saying if word got out that the newest Lady Hallowell went dancing along her wall every day.

The grass whispered under my bare feet as I set them down in the first movements of the form. I reached to the spark of my magic inside me and pushed that energy out through my body with the weaving of my hands. Every gesture I made called for protection, for shielding. I sent that energy up from me, all around the estate. The Frankfords might control some of my actions with the oath we'd taken, but I wasn't letting them get anything else from me. No magic of theirs was going to break through this barrier to spy on us. No sound would travel over these walls from more than a few feet away.

It would have taken hours for me to circle the entire estate with its extensive forested grounds. At the back I simply cut across the gardens, tying my protections to the farthest hedges. When we'd first returned here, I'd laid down a basic warding spell around the whole property. I'd bolster that once a month. The guys and Naomi knew not to say anything sensitive that far from the house, just in case.

My two guests... well, I hadn't been able to explain to them why I was setting up protections in any detail, but they'd gotten the gist. I didn't think they'd be shouting about their secrets in the forest anyway.

That forest used to be the part of the estate that gave me the most sense of safety. Back when it'd been just me and my father and the employees, I'd escaped the loneliness of the big old house to ramble among the trees with the guys who were now my consorts. Recently, while we'd still had to hide our relationship, we'd snuck out there to meet. So many fond memories were tied to those woods—and now the Frankfords' looming threat had cast a shadow over them.

I set that thought aside and focused all my

concentration on solidifying the magical wall laid over the real one.

By the time I'd made it back to the front gate, my muscles were trembling from the effort and sweat had formed on my forehead. I wiped it away, letting the strain fall from my body with an exhaled breath. I had a lot of power—Naomi said more power than she'd ever seen any witch use before—but not a lot of practice yet. An hour of concentrated magicking every morning should be doing wonders for my endurance.

I was just turning away from the wall, wondering if I might slip up to the garage-top apartment and pay Gabriel an early visit, when an engine rumbled up the road outside. Not one I recognized. I stepped closer to the wrought-iron bars of the gate, into the range where my voice would travel past it if need be.

The tan compact pulled to a stop just outside. The driver-side window rolled down. A woman with a wispy black pixie cut leaned her head and arm out. She didn't speak, her mouth set in a flat line, just flashed an ID with a crest I knew way too well. She was requesting entrance on the authority of the Assembly's Justice division.

I gave her a tight smile and pressed the controls for the gate. The Frankfords had sworn that they and their allies would see that the charges they'd encouraged against me were dropped and that they wouldn't pursue any further ones, but that didn't mean the rest of the Assembly couldn't take issue with what I did. I still had to play by their rules when they came calling.

The woman drove in and parked to the side of the drive just inside. The gate clanged shut behind her car. I stood there, fighting the urge to fidget, as she grabbed something out of the passenger seat and got out.

There was no way to know whether this particular Assembly enforcer was just a regular witch or one with ties to the Frankfords. I couldn't exactly ask her.

She shut the door and adjusted her leather satchel over her shoulder. "Investigator Ruiz on behalf of the Assembly," she said. "I believe you're Lady Hallowell?"

"That would be me," I said. "What's this about? I didn't know there was anything to investigate here."

One of her thin eyebrows lifted. "Two witches with no relation to your family have recently disappeared from their homes—and we've determined arrived here. Their families are concerned. I'm simply here to make sure there's no reason for that concern."

Oh. I should have expected this. I *had* expected a visit like this in the first few days after Lesley had turned up, but when no one had come calling, I'd assumed that was the end of it. Had it really taken the Assembly this long to figure out where she and Imogen were, or had their families been waiting for what they felt was the best time to prod me?

And if the latter, why had they chosen now?

I couldn't exactly ask Ruiz either of those things. I gave her another polite smile and motioned toward the manor. "There isn't anything to be concerned about, but why don't you come in so we can talk. You can speak with the witches you're here about too if you want. If they're not up yet, they should be soon."

Ruiz nodded and followed me to the house. I ushered her through the grand front hall into the less imposing sitting room off to the side. If it'd been a little later in the day, one of the staff would have ducked in to see if we wanted anything, but right now it was on me to act as full host.

"Can I get you some water or something else to drink?" I asked as Ruiz sat on the velvet cushion of the settee.

She waved her hand dismissively. "No need. I'd rather get out of your hair as quickly as possible. Let's get down to business."

I could appreciate that attitude. She didn't seem accusatory so far. I stayed wary, but my fingers unclenched as I sank into the armchair across from her.

She opened her satchel on the mahogany coffee table between us and took out a computer tablet that she flicked on. As she tapped through to whatever files she was looking for, the corner of my lips quirked up. Most of the witching folk I knew were still stuck on pen and paper. Kyler would have liked this one.

"So," Ruiz said, looking up from the tablet, "can you confirm that Miss Lesley Portsmith and Miss Imogen O'Brien are currently in residence on the Hallowell estate?"

"They are," I said. From the hum of the pipes overhead, at least one of them was currently in residence in the shower.

"And on what date did each of them arrive here?"

I thought back and told her. Ruiz typed on her tablet's screen.

"What reason did they give you for coming here?"

I paused. I didn't want to get my guests in trouble—or

Naomi, for putting out that whisper that the Hallowell estate was a good place to seek sanctuary.

"They didn't feel safe, and they thought they'd feel safer here," I settled on. "Maybe because I'm a young witch like them, managing the estate on my own? And because I made it through the trouble with my father." I didn't know how much the investigator knew about my arrest and the chase across the country last month, but Dad had been arrested by the main body of the Assembly. The Frankfords couldn't have erased their memories of that.

"That's all there was to it?" Ruiz said skeptically.

"I think if you want more details about their situations, it'd be better if you asked them directly," I said. "I don't know how much they'd want me to share. And that should be up to them, shouldn't it?"

Ruiz considered me for a moment. I thought I caught a flicker of a smile. "I guess you'd be proving them wrong for coming here if you said anything else."

"Is that a problem?"

She shrugged. "Not necessarily. I'll see what they have to say for themselves. You hadn't been in contact with them before they arrived here?"

I shook my head. "I met Lesley once or twice at functions in Portland years back when her family was visiting, but we never talked outside of that. I don't think I've met any of the O'Briens at all."

"And what have you done for them since they've arrived?"

"The usual things you'd do for guests?" I said. "Made

sure they had a place to sleep and food to eat. Other than that, they haven't asked for anything."

"Hmm. Have you told them anything to encourage them to continue feeling they're unsafe if they leave here?"

I'd told them I believed them, that I knew sometimes consortings were twisted for bad ends. I hadn't volunteered any specifics because the oath stopped me from doing that. "I don't think so," I said honestly. "But I wasn't going to turn them away when there's no reason I couldn't take them in."

Something in the cock of Ruiz's head sent an uneasy jitter through my nerves. I had the sudden suspicion that she was using magic right now, magic she'd put in place before she'd gotten out of that car, to help her judge my reactions. A lie-detector test of sorts. It couldn't be an official one, because she'd have needed my permission for that, so it wouldn't be incredibly effective, but she was gleaning something from whatever physiological responses she was tuning into.

Well, fine. I *was* telling the truth.

Ruiz looked at her tablet. Then she raised her gaze to meet mine again. "Regardless of what you know about Miss Portsmith's and Miss O'Brien's specific situations, have you seen reason to believe that there's some sort of malicious activity in the witching community that witches like them would need to be protected from?"

My spine stiffened. How the hell could I answer that? "What do you mean by malicious activity?" I asked, keeping my voice even. If she knew something already, maybe I could at least acknowledge it, even if I couldn't volunteer the facts.

The investigator's expression offered nothing. "I was hoping you could tell me."

"I..." The few things I could have told her, the bits of my own experience not covered by the oath, would have sounded crazy without proof. *I saw a demonic creature in a cave on a cliffside.* Yeah, that would go over well.

"I've seen reason to be wary," I said finally.

"*What* reason?"

"I'm sorry. I can't discuss it."

Ruiz's eyes searched mine, and in that moment I thought I saw real concern on her face. Something had slipped through the Frankfords' cover-ups, something had made her worry, and she wanted to stop it, not support it.

"Lady Hallowell, the Assembly can't help you or the other women here unless we know what we're dealing with. If you have a complaint to make, I'm here to take it."

My throat constricted. "I *can't* discuss it," I repeated.

I couldn't tell if my emphasis was enough. Ruiz studied me a moment longer and then leaned back. "You can always come in to the Justice Division if you have something to report. You can even ask for me directly. And if we find any evidence that leads back to you, we'll have to bring you in and insist on a full interrogation."

That last remark could have felt like a threat, but Spark help me, I wished they would find that evidence. That it didn't all hinge on me like it did right now.

"I know," I said, and couldn't help adding, "I'm sorry."

Ruiz let out her breath. "I suppose you'd better send down your guests now, if they're ready to speak with me."

* * *

Ruiz sent me out of the room while she talked with Imogen and then Lesley. They didn't look unsettled when they emerged, but Ruiz came out with a frown. When she left, after one last pointed glance at me, I went up to my bedroom and flopped on the bed. Emotion was tangled tight in my chest.

A minute later, the door eased open. Gabriel climbed on beside me. I turned, scooting closer into his embrace.

"Is everything okay?" he asked.

"For now," I said. "I think so. I guess it's possible the Assembly will decide I'm harboring fugitives or some other stupid charge and come back to arrest me for that." I didn't have a whole lot of faith in the Justice Division's version of justice these days.

"They'll see," he said, kissing my temple. "We'll expose the Frankfords and the rest of them, and the families like your aunt's will stand up and end this."

"I just wish we had more. All those files don't do us any good if we can't find verification somewhere else that the oath doesn't cover. They've been scheming for so long, drawing in so many people... We don't even know which women they've roped in, not for sure. Frankford was too damned careful even with his private files." There were records on those witches, of course, but under aliases I didn't know.

"We're making educated guesses, chasing down those

leads. Kyler's out near the coast right now looking into some things, isn't he?"

"Yeah." I didn't like that either. They've sworn not to hurt any of my consorts, but he was still so much more vulnerable than I was. "I wish that video you took had turned out better."

Gabriel had managed to film the demon and some of the confrontation with my father in the cave on a phone. But when we'd viewed it later, the image had been blurry, the audio distorted by a warble of the energy that had been pulsing from that portal. We weren't convincing anyone of our outlandish story with that as our only concrete proof.

"We'll get more chances," Gabriel said, hugging me tighter. "I know we will, because I know you, and I know there's no way you'd ever give up on this."

I hugged him back, tucking my head into his warmth. Having Gabriel's confidence meant more than I knew how to say to him. He'd lost his father because of how mine had treated them, tossing Mr. Lorde aside after generations of loyal service to the Hallowells. But he'd come back to me, supported me, sworn himself to me with more love than I ever could have asked for.

He kissed the side of my face, my cheek, heading toward my lips. I raised my chin to meet his mouth. But I only got to enjoy the heady heat of his kiss for a few seconds before the sound of the gate buzzer filtered through the door.

I groaned, but my pulse skittered at the same time. Maybe the Assembly *was* coming back to arrest me already.

"Do you want me to come with you?" Gabriel asked. If he'd been on duty, it'd have been him opening the gate anyway.

"Let me see who it is first," I said.

From the huge windows at the front end of the house, I could see down to the gate even from the second floor. A cherry-red Mustang was parked by the gate. And the young blond woman who was just stepping up to the bars was familiar enough that my breath caught in my throat.

Gabriel glanced at me. "You know her?"

I managed to nod. "That's Caroline Almeida. Her parents are some of my father's—and the Frankfords'—closest colleagues. What the hell is *she* doing here?"

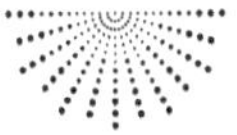

CHAPTER FOUR

Rose

Caroline Almeida sat primly on the same settee Investigator Ruiz used less than an hour ago. She looked so polished with her impeccably subtle make-up and the crisp cut of her blouse over her tailored slacks that it was hard to feel she'd take me seriously as lady of this estate. I was still in my dress that was rumpled from casting, my hair mussed after my snuggle with Gabriel. For a few seconds, I was taken back to those teenage years when I'd wandered around the witching get-togethers in Portland feeling gawky and out of place.

Then Caroline rubbed her mouth with a brisk motion of her hand, her eyes twitching away from me and back, and I realized at least part of the reason she looked so stiff was nerves. She didn't know what to expect from me either.

"Oh, hey, another visitor?" Naomi said, ambling in. "Nice to meet you! I'm Naomi."

Caroline went even more rigid, but she accepted Naomi's handshake. Her gaze shot back to me.

"She's my cousin," I said. "Anything you'd talk to me about, she can hear too." I turned to Naomi with a meaningful glance. "This is Caroline Almeida. Her parents have done a lot of work with my father." Then I added, to Caroline, "Do you want to tell me more about why you're here?" She'd been pretty vague when I'd gone to meet her at the gate, but intense enough with some sense of purpose that I'd let her in.

I knew from our stolen files that her family supported the Frankfords, but that meant they were bound by the oath not to harm us either. And *my* family, on my father's side, was linked too, so I couldn't make any definite judgements based on that. We'd just have to be very careful what we said around her.

And obviously she felt she needed to be careful with us. Fair enough.

"I just..." She hesitated, her hands clasping in her lap. "I've gotten the impression that there's some kind of conflict between you and my parents—and other people they do business with. I know they won't tell me what's going on. But I've heard enough that I'm worried. So I was hoping we could talk, and you could tell me your side of things, and that would at least give me a starting point."

Wow. What could she have heard that would have made her come to me instead of approaching her parents directly? Or maybe she had approached them and the way they'd dismissed her had made her suspicious?

I couldn't help thinking of the struggle I'd gone through accepting my father's guilt a month ago. But I'd accepted the truth in time.

"There's only so much I can say," I said. The oath prevented me from even mentioning there was an oath. "I'm not on the best of terms with several families in the witching community. I don't agree with certain things they've been doing. And my father tried to control my consorting in a way that would have really hurt me." *That* crime I'd uncovered more than a month before I'd taken the oath.

I braced myself for her to ask for proof. I couldn't have provided it to her any more than I could have to Ruiz. But she simply nodded. "These families had some kind of plan that you were supposed to participate in?" she said. "Or that you interrupted?"

"A little of both," I said.

"That faction had the enforcers loyal to them chasing her all the way across the damned country," Naomi broke in. "They almost—"

Her voice cut off before she could get into any actual criminal actions the Frankfords' people had taken. The oath I'd taken bound her too, just as much as it protected her and the rest of my family.

Caroline worried her lower lip under her perfectly white teeth. "But everything—everything got sorted out?"

Naomi and I exchanged a look. "Not exactly," I said. "But everything that's not, I can't talk about. I'm sorry. Believe me, I wish I wasn't in this position." I paused.

"Whatever you heard, it must have been pretty serious. Did you come all the way from Portugal?"

"We were staying with extended family in San Francisco for the month," Caroline said. "I guess that's why... They didn't realize the acoustics of the house..." She grimaced. "I don't know what to think. I hardly *know* anything. And if you can't tell me anything else..."

An idea lit in my head like an extension of my spark. "Your parents probably have more answers. Even if you're not comfortable talking to them, if you looked through their files—on paper, or on the computer—you might be able to put the pieces together. That's how I caught on to what my dad was doing."

She gave me a small wry smile. "I tried that already. As far as I can tell, Charles and Helen Frankford are in charge of whatever's going on, and they handle all the, ah, paperwork. It's sounded like they've tightened up their personal security even more in the last few weeks."

I might not be able to say much about the Frankfords, but my expression must have shifted. Her gaze sharpened. "You know about them too."

"I can't talk about it," I said quietly. It didn't surprise me at all that they'd have beefed up their security, though, after my unsparked consorts and I had breached it and nearly exposed their entire horrific conspiracy.

"Okay." She looked down at her hands and then back at me. "I think you might still be in some danger. I'm sure you're already looking out for yourself. And I don't know if my parents are involved in that at all—I hope not. I just wouldn't have felt right not saying something."

I blinked at her, suddenly touched. "Thank you," I

said. "I appreciate the warning. Was there anything specific you heard—"

She shook her head. "If there was, I'd tell you, I swear. It was just the general tone. The idea of the 'problem' needing to be 'resolved.' If I do hear anything specific, I'll reach out."

"That's the most I can ask," I said. My stomach had knotted. "I wish I could help *you* more."

"It's all right. The fact that you let me in at all says a lot." She sighed and got up. "I don't want to impose on you any more than this."

"It's all right," I said, standing with her. "I've already got two unexpected guests." I wasn't completely sure how I would have felt about her staying right here on the estate even after everything she'd said, but I wasn't sure I could turn her away if she needed somewhere to hide out either. I couldn't remember if she was consorted yet or not. Who knew what her parents might have arranged or be arranging for her?

"Thanks," she said with another small smile. "But I really should be getting back. It's a long drive... I told my parents I was visiting a friend. We're supposed to be heading back home in a few days anyway."

"Are you sure *you're* not in any danger?" Naomi said. My cousin knew how to get right to the point.

"Of course not," Caroline said. "I can't imagine..." A shiver ran through her. "No. It's nothing like that."

Was she really that sure? I grappled with what I could say and what I couldn't as I walked her to the door. "If you ever do feel like you need somewhere to go," I said. "I'd find a space for you here. Just so you know that."

"I don't think it'll come to that, but thank you." Her hands fidgeted with the hem of her blouse. Her nerves had returned, because of how she'd opened up with me or because of who she was heading back to, I didn't know.

Naomi and I watched her walk back to her Mustang. I pressed the control inside the door to open the front gate for her. My cousin set her hands on her hips.

"Well, that was interesting," she said.

More than just interesting. The things Caroline had said were still sinking in. She'd felt I was in danger— enough that she was willing to implicate her parents in telling me that. They were still talking about resolving the problem I posed, even though theoretically that problem had been resolved with the oath. I rubbed my arms, an uneasy chill running over my skin.

"We can't just keep doing what we've been doing," I said. "Poking at leads without even being able to say what we're looking for is getting us nowhere. We need to get real hard evidence. So what if Gabriel's video didn't work out? He wasn't prepared. If we could just get back to the cliff, show everything from where it is on the property to the cave itself, maybe even try to talk to that creature— We need to show people just how far the Frankfords and their allies have gone. Just what kind of monsters they're messing with."

"It wasn't that easy getting out there in the first place," Naomi said. "How do you figure we'd manage it?"

"I don't know. That's the problem. The Frankfords will have that property so much more heavily guarded than before. They'd expect us to try something like that." I bit my lip.

"Is there anything— I mean, I know you have more information than you're allowed to talk to me about. Is there something in there that might give you an angle?"

By all that was lit and warm, I wished I could talk to her about the files we'd grabbed. Frustration coiled in my chest. But in this case there wasn't much I could have told her anyway except, "Not that I've seen. We'd have jumped on that opportunity if we'd found it." I knew the history of the property's ownership, the calendar of their visits there, the old schedules the Frankfords had set up for rotating security, but they knew we'd seen all that. We couldn't go in blithely hoping they'd left everything the same.

"Well, you know you've got me on your side no matter what, cuz," Naomi said, slinging an arm around me. I hugged her back for a second, the frustration turning into an ache. She'd have to go home soon too. To her consort and the rest of my mother's family—including my other aunt, Irene, who didn't believe Naomi should be getting mixed up with me at all.

Somewhere in the depths of the house, one of our few landline phones rang. I shut the door and hurried to get it. It had barely rung since I'd gotten back—since the estate had become formally mine.

"Rose?" said the slightly familiar voice on the other end. "Oh, I suppose I should say Lady Hallowell now. It's Herbert Landry."

"Master Landry?" I said automatically. Most of my magical teaching had been done by James Courtland, who lived just outside town near us, but when I'd been particularly young, Landry had taken on some of my education. He'd moved down south—better for his old age, he'd said—and had only returned to Portland for occasional visits. I hadn't seen him in years.

He chuckled. "I think you're enough past being my student to drop that formality. I'm glad I reached you."

"Why's that?" I said. "What's going on?" I had only pleasant memories of Landry, but he'd never called to chat with me before.

"Oh, it's nothing terribly urgent, I merely— I just arrived in Portland for the week, and I dropped in on your father here. I hadn't realized you'd fallen out so badly. You've banned him from the family estate?"

My hand clenched around the phone. How *dare* my father bring other people into this conflict when he knew I couldn't properly accuse him of the things he'd done. "There are good reasons for that," I said, my voice tight.

"I have trouble imagining you going to those lengths otherwise," Landry said. "But in case there was any room for reconciliation... I've never seen him like this, Rose. He's a shadow of the man he was. If you can find it in your heart to even attempt to discuss the matter with him..."

"We've already discussed it at length," I said, only barely keeping myself from outright snapping. Landry didn't have any idea what I'd been through, the way Dad had talked to me during our last real conversation when he'd tried to justify enslaving my magic so I'd be forced into some sort of service with those demons... But right then I hated my former teacher for making me remember it, for buying into Dad's wounded act. "I don't want to talk about it with *anyone* anymore."

"All right, all right. Just a concerned friend of the family, you know."

"I know. I was actually in the middle of something. We'd better leave it at that."

"Well, all right," Landry said, and then I was hanging up.

I sagged against the wall beside the phone table and let out my breath. My stomach was twice as knotted as it'd been before.

Even if I'd wanted to follow the spirit of the oath as well as the letter, to live and let live and not care what happened beyond the walls of the estate, the Frankfords and my father and the rest of them clearly had no intention of letting me have that peace.

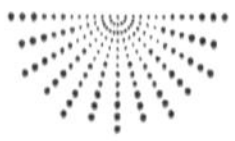

Damon

"I didn't like the idea of Kyler getting within ten miles of the place, and he's already out there," Rose said, sweeping a strand of her smooth black hair away from her face as she paced the room that had once been her father's office. The bunch of us had taken over the place while we hacked away at the prize we'd stolen—not that the contents of that hard drive had given us much prize-worthy stuff so far. "The last thing I want is you putting yourself anywhere near Frankford territory too."

As if going out there would be even half as much danger as she'd already put herself in to protect the rest of us. I couldn't say I was unhappy to still be breathing after she'd given in to the Frankford's threats and traded that awful oath for my and Kyler's lives, but there were a lot of nights when I couldn't sleep because my brain was too busy running scenarios where I somehow managed to break free and save the day myself.

This plan wasn't quite that epic, but it was something I could contribute that the other guys couldn't.

"It wouldn't be me putting myself out there, though," I said. "That's the point. I've been working with guys from this one gang for years. I know how to *work* them. I can get them to scope out the property for us, no sweat. And there's no reason the Frankfords would think those guys have anything to do with you."

"You don't think they could trace the gang guys back to you?" Rose asked. She propped herself against the edge of the desk, looking weary.

The sight of her, under strain all over again, jabbed me right in the heart. I stepped closer to her, cupping her face and leaning close. "Even if they do, which I don't think is very likely, so what? There's nothing in the oath about just looking at the place. I'll tell them hands off." I ran my thumb lightly over her cheek. "Let me do this for you, angel."

"I don't like getting more people involved in this mess," she said, but she leaned into my touch.

"They won't get that involved. I know to keep them at arm's length. Hell, I *can't* tell them anything they're not supposed to know, right? After what that girl told you, it sounds like we need to pull out all the stops. Get this done, take those bastards down, now."

"Yeah." She sighed and tipped her head toward me. I met her kiss, soaking in the gentle heat of her mouth. I still didn't know what I'd done so right to have a woman like her in my life, but now that I did, anyone who wanted to hurt her would have to go through me first.

"All right," Rose said when she'd eased back. "Keep it vague, and tell them whatever you need to say to make sure they don't get too close and raise any alarms with the Frankfords. The less they know about what we're doing, the better."

I saluted her. "Message received."

* * *

It wasn't hard to arrange a quick meet-up with my contact in Silvio's bunch, even though I hadn't been going out for the usual merchandise-sorting stints I'd used to schedule my weeks around, back when I'd been eager to make good with the big boss. I had larger priorities now. But I'd put in a lot of time over the years, and say what you want about small-time criminals, this group at least respected that kind of loyalty.

Markus and I were squeezed into a little booth in a bar that Silvio's people liked at the edge of the town. Silvio was friends with the owner or something. The place always smelled a little sour and I didn't love the metal music they liked to play, but the screeching guitars and the loud voices of the usual clientele covered up any criminally inclined conversations.

I downed the last of my beer and bent over the table toward the other guy.

"The property doesn't look like much," I said. "But you'll be able to tell they're storing something big there from all the security around the place. They're trying to keep it under the radar by not building up the house or anything too fancy."

"But *you* know what they've got stashed there?" Markus said.

"I do," I said. "Got a tip, figured Silvio would appreciate being in on it. I can't pull it off by myself anyway. But I want in. There are a couple things I know that you'll need to pull off the score."

"Sure, sure." Markus waved his hand as if to dismiss the idea that they wouldn't include me. His eyes had gone round in his broad face. "Absolutely Silvio is going to be glad you passed this on. But he's going to want more details before we actually go in."

"Don't worry," I said. "I'll lay the whole thing out once we're good to go. I'll know what timing we'll want to aim for when I hear back about their current set-up. Just make sure you don't catch their notice, like I said. We let them know we're interested, and they might move that stash before we get our chance."

"Not a problem. I'll be in touch when we've had a chance to scope out the place. Keep an open line." Markus clasped my hand with a brisk shake and a grin. Oh, yeah, I had him eating out of my hand with this story. Maybe we'd even be able to use Silvio's bunch to help us break back onto the Frankford's property with their special cliff.

The memory of that demonic face peering through the glowing portal in the cave made my stomach twist. I was *not* looking forward to facing that thing again. The first time had been enough to curdle all my insides. Whatever exactly that monster was, it didn't belong on this plane of existence. The horror that had run through every inch of my body had convinced me of that in an instant.

The sooner we shut down the Frankfords' associates and got the honest people from the Assembly on the case sealing up that hole, the happier I'd be.

A couple minutes after Markus had taken off, I headed out of the bar too. The evening air outside was hot, but not as stuffy as back there with all those half-drunk bodies crammed together. Maybe being around Rose was giving me a bit of a taste for the finer side of life.

I could swing by my mother's place with just a little detour on the way back to my crappy basement apartment. Give her an update on the job I was getting more committed to now. The apprenticeship Seth had set me up with, courtesy of an electrician who sometimes worked with his dad's reno business, was going better than I'd let myself hope. My new boss was a lot more boring than Silvio, but I also never had to worry he'd point a gun at my head. Boring had its upsides.

Besides, who wouldn't want to figure out how to get an entire building's power under your control? It was work that paid well... and that might come in handy somewhere down the line if our current plans to mess with the Frankfords didn't work out.

Mom hadn't been able to hide how overjoyed she'd been when I'd told her about the gig. She'd never made any comments about the other ways I'd earned money over the years, but I couldn't think of many mothers who'd have outright *approved* of the habits I'd fallen into.

I'd helped keep her afloat after Rose's dad had kicked

her to the curb without severance or even a reference. Made sure her apartment was at least a little less crappy than mine. Until Rose had come back to town, my mother had been the only person in this world I'd still given a damn about.

Going up the steps to her second-floor apartment, hearing the creak of the sagging wood, made me more depressed than usual. It was still a crappy place. Once I settled into this new job and we got rid of the witching threat hanging over us, maybe I could help her out more than I had before. Kick some extra cash toward a down payment on a nicer place. See if I could pull some strings to find her a better job than the one she had cleaning houses for that harassing jerk of a boss.

She was pretty much always home in the evenings. I rapped my knuckles against the door. "Mom? It's me."

It took longer than I expected before I heard the shuffle of her feet on the other side. Mom eased the door open. Her eyes had gotten a little sunken over the years, her dark brown hair strung with gray, but normally she brightened when she saw me. Today she gave me a look that was almost dour.

She stepped back to let me in, and I came inside with a frown. "Is everything okay? That asshole didn't try anything on you again, did he?"

"What?" she said, with honest surprise. "No. No, I just didn't expect to see you coming around here."

I stopped by the kitchen doorway, resting my hand on the counter. Her dinner dishes were already in the sink, rinsed, so I hadn't interrupted her meal. "Why wouldn't you expect me? I've been dropping in all the time since I stopped living with you. I mean, if you want me to start calling first, I can do that, you just always said—"

"No," she said. "I mean I thought you were too busy with that slut of yours."

My head snapped around. For a second I could only stare at her. I didn't think I'd *ever* heard my mother use that word, and I'd hung out with women in the past who openly embraced the label.

"Excuse me?" I said, my tongue stumbling.

"The Hallowell girl," Mom said, her dark eyes narrowing. "I know you've been seeing her. Everyone knows. And not just you. All sorts of young men she's luring into her home, isn't she? After what her family did to me... And now she's stealing you too, at least until she decides to spit you back out."

I groped for more words. "Mom—why are you talking like this?"

"Because I can't stand to see you turn into some kind of... of *degenerate*. You deserve better, Damon. You deserve to be better. I can hardly stand to look at you, knowing you've gone along with whatever whorish scheme she's caught you up in." She drew in a breath that sounded like a sob.

"*Mom*." Emotions wrenched through me, tearing me between fury that she'd talk that way about the love of my life and horror that I'd somehow disappointed and disgusted her so much. I grasped her shoulder. "It's not like that. I swear—"

Mom wrenched away from me and backed up to the table. "Don't touch me. Not with those hands that've been all over that whore. There's always been something wrong about that family. I should have known. I should have said something from the start."

"There's nothing to say," I said firmly, barely keeping my anger in check. "You can't talk about Rose that way. You have no idea— She's the kindest, strongest woman I know, Mom. There are no schemes. I care about her. I go out to see her. Anything else that happens is none of your business anyway."

"Of course you'd say that," she mumbled. "Of course. Get out. I don't want to see you, not when I know you're probably going running back to her the moment you leave."

"Mom."

"Go!" She pointed toward the door, her shoulders shaking.

God help me, what the hell was I supposed to do? I wavered and then went, catching the door a second before I slammed it. My pulse thumped through my veins like the steps rattling under my feet on the way down. I marched off toward my apartment, but that beat didn't settle. Queasiness pooled in my gut.

What the fuck had gotten into my mom? What had she heard to make her turn on Rose like that? How could she talk like that to *me*?

I sure as hell wasn't going to Rose with all this rage rushing through me. No, I'd prefer she saw as little as possible of this side of me.

And when I found out who was spreading this poison about her, I was looking forward to smashing their head in.

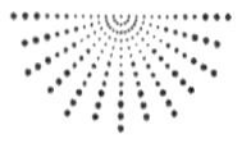

Rose

"Wow," Jin said as he stepped into the magicking room. His feet whispered over the polished hardwood floor. A glow from the skylight overhead streamed over us, and a whiff of the tangy incense used in one of my most recent magickings hung in the air. "This place definitely has atmosphere."

"I thought you'd appreciate that," I said with a smile.

"So, this is where the magic happens?" He turned, taking in the whole space. The room was empty other than the supply cabinet at the far end. "Literally?"

"Well, you know I can cast spells pretty much anywhere," I said. "But this room is the ideal environment. The walls are insulated so no outside sounds can distract me—and so anything I say won't carry out where the unsparked staff can hear. The colors are all neutral so I can focus on my internal purpose. And the floor is built for ease of movement while I'm moving through the forms. There's a smaller private one that's technically mine now as head of the family, but this is where I did most of my practicing growing up. I thought it'd be better to have the extra space."

"All those blank walls make me want to get painting," Jin said with a wink. "But I can see why you'd prefer them like this. *I'm* never going to be able to do any magicking, though, right? It's only ever the women, even in your witching families."

I nodded. "But there are joint forms for couples— they're supposed to help open the mind and emotions, to encourage an even deeper trust, so that the energy we create between us is even stronger. I figured... The Frankfords and their faction are so powerful. We know they've been using those demons to give them even more power." Though the files weren't completely clear on *how* the effects worked.

"So, the stronger your magic is, the better," Jin said. "Makes sense. How has it gone with the other guys?"

He asked the question so nonchalantly, taking it for granted that I'd tried this with at least a couple of my other consorts before him, that my heart pinched. Had I acted as if I relied on the others more than him?

"It hasn't," I said. "This is my first try. It seemed like you'd probably pick up the movements faster than anyone else—I saw how you danced at my little birthday celebration."

He turned to me with that slow flirty smile that always made my insides melt. "It's an honor to be the first, then, Briar Rose. Shall we dance?"

Suddenly I felt awkward. "I've never actually done this with *anyone* before. I mean, they're adapted from the single-person forms, and I read everything I could find on the dual forms in the library, but it's not quite the same…"

Jin took my hand and squeezed it. "We'll figure it out. Gotta start somewhere. How do we begin?"

My heart settled a little. Of course this would be okay. Jin didn't care if I looked a little silly. "The first form is the simplest. What do you say we go through it slowly and then chain it all together in a smoother flow once we have the hang of it?"

"Ready when you are."

The room might have been designed to minimize distractions, but there wasn't much that could have been more distracting than moving Jin through this sort-of dance. My fingers skimmed up and down his forearms as I showed him how to place his arms: around my waist now, across my shoulders next, his hand on my side, my hip, the small of my back. I leaned into him and then tugged him into me, supporting each other's weight in a symbolic way, and a totally non-symbolic heat kindled between us.

Jin's lips grazed the side of my neck as he bowed his head next to mine at the end of the form. I curled my fingers into my palms, fighting the urge to grab his jaw and pull those lips right to mine.

"You're picking it up fast," I said, knowing I sounded breathless. "Just like I figured."

"You know me well," Jin said with that same flirty smile. "I think I've got the shape of it down. Should we try speeding things up?"

"Let's," I said. An eager flush tickled over my skin.

We slipped around each other, bending and swaying and spinning together, like an expanded version of the forms I used on my own. After the first few movements, as those movements flowed together seamlessly now, I almost felt as if I had two sets of limbs, two torsos, moving in perfect symmetry. Jin and I hadn't done anything really intimate yet, but the spark of my magic flickered up in my chest, quivering eagerly. Each time our bodies connected, the warmth between us grew a little more.

"I can feel it," Jin murmured. "That's... That's amazing. Like we really are linked together with this sort of harmony..."

He trailed off as we launched into the final sequence. I dipped low, and he caught my shoulders. With a whirl of his arm, he swiveled me back toward him. Our feet stepped together, our legs twining and releasing and twining again. The quiver spread all through my muscles. I couldn't take my eyes off Jin's face.

When we finished, Jin pulled me into an embrace. He hugged me close. "That was fantastic," he said. "I felt the consort bond when we did the ceremony, but I'd never gotten this strong a sense of it since then."

The connection between us thrummed through my veins alongside that giddy quiver. I hugged him back, not wanting to let him go. "That's the point of the forms. To strengthen that bond. It won't feel like that all the time when we're not doing them, but it will stay stronger the more we practice the forms."

"And here I thought that bond couldn't get any stronger than it already was." He chuckled, his breath tickling over my hair. "You can call me in to practice any time."

"That's just the first one," I said. "You want to try something a little more complex?" I paused. "I'll need to use a little of my magic on you for the next one."

"Magic away," Jin said, so easily any anxiety I might have had about that component left me. I squeezed him tight before forcing myself to let go.

We started slowly again, trying out each movement and seeing how they joined together. At one point, in the middle of the form, I boosted Jin's feet several inches off the ground with a burst of magical energy. Then, at the end, I lifted us both in a quick spiral.

Jin was grinning when we touched down. "This is a fun one."

His confidence trickled into me, pushing back the looming fears about the Frankfords and whatever they might be planning. "Are you ready to try it faster?"

He clapped his hands. "Let's do this."

We moved through the flowing pattern, each touch and momentary hold spreading fresh heat over my skin. My heart swelled with the emotion coursing between us until I wasn't sure I could even hold it all. Jin's eyes shone as he gazed back at me.

The magical wind whipped around us into that final whirl. The second our feet hit the ground, I couldn't help myself. I reached for my consort's face, and he was already leaning in to claim my mouth.

Electricity seemed to shiver through me with that kiss. My whole body was alight from the closeness of the forms, and my spark leapt to flood every nerve with hot desire. Jin kissed me harder, his hands roaming lower down my body. I arched into his touch. I wanted more—I wanted everything. I wanted him to know how much I always wanted him.

My lips trailed across his jaw and down his neck. "Do you trust me?" I murmured, struck by a strange impulse.

"Absolutely," Jin said.

I nipped the bare skin at the crook of his shoulder, a slight graze of my teeth. At his encouraging sound, I bit a little harder. Not enough to break the skin, but enough to add a little spark of pain to his pleasure.

Jin's breath hitched. "Fuck me."

Before I could point out I intended to do exactly that, he'd drawn my mouth back to his. We devoured each other, sinking to the floor without breaking the kiss. Jin wrenched up my dress. I groped for the fly of his slacks. No time for teasing. No time for lingering in the moment. I wanted him in me now.

He slid inside me just as sure as the movements of our dance. A whimper escaped me at the welcome friction of his cock stretching my core. I raised my knees by his hips, urging him onward as our mouths collided again.

Pleasure spiraled through me in a swift wave. Jin plunged deeper and deeper with a groan. He cupped my breast through my dress, stroking his lithe fingers over the nipple until I was arching both chest and hips toward him in turn. My spark flared through me, so bright I thought it might consume us both.

He slipped his hand under my ass, angling me higher to meet him. I moaned as he filled me even more completely. All I could do then was cling to him, skin to sweat-damp skin, rocking with the force of his thrusts. His cock hit that glorious spot inside me again, and again, and—

I tipped over the edge with a burst of light behind my eyes. Bliss raced through my body, curling my toes. Jin came a moment later, with a ragged breath against my cheek. His release was another sear of heat through my core.

He eased to a stop over me, beaming down at me. I smiled up at him as the last ripples of pleasure radiated through me.

"You're a fucking wonder, Rose," Jin murmured. He nuzzled the side of my face and rolled us over, his legs tangling with mine. "How's that for solidifying a bond?"

I giggled. "I think we passed with flying colors. Do you still feel different?"

"You mean other than the amazing high of just being with you?" He ran his hand over my hair. "There's something about it—the sensation when I think about you, it's... fuller, somehow? But, you know, it was pretty intense before, so I'm not sure it can get *that* much more so."

"Even a little could make a difference if it comes down to a real fight." Not just against a handful of lackey enforcers, but against all the witches who stood with the Frankfords—and maybe against those demonic creatures too?

The worries crept back in. I buried my face in Jin's shoulder, but I couldn't escape them completely. Jin kissed my forehead.

"You've got us," he said. "You'll always have us. And that means you'll always be stronger. Do you know— You remember when Gabriel first showed up with that page from your book, the one you gave each of us before you left the estate the first time?"

"Yeah," I said. The memory of Gabriel's return was etched clearly in my mind. That and the moment when I'd given the guys those pages. I'd torn them from my favorite childhood novel, *The Lion, The Witch, and The Wardrobe*, as a sort of token when my father had decided to move the family to Portland—mainly to force an end to my friendship with the unsparked guys he'd deemed unsuitable companions for a thirteen-year-old witch.

"I still have my page too," Jin said. "Tucked in with my favorite art supplies back home. Any time I left for more than a day, I'd slip it into my wallet. Like it was for luck or something. Or in case it'd somehow let our paths cross. You've always been with me, Rose, and I'll always be here if you need me. You can trust in that."

My throat choked up. I tipped my head to kiss him. His hand rose to my cheek, and we might have fallen back into each other all over again, except a frantic knocking reverberated through the door right then.

"Rose!" a muffled voice said from right outside. "I think you'd better come. There's someone at the gate—he says Charles Frankford sent him."

CHAPTER SEVEN

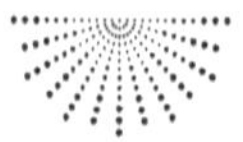

Rose

Jin followed me down to the front door. "Stay behind me," I told him. "And hang back a bit. I know you want to help, but... we don't know what to expect from this guy."

Jin made a face, but he nodded at the same time. "I've got your back." His voice turned sly. "He definitely doesn't want to mess with you after the boost your spark just got."

In spite of the stressful situation ahead, I might have been a bit flushed when I started down the front drive.

There was indeed a guy outside the gate, waiting there with his arms folded loosely over his chest. He wasn't much taller than me, but he was burly, with hard lines to his nose and his jaw that made him look imposing. From the lines at the corners of his eyes and the silver cast to his light brown hair, I guessed he was about my father's age.

He tapped his foot in a slow but forceful rhythm as I approached. I couldn't see his car, though I doubted he'd walked here. He must have parked it farther down the road. Because he was worried we'd do something to it? That our seeing it would be a bad thing?

Hard to tell whether it was reasonable sneakiness or just paranoia.

"Hello," I said, coming to a stop a few feet from the gate. The guy didn't look as if he were carrying any of the magical weapons the male enforcers sometimes used, but after what I'd seen in the last few weeks from his people, I didn't trust myself to be able to spot every potential threat. "You wanted something?"

"Is this how you usually greet visitors, Lady Hallowell?" the man said with a gravely edge to his voice.

"No," I said. "But visitors usually call first, or at least they don't demand my attention the second they arrive, after they've announced they're coming sent by someone who specifically swore to leave me alone."

The guy shrugged. "I'd think your dealings with my boss would make you more inclined to tread carefully."

"Your opinion has been noted," I said, folding my own arms in front of me. "Are you here to judge how welcoming I am, or is there some other reason you came by?"

He patted his hand against the bars of the gate. "Can I come in so we can talk?"

I barely held in a snort of derision. "No. My 'dealings' with your boss have made me inclined to keep a wall between me and anyone associated with him if at all possible."

Jin let out a muffled snicker behind me. The guy glowered at him and then at me. "This isn't really how I'd like to have a conversation."

"Well, if you don't really want to talk, you can go, and I'll get back to what I was doing."

His jaw worked. He sighed, dropping his arms. "Fine. Mr. and Lady Frankford would like to confirm that you're following the terms of your agreement with them."

"I don't really have a whole lot of choice in the matter, do I?" I said. "I'd be curious to know if *they* have."

Their lackey ignored that jab. "You had a visit from Caroline Almeida," he said.

My back tensed. They *had* been monitoring the estate, then. She'd obviously covered her tracks with her parents, so it wasn't from them that the Frankfords would have found out. I hoped she hadn't gotten in trouble for coming to me.

"Are you jealous because I invited her in and not you?" I asked.

"I want to know what business you had with her."

"Well, first," I said, "that's none of *your* business, because I didn't say a word about your boss to her." Which was true. She was the one who'd mentioned the Frankfords. "She simply happened to be in the neighborhood and wanted to drop in. We hadn't seen each other in a few years, you know."

Caroline and I had never been particularly friendly with each other, but it wasn't as if we'd been at each other's throats either. I didn't think the Frankfords could say I had to be lying.

The man's eyebrow arched. "That's all? You caught up over tea and sent her on her way?"

"What do you think I'd tell her about?" I fixed him with a hard smile. If he said anything incriminating, I *could* tell people about that. It wouldn't have come from the files.

"Never mind that," he said. "If Mr. Frankford finds out you've been looking for loopholes in your oath—"

"He'll what?" I broke in. "Break his end of the oath and do something to hurt me or my family?"

The guy narrowed his eyes. "For an oath to be broken, it must be agreed on both sides."

"Which means he knows that hasn't happened. Is that all you wanted to ask about? I've got nothing else to tell you about Caroline Almeida. You can always talk to her directly, you know." I kind of hoped she was already out of the country by now.

"What about the other two witches who've joined you here?" he prodded, shifting subjects with about as much grace as a bull. "What did they want here? Why have you let them stay?"

"They told me they needed somewhere to stay," I said evenly. "I have plenty of room and nothing against either of them. Why would I turn them away?"

"Because you know you're not supposed to be spreading around word of what you've been doing, about your perverse relationships." He gestured toward Jin with a disgusted curl of his lip, and my temper flared.

I managed to tamp it down—for the most part. "I

haven't volunteered any information about my consorting with them," I said tartly. "As I swore not to. If they draw their own conclusions, I can't help that. I should be allowed to spend time with whoever I want on my own estate."

"It just doesn't seem right, you witches gathering together like this," the guy said. "You don't want to make Mr. and Lady Frankford uncomfortable, thinking you might be brewing some sort of conspiracy."

They were worried about *me* conspiring, when they'd been carrying on a massive conspiracy against all witching society for decades? I would have rolled my eyes if I hadn't been so on edge.

"There's no conspiracy," I said. "My guests just want to live in peace. Which is all *I* want to do too. You coming around here harassing me about things that have nothing to do with you or your boss doesn't help with that."

The guy shook his head. "No harassing here. Just making sure you remember what's good for you."

Now I was really bristling. "Look," I said, taking another step forward and summoning a glow of magic into my hand with a flick of my wrist. "What would be good for me is if you got the hell out of here and all of you left me and the rest of us alone. Tell the Frankfords they should remember what's good for *them*. Or maybe you should just think about what's good for you."

The man's gaze jerked to the quavering light dancing around my fingers. A fire I could have called all the way into being and thrown at him if I'd really wanted to. It'd have been more for show than functional, but it still could have burned.

"Rose." Gabriel's voice carried across the yard like a warning. He'd come out of the garage apartment. He glanced from me to the guy and strode over to join us. "You heard her," he said tightly. "Lady Hallowell asked you to leave."

"I'll leave when I'm damn well ready—"

An engine rumbled on the road. A pick-up truck pulled up just behind the guy. Seth frowned at him from the driver's seat as he leaned out the open window. "Is there a problem?" he asked me. The muscles in his shoulders had flexed.

The Frankfords' lackey might be burly, but Seth had at least half a foot on him, plus a little extra muscle besides that. Not to mention the truck. He'd left the engine running at a low growl.

The guy looked from me and my two consorts behind me to the one in the truck and seemed to decide he'd finally outstayed his welcome. "Mr. Frankford isn't going to be pleased that you handled the situation like this," he said, turning to go.

"You can let him know I'm not pleased he sent you at all," I called after him.

I waited until the Frankfords' man was well down the road before I opened the gate for Seth. Not that I really thought the guy would try to dash in—what would that even accomplish?—but caution seemed wise. I'd gathered the magic I'd sent to my hand back into my body, where it thrummed at an agitated key.

"Are you okay?" Seth asked, jumping out of the truck. "Who was that guy?"

"Some jerk the Frankfords sent to poke around," Jin

said. "Our Briar Rose brought out the thorns." He grinned.

"I'm fine," I said, but I leaned into the embrace Seth offered anyway. Few things made me feel quite as secure as his solid body against mine. "I just wish they'd back off." I paused, straightening up again, and motioned the guys away from the gate. The three of them followed me around the other side of the garage.

"You know not to talk about any of this, even with each other, outside these walls, right?" I said quietly. "From some of the things he said, it's obvious they're monitoring what goes on around the estate, like I thought they might be. I can block them from spying right inside, but to try to push those protections farther..."

"You shouldn't strain yourself," Gabriel said. "We've had a lot of practice keeping our mouths shut in the last couple months. You don't have to worry."

"Even Ky and I don't talk about anything to do with you or the rest of it when we're not here," Seth said. "Sometimes it's hard, but—better than the alternative."

I let out my breath. "Okay. Okay. Damn it!" Every time I started to think I'd gotten a handle on things, every time I found a new strategy to pursue, the Frankfords pushed back a little harder. And I hadn't even started to really push at them yet. If they'd wanted to make me feel hemmed in, they'd succeeded.

"He's gone now," Jin said. "You put him in his place. I was ready to start applauding."

"But he'll come back, or they'll send someone else—or something else." I paced to the side of the garage and back again. "I thought we'd have more time than this. Do they even think about what they're doing? I promised not to talk about them or share what we found. *I* never promised not to hurt *them*."

"Rose." Gabriel caught my arm, turning me toward him. His bright blue eyes searched mine. "You don't really mean that," he said.

The concern in his tone deflated some of my anger. Only some. "I don't," I muttered. "Not that I'd be all that sorry to hear it if something happened to them another way. I wouldn't go calling down their wrath on us like that."

His gaze stayed on me, the corners of his mouth tensing in a way that made my chest clench up a little, even though I wasn't sure what was bothering him.

Jin motioned toward the house. "You know," he said, "I've been thinking, if you don't mind me messing with the décor... I could do in the house what we did with that tour bus we drove back from New York—paint glyphs on the walls to help support all that protective magic you're doing. I could probably blend it into a sort of trim along the ceiling so it looked like a quirky design, not anything your staff would associate with magic."

Something in me twisted at the idea of shaking up the traditional look of my childhood home just to fend off villains like the Frankfords. But we did have to fend them off. And... maybe it wouldn't be so bad to change the house up a little anyway. It held a lot of good memories, but there were a lot of bad ones in that place now too.

"All right," I said. "That's a great idea. Let's really make the place ours."

CHAPTER EIGHT

Rose

I wasn't sure what time it was when my phone started ringing, but I'd been asleep for just long enough for my head to feel muggy as I woke up, and the sky outside my bedroom window was completely dark. Seth, who'd stayed for dinner and ended up spending the night, stirred next to me. He hugged me where his arm was looped around my waist as if encouraging me to stay put.

My heart was already thumping too fast for that. Why would anyone be calling me this late unless it was an emergency?

Reluctantly, I scooted out of my consort's embrace and grabbed the phone off the bedside table. The number was Imogen's. I stared at it for a second, dazed, trying to figure out why the hell one of the witches staying under my roof would be phoning me instead of walking across the hall if she wanted to talk. Then I shook myself a little more awake and hit the talk button.

"Imogen?" I said, managing to sound reasonably conscious.

"Hi, Rose," she said in her usual bubbly tone. "I, um, I'm sorry to be calling this late. I just—I'm in a bar in the town, and they're closing soon, and I'm starting to think I probably shouldn't drive myself back."

The more she talked, the more I noticed the slight slur to her words. She giggled as she finished that statement. One of the guests I'd been trying to protect had flown the coop and gotten drunk? When had she even left?

"Okay," I said, sitting up and rubbing the last bits of sleep from my eyes. "What's the bar's name? I'll come get you."

"Ummm... Oh, here, it's on the coaster." Imogen giggled again. "The Caravan. You know that place?"

I couldn't say I'd ever gone drinking in town, but it was small enough that I'd at least passed by most of the businesses. The Caravan was just off the main square, about a block from the cafe that Seth and Kyler's mom baked for.

"I do," I said. "Stay put. I'll be there in ten minutes."

I shoved myself out of bed and cast about for something to wear. Seth straightened up as I pulled on a pair of jeans and a T-shirt that were the first things I'd been able to lay my hands on. "What's going on?" he asked, his drowsiness fading quickly behind his concern.

"Apparently Imogen went out bar-hopping," I said.

"I'm picking her up from The Caravan. It shouldn't take very long."

Seth made a dismissive sound and reached for his own clothes. "I'll come with you."

"You don't have to."

He shot me a look. "You really think I'm going to get a lot of sleep lying here alone wondering how the drunks in town are treating you?"

I wrinkled my nose at him. "They're not going to be *that* bad, are they?"

"It doesn't matter how friendly people are when they come in; there are always at least a couple who've turned into assholes by closing time. We'll take my truck. You can focus on Imogen if she needs it."

"Fine, fine."

We slipped downstairs and out to the driveway where Seth had parked the truck. At least taking it out would make less noise than opening up the garage. No need to wake Gabriel too. Seth hopped into the driver's seat, and I climbed in beside him, clutching my purse. Imogen hadn't phoned again. I wanted to think that was a good sign.

I kept the window down as we drove into town, letting the cool night air wash over me. Most of the buildings were dark, no illumination on the roads except the glow of the streetlamps. When we turned the corner by the bar, its door was open, strains of music and yellow light spilling out.

Seth parked outside, and we headed in together. Imogen was sitting at a table right by the door, her freckled face flushed almost as red as her hair and her shoulders hunched. The few guys still perched at the bar glanced over at us but stayed put.

"Hey," I said. "Ready to go?"

She nodded and got up. Her first step was wobbly, but then she found her feet. I took her forearm just in case. Seth nodded to the guys at the bar. A couple of them nodded back, but one, a young-ish man with coarse black hair, grimaced.

"Your friend is a real tease," he said. "Maybe she should stick to drinking at home if she doesn't like company."

"We're taking her home now," Seth said evenly, but his shoulders tensed.

"I'm sorry," Imogen said when we got outside. "I just... I couldn't sleep. I was feeling so restless. I figured it couldn't hurt to just drive into town and see what was going on down here. Enjoy myself a little."

"It's okay," I said. "I don't know what that jerk was talking about, but you don't owe anyone anything."

I got into the back seat with her, watching for any sign that she was going to need a stop at the side of the road to empty some of that alcohol out of her. But she didn't seem incredibly drunk, just pretty tipsy. She leaned her head against the glass of the window as Seth started the engine.

"How long have you been down here?" I asked her.

"A few hours. I didn't want to bother you. It's such a short drive. I guess I'll have to come back and get my car tomorrow."

"I can come get it," I said. "It's a short walk too. You know it's not that there's anything wrong with the town, right? It's just that you're not as protected outside the estate. If you do want to get out and see the sights, it's better if you wait until I can go with you. Or even Lesley." At least the older witch had some magic of her own.

"I just wanted to see what it'd be like," Imogen murmured. Her eyes closed. For a few moments, I thought she was dozing off. But then she added, "I thought maybe I'd know what I want to do if I could just light my spark, even a little bit."

I glanced over at her. "*Did* you light it?" I asked. That guy had called her a tease. Maybe she'd made out with him a little, and he was peeved that she'd stopped things there.

She shook her head with a jostling of her curls. Her voice turned almost dreamy. "I meant to. We were talking, and he seemed like a nice enough guy. Kind of cute. I could have kissed him. I could have done lots with him. I was thinking about it. But then he leaned in and put his hand on my knee, and I just..." She stopped, her brow furrowing. "What if it ruins me? Being with someone like that. Someone unsparked."

The corner of my mouth quirked up, but my stomach knotted at the same time. "It can't ruin you," I said. "A lit spark is a lit spark. It's not as if the magic can tell who helped you wake it up."

"But who's going to want me?" Imogen said, starting to slur again. "Who's going to want to be my consort if I've been messing around with men who aren't even witching?"

"Anyone who counts won't care at all," I said, but that

wasn't the whole truth and I knew it. I remembered the way my ex-fiancé had sneered when he'd caught me with two of my consorts. How my father had talked about them. Most of the witching world looked down on anyone unsparked. If her aunt and uncle caught wind of a dalliance like that, they'd have one more thing to harangue her about. "You wouldn't have to tell them anyway."

"No. I guess not. But *I'd* know."

She fell silent as we pulled past the gate. We parked close to the house.

"Thank you for picking me up," Imogen said. "I'm sorry again about the trouble. I can get myself to bed— you don't have to worry, really."

She headed to the front door, swaying a little but steady enough that I let her go. I closed the truck door and leaned against it, sweeping my hands back into my hair.

Seth came around to my side and propped himself next to me. "Are you okay?"

"Of course," I said. "It was fine. I told you it would be."

"I just meant the stuff she was saying— I'm sure she wasn't trying to criticize you."

It hadn't even occurred to me that she might be. "I know," I said, feeling suddenly twice as tired. "She was just saying what most of the witching world thinks."

"We don't need to worry about the rest of the witching world," Seth said. "We're fine right here, aren't we?"

"We are." But Imogen's stray comments gnawed at

me all the same. The unfairness of it—that I'd had to fight so hard for my consorts, that even after I had, even if we brought the Frankfords down and could live without that threat hanging over us, there would always be more of the same if on a smaller scale. People in my society lived and breathed those prejudices with about as much thought as they gave to the air around them.

I didn't need the oath to stop me from broadcasting the truth about my consorting. I wouldn't have thought it was smart to shout it out widely anyway.

Even with witches coming to me for shelter and support, when it came right down to it, I was alone.

I shook off that thought. I knew that wasn't literally true. Naomi had never acted like she judged me. And I had my consorts. That was enough.

I twined my fingers with Seth's and walked back to the house with him, wishing I didn't feel as if somehow the Frankfords had already won in the ways that mattered most.

CHAPTER NINE

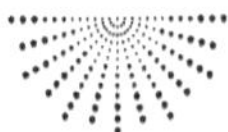

Jin

I wasn't sure I was ever going to feel totally comfortable in Rose's manor house. The place felt too much like the historic buildings I'd wandered around in when I'd traveled across Europe, tagging along on my dad's tours, and nothing at all like the places I'd actually lived in. But adding my own touch in the narrow mural I was painting along the top of the walls got me partway there. The pungent smell of the paint fumes and the streaks of bright color against the reserved beige and ivory brought a little of *me* into the space.

Rose's cousin Naomi was working on the other side of the room, imbuing the glyphs with protective magic. Rose had handled the bedrooms herself, and she would have kept going if Naomi hadn't insisted she take a break.

"One last way I can pitch in before I head back to New York," she'd said. She was leaving this afternoon.

Now, as I dabbed a last bit of paint to the final corner, she stepped back from the wall and sighed. "We don't need this kind of protection back on the Levesque property, but I've got to say, it looks so gorgeous I'm tempted to hire you anyway."

"Hey," I said. "The next time we're out that way, let me know and I'll bring the paints. It probably couldn't hurt to have some extra security, right?"

"I suppose not." She paused, a shadow crossing her expression. "Maybe we're not all that safe. Rose said we shouldn't need to worry... but she didn't think you all would have to be taking precautions like this after whatever she agreed to either, did she?"

"After the way Frankford's guy was poking around, and hearing that the witch from one of the other families had heard something that sounded threatening, she doesn't want to take any chances." I rinsed my brush and carried my set-up carefully down the tall step-ladder. "No one's made any kind of attack since we've been back. And it's been almost a month now."

"But it feels better having as much security as possible in place, doesn't it?" Naomi said.

I didn't like to think of my life that way—like a cage we were building around ourselves to keep the bad guys out, but also in some ways holding us in. But after the battles we'd had to fight just making it back here alive, I couldn't deny we needed it.

"It does," I said. "If you want, I could make some portable pieces, ones you could take back on the plane and hang in whichever rooms you'd want them the most."

Naomi flashed me a grateful smile. "Thanks. That's

really lovely of you to offer. I don't want to distract you from the work you're doing here, though. You're the ones really under fire. And I don't know how much we can trust my Aunt Irene. She'll be poking around after I get back home—you can be sure of that. If she's passing information on to the Frankfords or whoever, trying to stop Rose so the rest of the family doesn't get implicated..." She grimaced and shook her head.

"She still hasn't owned up to tattling on us, huh?" I said.

"Nope. She acted all offended when I even suggested it. But the timing of when she saw my message to my mom and when the enforcers found us... And she really wasn't happy about me going with you guys at all. It makes me sick thinking about it, but what can you do? She's always been a hard-ass. I just figured she'd have more loyalty to Rose as part of the family."

"Family's a strange thing," I said, sorting my supplies back into the larger carrying case I was storing them in at the manor. "People are always making decisions about who counts and who doesn't. I've got a few relatives who don't see me as a full Lyang because my parents raised me totally Americanized. I don't follow fast enough when they're speaking in Korean; I haven't been over to visit the relatives 'back home' often enough. The way I look at it, you pick the people who show they're really going to act like family, and the rest, well, their loss."

"Yeah," Naomi said quietly. "It just hurts. You always want to think your family has the same values you do. For her to not only let this slide but actively help them..." She shuddered. "And I don't even know half of what's going on."

"It's a pretty crappy situation all around."

"I wish I had a better idea what we're up against. Knowing there's this stuff you all know that you can't tell me about, with all the things I already know... It's hard to feel safe like that."

She looked so uneasy right then that I was hit with a pang of guilt that I couldn't tell her more. But I was bound by the oath just as much as Rose was.

"If Rose finds a way around it, you know you'll be the first person she goes to," I said. "There's one good thing that came out of this mess, right? I don't think she's had anyone she can count on outside of us before you two reconnected."

Naomi's smile came back, softer this time. "It's hard to be upset about that part. I'd stay longer, but *my* consort is going to start thinking I've set up my own little harem over here without him."

I chuckled. "You could always bring him along next time. He could join in with your new harem."

She laughed too, her mood lighter. I went to wash my hands with more of a sense of accomplishment.

I had my own family obligation today, but one I didn't mind fulfilling. I'd only seen my mother once since we'd gotten back from our unexpected road trip of sorts, and then just for a chat. We were supposed to be acting like everything was normal. I knew the other guys, the ones with family in town, had been making a point to keeping in regular contact. So when Mom had texted me asking me over for lunch, I'd told her sure.

I'd talked to my dad on the phone, but who knew when I'd see him again. He'd wrapped up his South American tour with the band he was playing bass for and then he'd scored a new gig that had him in an L.A. recording studio on a tight schedule. For as long as I could remember, he'd been out of town at least as often as he was here.

On my way through town, I swung by the bakery and picked up Mom's favorite rye. She'd left the inner door of her bungalow open so the breeze could come through the screen door. I gave it a light rap and stepped inside.

"Hey, Mom."

"Jin!" she called from the kitchen. "On time for once, hmm?" Her tone was gently ribbing.

"And I even brought the bread," I said, ambling over and setting it on the table.

"Oh, perfect, I was just getting down to the heel of my last loaf." She tucked her short bob back behind her ears and ducked to retrieve the fixings from the fridge. "I was thinking we could sit out back on the deck, it's so nice out. The wasps haven't been too bad this year."

"Works for me."

We assembled our sandwiches in tandem, and I carried both plates out to the patio table on the small deck that overlooked the yard, which was half vegetable garden, half flowering extravaganza. Dad might not be here all that often, but his gigs paid well enough that Mom hadn't bothered going back to full-time work since the Hallowells had fired her from their gardening staff. That meant she had plenty of time to work on her own gardens.

Mom brought out iced tea and poured us both a full glass. We sat back and dug in, not saying much at first, just enjoying the meal and the view. The scent rising off the flowers was a perfect perfume, which I guessed was why the wasps liked to hang out back here lots of the time.

"You've talked to your father recently?" Mom said after a while.

"Yep. Sounds like he's having a blast even with how busy they're keeping him in the studio."

"He's always happiest when he's creating something." A fond smile lit Mom's face. Watching her, my gut twisted a little. She never seemed unhappy with the way their relationship worked, but I found it hard to believe she never got lonely, never wished he loved her a little more and the music a little less. The way I felt about Rose, I'd never have gone off without her for months every year.

"You used to be the same way," she added, glancing over at me with a slight narrowing of her eyes that put me on instant alert. My mom had been pretty easy-going in general when I was growing up, but I could spot her strict side coming out in an instant. She didn't usually try to pull it on me these days.

"I still am," I said easily. "I was just doing some painting today." I held up my hand, displaying the flecks of color I hadn't quite managed to wash off.

"Not the way you used to," Mom said. "Don't think I haven't noticed. You've changed in the last couple months. Ever since Rose Hallowell got back into town."

The bread I'd been chewing turned sour in my

mouth. I swallowed it. Mom had never even hinted she had a problem with Rose before. "I don't think Rose being back has changed anything."

"Your father told me you turned down the chance to travel with him like you two used to."

"It was last minute, and I had other plans," I said. Like making sure Rose's asshole ex-fiancé and father didn't take over her life.

"How many of those plans had anything to do with your art?" She peered at me sideways. "I've been by the gallery, and you haven't had it open that I've seen in at least a week."

One of the downsides to having set up shop just a few streets away from my parents' home—it was way too easy for her to keep an eye on my comings and goings if she decided to.

"I'm taking a little time off from the public side," I said. "I'm still *painting*. I'm still working on my art. I couldn't not do that."

"Maybe not," she said. "But have you been pouring your whole heart into it the way you used to? The way your father does with his music?"

No, I hadn't really sat down and lost myself in my studio the way I used to all the time in the past. But I'd had other things on my mind. Sometimes you *had* to let other parts of your life take priority. Did she really not understand that?

"I haven't set it aside," I said. "I just have other things in my life that are important too."

She shook her head. "It worries me, Jin, that's all. To see you losing your artistic passion like that, all for a *girl*."

"I haven't lost anything," I said. My hand tightened around my glass. I set it down without taking another drink. "Mom, I don't want to talk about this anymore. You're making up some huge problem where there isn't one."

She tapped her finger against the table. "It's my job as your mother, no matter how old you are, to watch out for you. And I don't think all the attention you're giving to Rose is good for you. That's all I'm saying."

"Okay," I said, standing up. "I heard you. I don't agree. And I really don't want to keep listening to you talk like this. I'm happy, Mom. That should be what matters to you."

She just stared back at me, unwavering.

I sighed. "I'll talk to you again soon. Hopefully you'll be in a better mood then."

Even though I was pissed off, I still brought my dishes back into the kitchen. Some expectations of behavior were hard to shake.

Outside, I hesitated, not sure where I wanted to go now. Maybe I didn't agree with Mom, but I might have been spending more time at the Hallowell estate than was a good idea in general, as far as murmurs around town went. I could open up the gallery for the rest of the day. Why not? It would make for a good change of pace.

I set off for the two-story building that housed my independent art gallery, composed partly of my works and partly of those by local artists I enjoyed, and my second-floor apartment. An acrid smell tickled my nose. I frowned, glancing up, and noticed smoke streaking across the sky.

What the hell was that from? I grabbed my phone, ready to dial the emergency department, as I hustled over. My eyes started to water with the thickening smell. The streak of smoke turned into a billow.

I rounded the corner and stopped dead. An icy knife of panic cut through me despite the heat wafting through the air.

Flames were leaping from two buildings side by side at the other end of the block, their faces already charred. And one of those buildings was my gallery. My home.

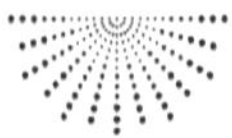

CHAPTER TEN

Rose

"It can't be a coincidence," I said. My stomach churned as I looked at the photographs Ky was flipping through on his laptop. We'd all gathered around the dining room table to go over his findings. He'd hacked into the various networks to nab the fire and police departments' records on the fire at Jin's gallery—the gallery that now wasn't much more than a blackened shell. "There hasn't been a fire that bad in town in the entire time I've lived here. Now there's a huge one, and it just happens to hit Jin's home and workplace? Right after the Frankfords were making those veiled threats?"

"Those bastards," Damon muttered, his hands balled at his sides.

"They shouldn't be able to do anything like that, should they?" Jin said. His usual playful energy was subdued, his expression drawn. Seeing how the loss of all that work had shaken him made me even more queasy. "They swore in the oath not to do or order anything that would hurt us—including our happiness. It's not like it takes much thinking to realize that a person's happiness is partly tied to their home and the things they've made."

He'd lost all the paintings he'd been keeping in his studio and displaying in his gallery. Dozens of pieces of art, some of which I'd never even gotten the chance to see. My jaw clenched.

"What do the reports say?" Seth asked Kyler. "How did the fire start? Are the police thinking arson?"

"They always consider that possibility when an insured property burns," Kyler said. "It looks like they determined it was a freak accident. No one could find any cause of the fire, but it started with a couple of wires inside the wall of the neighboring building. The guy who owns that place just had the wiring inspected six months ago to make sure it was all up to code."

Anger started to burn through my nausea. "That's it," I said. "That's how they got around the oath. They sent a witch to work some magic on the building next door, and the oath didn't stop them because technically it wasn't directly harming us. The witch who did it probably didn't have any clue what the real target was. Those cheating assholes!"

"We can't know for sure that's what happened," Gabriel said in a low voice. "It *could* have been a freak accident. These things happen."

Damon spun on him. "Oh, come on. You can't really believe that these fuckers didn't set this whole thing up."

"I've got to say, I agree with Damon on this one," Ky

said slowly. "I also found..." He clicked through to a different set of photographs of a silver sedan. "I checked the traffic cams at the intersection where people usually come off the highway heading east. This car came into town about an hour before the fire started and headed back just a half hour later. I ran the plates. It's registered to a woman on Frankford's employee list."

For a second, I was so furious I couldn't breathe. "There you go. We couldn't ask for more proof than that. What else would she have been doing popping into town?"

"Checking up on us?" Gabriel suggested, but he didn't sound all that convinced. "It looks bad. But we knew they might try something. Now we need to figure out what we can do for Jin—and how to make sure nothing like this happens to anyone else."

"Other than the art, nothing in the building was irreplaceable," Jin said. "I had back-ups on the cloud of all my important info. I even have pictures of the art I lost."

Not that a photograph was quite the same as having the original paintings and sculptures. I looped my arm around his and leaned my head against his shoulder.

"That doesn't make it okay. They swore that oath. We haven't done *anything* to them, and they're still trying to hurt us any way possible. They—"

My throat closed up with a magical pressure. Someone who wasn't meant to hear the terms of that oath must be nearby. I gritted my teeth and strained to say the words anyway, but my vocal chords wouldn't budge. The oath bound me too tightly.

Footsteps whispered outside the room. Lesley poked her head in. "Is everything all right?" she asked, her eyes widening when she took in our assembled group and our dark expressions.

My stomach twisted tighter. What about her and Imogen? The Frankfords hadn't sworn to leave them alone at all. If they were willing to go this far without even being provoked, where would they stop?

Witches had been killed to cover up their conspiracy. Even witches who'd once been a part of it, like my stepmother.

"We're figuring that out," I said, trying to keep my voice relaxed enough not to worry her more. "No matter what happens, we should at least be safe in here." Between my morning routine of magicking and Jin's new decorations around the house, I didn't think any witch could threaten us without us having plenty of warning to fight back before they did any real damage.

But that didn't protect anything or anyone we cared about outside these walls. I couldn't expect them or us to live inside the estate for the rest of our lives. What about the staff? Were the Frankfords going to target those totally unknowing unsparked people too?

Lesley was still wavering in the doorway. I went over to her, showing as much calm as I could manage even though my emotions were running wild. "Stay in or close to the manor for now, and you'll be fine. If you want to go somewhere else, just let me know, and I'll work out the safest way to do that. All right?"

She gave me a nervous smile. "If it's like that out there, I'm happy staying in here, Rose. Thank you."

She ducked her head and turned back to the hall. I waited until I'd heard the steps stop creaking on her way upstairs, and then I whirled to face the guys. My earlier anger rushed up through the calm front I'd been holding in place.

"It isn't enough," I said.

"What, Rose?" Seth said, reaching to rub my shoulder.

"What we've been doing. Even the new plans we've been making. It isn't enough to just expose them. If we wait until we can do that properly, who knows what they'll do, how many innocent people they'll hurt, in the meantime."

Gabriel had gone still. "Where are you going with this, Sprout?"

The use of his childhood nickname for me cooled my temper for a second—but only for a second. Had they tried to burn down my home here first? All *our* history could have gone up in flames so easily if I hadn't been prepared for them to launch some sort of attack. I'd known I couldn't trust them. The demons in the cave had been monsters, sure, but the real monsters were the people who'd summoned them, who'd used them, who'd trapped other witches into being a part of those schemes.

"They're going to play dirty?" I said. "We can too. We have to fight back, any way we can. Let them see their homes burning to the ground. Destroy the entrance to that damn cave so they can't even get to the portal. *Stop* them, as quickly as we can. Make them regret ever stooping this low."

Damon cracked his knuckles. "We can, right? We never promised not to tear them up like that."

"Rose." Gabriel grabbed my hand. "We'll make them regret it. But we don't have to stoop to their level. You're better than that."

I squeezed his fingers and let them go. "That's what they're counting on. No. They have to see there'll be consequences if they come after us. I won't find a way around the oath like they did. I'll hit them where they never even expected it."

His expression was so fraught I had to add, "I'm not going to *kill* anyone. I can..."

The idea sparked in my head as I looked at that picture of the damp charred ruins of Jin's gallery. I spun around and hurried for the stairs. The guys trailed after me, Kyler closing his laptop with a snap and bringing it with him.

I strode into my father's former office and pawed through the books on the shelves. He had one section where he kept documents and books that were from his various colleagues' external endeavors. I knew he'd shown me it when he'd first gotten it— There.

I grabbed the booklet and slapped it down on the desk. A brochure for an upscale clothing boutique in downtown Portland.

Damon looked at it and raised an eyebrow. "Uh, I'm not sure dress shopping is going to make much of an impact on these bastards."

I rolled my eyes at him. "That's Helen Frankford's shop. The business she runs. She's spent years building it up, cultivating the richest clientele in Portland.

Unsparked dollars count to them even if unsparked people don't. And based on what we've seen in their files, I'd guess she cozies up to anyone who seems to have the sort of business or political influence they need at any given time."

"What are you going to do with that?" Kyler asked.

I tapped the photo on the front of the brochure. It showed the storefront, sleek dresses and a trim suit visible through the glass. "I've been there a few times. I have a good sense of the place. Between that and the picture... I think I can work a magicking from here to there."

"It's the middle of the day," Gabriel said. "Those 'unsparked' people are probably shopping there right now."

And I didn't have any plans to hurt them. My hands clenched and opened. A smile crossed my face. "That's fine. I have the perfect approach. I'll just put out the fire they started. There's a sprinkler system. I can flood the place." Freak out all those posh clients. Destroy all that sensitive fabric. Yes. It didn't come close to paying them back for what they'd done to Jin, but it was the best I could do from here, right now.

If I could do it.

"I'll need space," I said, spreading out my arms. "This is going to take a lot of work." I'd never done a magicking like this, transmitting the energy of the spell through a token like the picture. But it should theoretically work, the same way you could use a voodoo doll to harm a person if you connected it to them properly.

The guys stepped back to the edges of the room. I picked up the brochure, staring hard at the picture, and then clasped it to my chest. Closing my eyes, I summoned the memories from my visits to that place. The faint jasmine scent always drifting through the cool air. The rustling of the dresses as other patrons shuffled through them. The lilting classical music Helen liked to play.

"From me to there," I murmured, my fingers tensing around the brochure. "From me to there."

I swept into the form, picking each move just a step beforehand, finding my flow as I focused on my purpose. All those pipes running through the ceiling. The pressure of all that water. As my spark flared inside me, I imagined it rushing from me into the sprinkler system's trigger point. Wrap around it. Hold it tight. More and more. I wanted to send enough that it would keep that water gushing until the entire space was drenched through.

My feet spun me on the hardwood floor. The power sang through every inch of my body. My lungs seared, my breath stuttered.

Then I jerked to a halt and smacked my hands together with the brochure in between them.

Magic crackled through my veins with a faint popping sensation in my ears. All the energy in my body seemed to wrench away from me. My legs wobbled as a wave of exhaustion surged over me in its wake. But then, just for an instant, I could hear the distant shrieks as the spray poured down on customers and clothes alike.

I sagged, catching myself against the desk. A laugh burst from my mouth. We'd gotten one small sliver of victory.

And this would be only the beginning.

CHAPTER ELEVEN

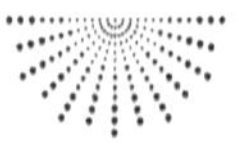

Rose

I spun around Gabriel, sending out a lick of magic to pull him with me, and came to a stop on the magicking room's polished floor at the end of the form. My chest was heaving from the physical exertion, but my spark blazed joyfully in my chest. The strength of our bond, the one between me and my most recent consort, hummed in the air around us.

Gabriel set his hand on my waist and tugged me closer so he could bow his head over mine. His dark red hair was damp along his forehead. The smell of him, darkly mossy with a hint of sweetness, filled my nose. "Are you sure you should be pushing yourself this hard?" he said.

"It's good," I said. "You can feel it, can't you? The way the magic wells up even faster between us?"

"Oh, I can feel it." He dipped his head a little lower,

his lips brushing the sensitive skin between my eyebrows. "I just mean after you extended yourself so much the other day..."

Two days ago, when I'd called down a torrent of rage on Helen Frankford's prized business. It'd taken so much energy casting that spell that I'd been wobbly the whole rest of the day. But I'd felt pretty much normal by the next morning. Better than usual, really, when Kyler had brought me the news reports mentioning the apparently spontaneous flooding at the shop.

All the merchandise ruined. Store closed until further notice. It wasn't half the damage she and her husband had done to Jin, but it should remind them that I knew how to hit back—and I wasn't bound by any promise to protect anything except that one secret of theirs. Maybe while they were scrambling to deal with that loss, they'd have less time for conspiring against other fledgling witches.

"This kind of practice will just help me bounce back faster if I need to cast another spell like that," I said. "Come on. You want to try another one?"

He chuckled. "All right, but I think one more is about all I have in me for today. Are you working all of us this hard?"

"It wouldn't be fair if I gave you special treatment, now would it?" I said, gazing at him through my eyelashes.

Heat lit in his bright blue eyes and where his hand rested against my side. But there was something hesitant under the teasing note in his voice. "Trying to beat us into shape like a little army, are you?"

The words made *me* hesitate for a second, but they weren't exactly wrong. "Anything that makes my magic and our bond stronger... I need to be able to call on as much power as possible, maybe without much warning, if we're going to tackle the Frankfords."

"You're talking like we're going to battle with them instead of trying to expose them. Wasn't destroying her store enough?"

"If it makes them back down. We don't know that yet." I leaned into him, wishing I could completely lose myself in his warmth, that the worries wouldn't follow me there. "And... maybe I've been going about this wrong from the beginning. Always trying to do things as much by the rules as possible. Trying to rely on justice and fair play. It's never worked. I gain a little ground and then they hit back even harder."

"But we've won," Gabriel said. "*You've* won. Eventually we'll win the whole war, without it becoming an actual war."

"How long is that going to take, though? It's not just me. All the other witches they're hurting or might be, while we're poking around at files, doing our best to scrounge up even a little evidence we can use... I'm not saying I think we should do anything *cruel*."

Gabriel's hand stroked up and down my back. "What are you saying, Rose?"

"I guess just... I want to be ready. For *anything* I might have to do. I'm just one witch, and Frankford has a couple dozen families on his side, some of them powerful ones, not to mention the demons and whatever power they offer."

"It's not just you," he said gently. "You have the other witches who've come here. They'd help if you asked them. And you have us. You always have us."

My throat tightened. I hugged him and tipped my head up for a kiss. He offered that without hesitation, his fingers teasing into my hair as the heat of his mouth washed through me. I gripped his shirt and eased up on my toes to kiss him even harder.

The memory of kissing another guy in here tickled up in the back of my head. The things I'd talked about with Jin, after. When we eased apart, just a few inches, I asked, "Do you still have that page from my book? The one I called you back here with?"

Until he'd shown up that day, I hadn't known for sure he even still had that token I'd given him. While the other four guys had stayed in town, Gabriel had been gone for years when I'd first gotten back. It'd been too painful for him to stay after his father's depression and suicide.

But he'd been missing from a group, like a hole no amount of closeness between the rest of us could fill. I'd reached out to him, urging him to return to us, with the faint glow of magic I'd managed to kindle with the other guys before we'd been officially consorted. And he'd shown up a couple of weeks later with the folded page in his hand.

Jin didn't have his page anymore. It would have burned up with everything else in that fire. That thought sent a jab of bitterness through me. I hoped I'd ruined at least one thing really dear to Helen Frankford's heart too.

"Of course I do," Gabriel said. "It's tucked away in

my wallet right now. What, did you think I was going to throw it out?"

A blush warmed my face. "Well, no."

He kissed my cheek. "It brought me back to you. I'd like to know it always could again."

I cupped his face and brought his lips to mine. A sharper desire rang through me as our mouths melded together. Making love with more than one of my consorts together was something special, but sometimes it was a thrill to focus all my attention on just one of them.

"Maybe more practice can wait," I murmured. "Would you care to join me in the master bedroom? I have an, um, engine that could use revving."

Gabriel cracked up with a sputter of startled laughter. Before I could join in, he was kissing me again. "You," he muttered affectionately. He swept me off my feet into his arms as if he planned on carrying me to the bedroom.

"Gabriel," I said, half pleased, half protesting. We did still have to keep in mind appearances for the staff.

"I know." He stopped when he reached the door, kissing me up against it, his hand easing over my hip. Then he set me down. "Let's make sure the coast is clear."

I edged open the door and peeked out. No one in the upstairs hall. No sound of anyone puttering around up here. I grinned and grabbed Gabriel's hand, pulling him with me.

We were two steps from the bedroom door when the buzzer for the gate sounded from below.

I stopped with a groan. The chances that whoever

had come calling wanted to see anyone other than me were slim to none.

Gabriel kissed the top of my head. "We'd better go find out who it is," he said, his voice easy but his body tensed. It could be someone Frankford had sent again. It could be another investigator from the Assembly. The list of bad possibilities was a lot longer than the list of good ones.

I peered down the drive from the window at the front of the house, but I didn't recognize the car: a navy sedan with styling that looked at least ten years out of date. Whoever had reached out to signal the buzzer was hidden behind the reflections on the windshield now.

Frowning, I headed downstairs. Gabriel came with me, falling back at the sight of the single member of my current cleaning staff just emerging from the living room. Imogen bounded out of the kitchen a moment later.

"Who's here now?" she asked, her bright red curls bouncing around her face.

"I don't know," I said. "Why don't you stay in here until I figure that out?"

The younger witch nodded sharply. We'd had a brief talk earlier about which places were and weren't necessarily safe. I worried about her more than Lesley, who could have defended herself magically at least a little. I wasn't sure how brightly the other witch's spark was still lit since her consort's death, but it was at least kindled. Imogen had never been consorted at all.

The camera feed by the gate control, which had blinked on at the buzz, showed our visitor was still in the car. Bracing myself, I pushed open the door and hurried down the front drive.

She got out when I was halfway there: a tall skinny woman in a slim pantsuit, her posture elegant but a little stiff. A few streaks of gray wove through her cloud of frizzy brown hair. She bit her lip and then seemed to catch herself, releasing it, as I got closer. She looked about as old as my Aunt Ginny, Naomi's mother: mid-forties, maybe. But there was a weariness in her eyes that struck me as much older than that. My chest clenched.

"Can I help you?" I said.

Her gaze burrowed into me. "Lady Hallowell?" she said. "You're the one taking in witches who need asylum?"

No one had put it that way before, but I guessed that was what I was doing. "Yes," I said. "Is that what you're here for? Are you okay?" The longer I looked at her, the more I got the impression that the stiffness in her stance was the only thing holding her upright—that if she'd relaxed for a second, she might have collapsed.

She hesitated, and then she said, "Yes. Yes, I think so. I think I'd better come in— If it's all right."

I couldn't see anything threatening about her. But recent events made me even more cautious. "I just need to be sure—will you offer a truth-magicking? Just to confirm why you're here."

She nodded as if she'd expected that. A hint of power crackled into her next words. "I give my oath that I mean no one here any harm. I'm here because I had to get away from... from what was happening to me."

The magic twanged off-key with those last words in a

way that jarred against my nerves. I swallowed hard. She had a spell binding her from talking about "what had happened"—I could feel it. A sudden certainty swelled inside me.

"They've used you, haven't they?" I murmured. "At the Cliff..."

A flash of panic crossed her face, so stark and raw I almost wished I hadn't said anything. That was confirmation enough. I hit the control to open the gate.

"Thank you," she said, sinking back into the driver's seat. "I don't want to cause you any trouble. I—I cast a spell to cover my tracks. They shouldn't be able to tell I've come here, even if they're watching."

So they couldn't bring her back to more of whatever they'd already done to her. "It's no trouble at all," I said firmly. I backed up to give her room to drive in, horror reverberating through me.

They'd used her a lot, the Frankfords and their faction. Drained her almost dry. How often had she faced the demons in the portal, been forced to contend with their nausea-inducing power?

That could have been me. If Dad had succeeded in his plans, if he'd managed to rope me into that deadly consorting with Derek or anyone he'd found to replace him... In another twenty years, I might have looked like she did now.

I glanced back at Gabriel, who'd been waiting near the garage. The same understanding was etched on his face. "Maybe I'd better talk to her alone," I said. After the way her consort must have treated her, I didn't know how much she'd want to see any male face.

He bobbed his head. "I'll be in my apartment if you need me."

I waited close by the car as the woman got out in case she needed any physical support. She walked toward the house at a slow and stiff but steady pace. A few times, her head twitched around to check the gate now closed behind us.

"I'm not sure..." she said. "I think the spell I worked will be enough. But you never know. They have so many ways..."

"It doesn't matter," I said. "You're here now. They can't do anything about that. What's your name?"

"Thalia Ainsworth," she said.

I stopped in my tracks at the bottom of the front steps. "Ainsworth?" I said. "You're not—Tom Ainsworth's wife?" He was another of my father's associates, not as close as the Frankfords or the Almeidas, but he'd been at many of our Portland gatherings. His wife and consort, he'd always claimed in a fond sort of way, preferred to stay home and read, she disliked socializing so much. I'd envied her. But that wasn't why he'd kept her out of the public eye, clearly.

I should have realized. I'd seen his name in the Frankfords' files but not his consort's.

Her lips pressed into what was only a smidgeon of a smile. "That I am. At least until I can sever that bond officially."

She'd started to sway a bit where she was standing. I grasped her elbow to usher her up the steps. "Okay. Why don't you just rest for a bit, and then we'll figure out what we can do for you?" Imogen poked her head into the hall as we came in, and I motioned her back. I wasn't sure how Thalia would react to meeting more strangers right now.

"There isn't much to do," Thalia murmured, almost dreamily. "They take the power... They want to be like us. Men aren't meant to be witches."

I almost halted again in shock. Was she saying that the men were trying to take—or did take—the demons' power right into themselves? So they could work a sort of magic of their own?

"Is that what they do in the cave?" I said cautiously.

She opened her mouth and winced. "I can't... I can't really talk about it."

I knew that feeling too well.

"I know. I'm sorry. Here, we've got another bedroom free upstairs. We'll see how much we can talk when you're feeling up to it. For now, just focus on recovering."

If she even could recover from what they'd put her through. As I helped her up the stairs, the emotions churning inside me squeezed into a hard ball of fear —and rage.

How dare they do this to any witch? And every second I let it continue, I was helping *them*.

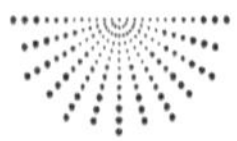

CHAPTER TWELVE

Seth

Maybe fixing up other people's houses wasn't how I wanted to spend the rest of my life, but there was still something comforting about the smell of pine sawdust and the feel of the solid wood against my hands. I hefted another board into place, holding it while my father drilled in the screws. He stepped past me to the other side to repeat the task and then nodded.

"There. That's the end of that." He motioned to the truck parked in the driveway. "Would you grab the first packs of insulation?"

"Are you using that scratch as an excuse to slack off?" I said jokingly. A bandage was wrapped tight around his left wrist. The truth was, from what I'd heard, it was more than a scratch. He'd needed ten stitches where he'd lost his grip on the saw for a second. If his reflexes had been any slower, he could have lost his whole hand. But he'd ribbed me enough growing up that I figured it was my job to pay him back when I could.

He grinned at me. "Doctor's orders! I have to admit it's easier to take it easy when you're around."

His voice was light, but a prickle ran through my chest at what he'd left unsaid. I hadn't been there to actually see his accident because I'd dropped down to three days a week working with the family business instead of five. The other free days I'd been spending my usual work time visiting property offices, checking out blueprints—basically digging up everything I could about every property the Frankfords and their known associates owned. If there was a gap we could exploit to expose them there, I was going to find it.

But that had meant Dad was relying a little more on the apprentice he was training in.

I hefted a bale of insulation out of the truck and carried it over, setting it with a thump by the frame of the addition we were building. Right now the structure didn't look like much more than a wooden skeleton, but when we were done, the Nelsons would have a whole new family room off the back of their house.

They'd scheduled the reno for while they were visiting relatives out of state so they didn't have to deal with the noise and the mess while we did our work. There were positives and negatives to absent clients. No spontaneous offers of free coffee or donuts, sure. But also no one peering over our shoulders making suggestions based on approximately zero knowledge of construction.

"What have you been up to the last few days anyway,

Seth?" Dad said as he joined me. "I know something's obviously keeping you very busy."

I weighed my words before answering. Kyler had mentioned our mom laying into him a bit about the time he'd been spending with Rose—and that he'd hinted I might be seeing her too. She'd probably passed that information on to Dad. But he wasn't the type to outright pry about my love life.

"Just some independent projects," I said. "Pretty intensive stuff, but mostly research and planning at this stage."

"Not anything you can discuss with your old man?" he said a little teasingly.

"That's right," I said, matching his tone. "Top secret. If I told you, I'd have to kill you."

He laughed and pulled up his mask as he leaned over the bale of insulation. It muffled his voice, but I could still hear him clearly enough. "Well, I'm glad you've found something of your own to occupy yourself with. I can't imagine you really wanted to spend the next twenty years with your dad for a boss. But I do miss having you on hand for some of these jobs. You're still the best employee I've ever had."

A knot of emotion formed in my chest. "You've been a damn good boss too," I said. "The whole dad thing aside. But do you really figure you're still going to be at this in twenty years? What about retiring?"

He laughed. "Oh, Lord, can you imagine? I'd be so bored—I'd drive your mother crazy around the house. I can already picture it. No, I'll make it thirty more if I can still handle the tools well enough when I'm eighty."

I rolled my eyes at him with a shake of my head, but I was smiling behind my own mask. It *was* hard imagining Dad just sitting around at home without anything to build or remodel. He'd probably end up refitting the whole house. They'd end up with five stories and ten additions and no more back yard.

We worked in silence for several minutes as we fitted the insulation into place along the one wall. The sky was overcast but not too thickly clouded—just enough to press the summer heat down on us. My breath turned the air inside my mask even more humid. Sweat trickled along the side of my face and down my back, only cooling me a bit in the sluggish breeze.

"We'll want to cover this whole area up before we leave tonight," Dad said, stepping back to survey our work so far. "That haze could turn into storm clouds in a blink."

"The extra tarp is in the truck," I said.

He pointed a playful finger at me. "This is why I need you around. You think of these things."

He took another step backwards, turning to where the new back door would be, and the frame shifted with a sharp cracking sound.

"Dad!" I leapt toward him instinctively, but the whole back end of the addition was already collapsing in on him. Several pounds of hard wood battered his head and back. He lurched and crumpled under them.

One of the boards clipped my shoulder. I dodged and threw myself forward again, grasping the fallen slabs at the top of the heap. The splintered ends rasped against each other.

Dad groaned. I tossed one and then another board aside, heaving them off him as quickly as I could. My lungs were so clenched up I could hardly force air into them. "Dad, are you okay?" I called.

He didn't answer me. His face had gone slack where he was slumped on the ground. His chest was still rising with halting breaths, but blood was seeping from a blow to his temple where his head had hit the concrete foundation, and more was trickling through his hair from wounds I couldn't see. My heart stuttered painfully. No. Fuck, no. We'd just been talking about thirty more years.

I hauled the last few boards covering him out of the way. He still hadn't moved. I moved to kneel beside him, to grasp his arm, and then hesitated. What if I hurt him more by accident?

I fumbled in my pocket, almost forgetting to yank down my mask before I whipped my phone to my ear. 9-1-1. I'd never needed to use that number before today.

A responder answered with a decisive even voice. "What is your emergency?"

"My dad. We were doing some construction work, and a bunch of the frame fell on him. He's unconscious—bleeding..." I couldn't tell if I was making much sense.

Her next words drifted through my head as I answered her questions automatically. There wasn't room for much in there except for the thudding of my pulse and the image of Dad sprawled motionless beside me.

"Don't try to move him," the woman said. "That could exacerbate any injuries. It's a good sign that he's breathing. If you've got something reasonably clean you can press to any wounds that are bleeding to stop the flow, do that. Otherwise, hang tight and be ready to reassure him if he comes to. Don't let him try to get up until the paramedics arrive. The ambulance is on its way."

A good sign that he was breathing. I held onto that as I squatted down next to my father. I wrapped a spare shirt from the truck around his head as tightly as I dared, and then I couldn't do anything for him except wait. Wait and watch his chest hoping it kept rising.

My gaze slid to the remains of the addition's frame. How the hell had that collapse even happened? Dad was incredibly careful about the wood he used, and he had a good supplier. I couldn't believe we could have built that whole frame without noticing there was something wrong with our materials.

Looking at the strewn boards around us, I couldn't see any sign of a flaw in them. No lines of rot, nothing mis-cut. They should have been perfectly sound. There was no way it made sense for them to have just snapped like that.

A chill washed over me. No, there wasn't any way in the regular world they should have broken like that. But I knew now that the world I'd used to live in wasn't the only one that existed. A witch had come into town last week to start a freak fire next to Jin's gallery. I was willing to bet everything I owned that there was some spell that could make wood act like it'd rotted through.

The Frankfords again. Who else could it be? How had they skewed that spell to avoid showing they were targeting us?

A deeper sliver of cold pierced my gut. Had Dad's first accident with the saw even *been* an accident, or had they meddled there too? It was the first injury bad enough to require a doctor that he'd had in at least a decade.

That'd happened before the fire. They hadn't managed to really hurt him, so they'd tried again, weaseling their way around their oath one way or another? The more I thought about it, the more that idea rang true. My jaw tensed.

They still hadn't won. He was hurt, but he was alive. The doctors would patch him up at the hospital.

I *had* to believe that.

The wail of the siren sounded in the distance. I glanced at the phone I was still clutching. I needed to call Mom so she could meet us at the hospital. And Ky?

I hesitated. There wasn't any reason to worry him yet. What could he do anyway? I'd listen to what the paramedics said. If it seemed really serious, I'd call him over. Otherwise, I could at least save him some of the stress.

The ambulance screeched to a halt outside the Nelsons' house. Feet thumped up the drive to where I was crouched. Two of the paramedics were carrying a stretcher. I pulled back as they knelt around Dad, checking him over.

"He's been unconscious since the accident?" one of them asked me.

I nodded, my jaw tight. "He hasn't moved at all."

I restrained a wince as they lifted him onto the stretcher. No one was saying anything about how serious they thought this was. One of them waved to me as they hefted Dad up.

"Are you riding with us?"

"Yeah," I managed to rasp.

"Then come on. The faster we get him to emergency, the better shape he'll be in."

I followed them into the back of the ambulance and listened to the doors swing shut with a clang that sounded way too final.

CHAPTER THIRTEEN

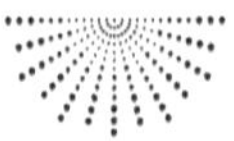

Rose

I looked at the grandfather clock farther down the hallway. Its steady ticking echoed through the wide space. It was twenty minutes past the hour.

"Seth isn't usually late," I said. If anything, he was the most punctual of the guys. Jin and Kyler were prone to getting absorbed in whatever they were working on, art or some new line of research. Damon liked to flaunt social norms. And Gabriel didn't have to try all that hard, since he lived just across the driveway.

Ky checked his phone. "I texted him, but he hasn't replied. He's probably on his way right now. He's a stickler for leaving the phone alone when he's driving too."

Damon shifted his weight from one foot to the other, his shoulders slightly hunched in his loose tee. "Do you think we should get started without him? You snooze, you lose."

Gabriel shot him a half smile where he was leaning against the wall. "I think that would kind of defeat the purpose of the get-together. The whole idea is to see if we can work those practice forms with all of us together instead of just one-on-one."

"We made do with four before you came along, in case you don't remember," Damon said archly, but there was no venom in the comment. Gabriel just shook his head.

Jin was rolling his shoulders, his lean muscles flexing where his paint-flecked tank top bared them. "Are you getting stiff from the painting?" I asked him.

"A little," he said. "But I think those extra touches I added were worth it. I was wondering if there's some way I can start working on the wall around the estate... But I guess any paint on the stones would stand out as something strange."

I considered that possibility. "True, but we could do tokens like we have before. I could bury them around the property. That would give my protections an extra boost without anyone even seeing them. And we could make them really simple since no one will see them, so you wouldn't have to work too hard."

"Perfect!" He pointed a finger at me. "That's tomorrow's project, then."

Ky glanced at the door and then his phone again, frowning. A nervous twitch wriggled into my stomach. I pulled out my own phone to scroll back through my messages. Yes, I'd checked with Seth that he could get here at six. He'd said it'd be no problem, that he should be finishing his shift with his dad at five.

What if something had happened to him? Something that had left him so incapacitated he couldn't even contact us?

"Can you try your dad?" I said to Ky. "They were supposed to be working together most of the day. At least then we'd know he was okay until recently."

"I already texted him too," Ky said. "No answer there either. But that's less surprising. Dad still hasn't gotten totally used to the whole cell phone thing. We're lucky if he's got the battery charged half the days of the week."

I paced from one end of the hall to the other. "If they've hurt *him*..."

"We don't know that's what happened," Gabriel said in a low, smooth voice. "They shouldn't be able to do that. He's only a little late."

Damon's head jerked up. "Hey," he said. "That oath —does it cover your father too? He shouldn't be able to hurt any of us, right?"

A cold prickle shot down my back. "It should cover all the families allied with the Frankfords. Even if they were sticking to the barest letter of the law, that would include everyone named in the files. My father's in there."

His shoulders came down, but not completely. "What about that Courtland guy?"

Master Courtland, my former tutor, had been conspiring with my stepmother, sharing research on how she might twist my consort ceremony so the fiancé she and Dad had chosen would have direct control over my magic. I didn't know what Master Courtland's stake in the conspiracy was, or if he even knew the full extent of it. His name hadn't come up anywhere else. But Dad clearly had the older witching man in his pocket.

"My father couldn't order him to do anything that would hurt us directly," I said. "And neither of them have any magic of their own to attack us with. Why are you asking about them?"

"I just remembered," Damon said. "Yesterday I was cruising by the old guy's house and I saw him in the yard with your dad. Just talking, but it's not like I trust anything they'd be talking about."

Before he'd even finished speaking, I'd bristled. Snuff my spark, what was my father doing around town?

He wasn't forbidden from visiting a friend near the estate. Technically he wasn't even forbidden from coming here and requesting entrance—he just couldn't waltz right in like he owned the place, because he no longer did.

Like Damon, I couldn't imagine any good reason for him to be poking around. If he'd wanted to see Master Courtland, he could have invited him somewhere else. How long had he spent in town? Was he *still* here, just a few minutes' drive away?

"If you see him again, it's fine with me if you make it clear he's not welcome," I said. "However you feel like doing that."

Damon grinned sharkishly. "Oh, angel, that's an invitation I'm not likely to turn down."

Gabriel raised his eyebrows. "Is that really a good idea?"

"It's a horribly bad idea for him to come anywhere near here," I said tersely. The memory of the last time I'd talked to my father swam up—the way he'd talked as if what he'd tried to do for me was beyond his control, not taking any responsibility—the way he'd sneered at my consorts as if *they* were unworthy of me.

The way he'd looked at me when I'd bluffed that I'd release the demon to do whatever it wanted with him, as if he'd really thought I was that stupid and that sick-minded.

Suddenly I felt nearly as queasy as I had in the cave with that thing and with him. Why couldn't he just leave me the fuck *alone*?

Imogen appeared at the bottom of the stairs, which she must have descended more quietly than usual. "Rose?" she said hesitantly.

"We're in the middle of something," I snapped. A jab of guilt hit me immediately, sharpened by the way her eyes widened. Most of my anger deflated. I stepped toward her. "I'm sorry. What is it?"

"I just... I was hoping I could talk with you." Her voice was unusually quiet too. Now that I was paying more attention, it was hard not to notice how subdued she was in general. Even her bright red curls hung a little limp against her shoulders. "If now isn't a good time, though, it can totally wait."

"No. I—" I glanced at the guys.

"Go ahead," Gabriel said. "We're still waiting for Seth anyway. If he hasn't shown up soon, we'll split up and scout out the roads between here and the house and wherever he was working."

I smiled at him with a rush of gratitude and motioned for Imogen to come with me into the parlor. Having seen how nervous she looked, I closed the door behind us for privacy.

"What's going on?" I asked. "Did something happen?"

"Sort of." The young witch slumped into one of the armchairs, her elbows splaying over the sides. "My aunt and uncle have been blowing up my phone since I left. I was just ignoring them... But my aunt sent a text saying there was some kind of emergency with my sister."

My pulse stuttered. "Is she okay?"

"Yes." Imogen grimaced. "I ended up calling her and asking what was going on, trying to get her to let me talk to my sister—*she's* not the problem there, she's only fifteen; if I could have, I'd have brought her with me. It turned out my aunt was just making shit up to try to convince me to come back. And then once she had me on the phone she went on and on about how I'm embarrassing the family and I should be grateful for all the time and energy they've put into finding me a match and what am I even doing with myself and..." She pressed her hands over her ears as if to block out the voices she could no longer hear anyway.

"That's tough," I said quietly, wishing I could say more. "You're sure there was something off about the potential consorts they were bringing around, though, aren't you?"

"I don't know. Maybe I was just being too picky. I mean, Aunt Florence and Uncle Sherman have never acted like they cared about me like parents, but they're *not* my parents, so... They got saddled with me and my sister when I was only nine and she was just two. They weren't planning on having kids. What if they *are* just doing the best they can?"

"I don't know." I propped myself against the side of one of the other chairs. "I don't think someone with totally good intentions would try to use your sister's well-being as bait."

"True. But, I mean, I am going to have to find a consort sooner and not later. If I look like an ungrateful hysteric, that's not going to make it easier." Imogen let out a huff of a sigh.

Spark help me, if only I could have brought her up to the room where Thalia Ainsworth was still recovering—hardly talking, mostly just sleeping restlessly and eating and expressing how thankful she was to be here—and told her that was the future her aunt and uncle had planned for her.

I gritted my teeth and then forced my jaw to relax.

"Look," I said. "Everything you've told me about the two of them gives me a bad feeling. It reminds me of how my father and stepmother were acting—and they were trying to tie me to a consort who would have used me for his and their selfish ends. I don't want that for you. What you do, whether you stay here, is up to you, always. But you have to know I don't think you're the slightest bit wrong to be worried. I'd say get your sister out of there as soon as you can too."

Imogen gazed back at me thoughtfully. "And where do I go from there? I just live here with you until I hit twenty-five and lose my magic?"

"That's up to you," I said. "But you could still look for a consort yourself. I'd be happy to help any way I can. It doesn't have to—"

It doesn't have to be a witching man, you know, I'd wanted to say. But the oath clamped my throat shut around revealing that.

Of course, Imogen had been living here. She had eyes, and while I wasn't allowed to discuss the status of my relationship with my consorts, I hadn't tried to hide it from her or the other witches under asylum like I had the staff. Her comments after she'd gone to that bar showed she'd figured out that an unsparked guy would light at least a little magic in her.

"The five of them, they're *all* your consorts, aren't they?" she murmured. "And they're just regular guys from the town? Not witching families at all?"

I wet my lips and gave her a meaningful look. "I can't talk about that."

For a second, hope lit her face. Then she sagged back into the chair. "I don't know. I just don't know. If I leave my aunt and uncle for good, then I've got no claim on their estate either. Consort with an unsparked man? Moldy cinders, I might as well be unsparked too, for all I'd be part of witching society then."

That was true. Maybe I'd been too harsh on her, blaming her hesitation completely on prejudice. I hadn't thought through all the consequences she'd face. I'd had an estate waiting for me, enough properties in the family that I could simply shunt my dad off to one that was hours away—not that he'd stayed there. For someone with so much less means...

"You'd figure something out," I said. Anything was better than ended up drained and haunted like Lady Ainsworth. "*We'd* figure something out, if you stayed here. There have to be better options."

Imogen gave me a small tight smile. "It's easy to say that," she said. "Not so easy to just make those options appear. Sometimes your only choices are not-so-great ones. I guess I just have to pick which not-so-great one I can stomach."

My stomach balled. *No*, I wanted to say. *Don't give up*. But who was I to tell her that when I had so much more than her and I still couldn't keep my consorts and their families safe?

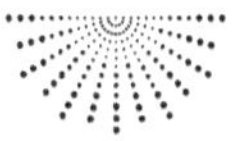

CHAPTER FOURTEEN

Gabriel

I watched the door close behind Rose and the younger witch with a twist in my gut. She'd simmered down, but for a few moments there... I'd hardly felt as if that was the woman I knew.

"I've never seen Rose snap at someone like that before," I said, keeping my voice low.

Damon shrugged. "She's got a lot of crap to deal with right now. Who can blame her?"

"I know she's stressed, but..." I glanced at him. "Did you think you'd ever hear her encouraging you to go off on someone like that? Don't you remember how she freaked out when you had your friends rough up Derek?"

Damon's face darkened for a second. "That asshole deserved it. And they're not my friends. They're hardly even work associates at this point."

I raised a conciliatory hand. "That's not what I'm

talking about. I'm not getting on your case about what you did. My point is, back then she was horrified that you took things that far. Now she's saying go ahead and do whatever you want to scare off her dad?"

"Desperate times call for desperate measures."

Kyler's frown deepened as he looked up from his phone. "No, Gabriel's right. We've been through a lot of crap, sure, but it's getting to her more than it used to. I don't like hearing her talk that way either. But—maybe that's how cutthroat we all need to be thinking right now?" He let out a sharp breath and rubbed his forehead. "If I could just find a point of leverage we could really use to end this, it wouldn't matter anymore. You'd think with all those files there'd be *something* I could work with."

"You're doing everything you can," Jin said. "And so is Rose. I trust her judgment. This is her world a lot more than it is ours."

"It is." I hesitated. "I just never imagined I'd see Rose be that vicious. You weren't there in the cave the last time we saw her father. She trapped him in there with that demon, with no way to call for help. He could have died in there if he hadn't been found. And she didn't seem to care at all."

"Why should she care about that prick?" Damon said. "He tried to force her to be chained to that thing somehow, doing whatever he and the rest of those shitheads want."

"There's a difference between not caring about someone, even being furious with them, and actively doing something that could kill them," Kyler said.

"Exactly," I said. "I know she's been under a ton of pressure. I just hate that it seems to be pushing her into becoming someone who'd be that cruel. That can't be what she'd have wanted."

The first time Rose had tried to take on her father directly, she'd come to me freaking out that she might be enjoying the thought of briefly hurting him and his colleagues too much. Worried about the darkness her power might bring out in her. Back then, I'd reassured her that she was justified, that it made sense for her to want to hit back, that I knew she'd never take things so far.

That'd only been a handful of weeks ago. Could I have said the same thing now? She'd done things since then that I never would have believed her capable of.

That uncertainty sat like a jagged lump in my stomach.

"We end this fast, and then she won't be under all that pressure," Damon said. "Simple as that."

"Simple enough to *say*..." Ky said. He checked his phone again. "Still nothing from Seth. Maybe we should head out and look for him like you suggested, Gabriel. He's more than half an hour late now. Not even a message—that's not like Seth at all."

I nodded, setting the other more ephemeral worries aside. "Do you know where he was working with your dad before he was supposed to come here?"

"Yeah, the Nelsons' place, over on Haven St. I can swing by there."

"I can go around by his house," Jin said. "Check things out there."

"Maybe we should pair up," I said. "It'll take a little

longer to cover as much ground, but when we don't know if he might be in some kind of trouble, extra manpower seems like a good precaution."

My hand lifted to brush over the token Jin had painted and Rose had imbued with magic, which hung from its leather string around my neck. We all still wore them under our shirts as another precaution—a little extra magical protection. They couldn't protect us from everything, though. We'd gotten hurt in the skirmishes on the road last month.

No wonder Rose felt as if she had to take on the Frankfords and their allies all by herself. How much *could* the rest of us even do?

Damon looked like he was about to argue—I wasn't sure he knew how to take suggestions without automatic resistance—but Ky was already nodding. He started toward the door. "That makes sense. We don't want to get careless. Rose *needs* us."

Those last few words shut Damon up. He loped to catch up. Kyler was just reaching for the door when it swung open from the outside.

Seth stepped into the hall. His T-shirt and jeans were so dirt-streaked it was obvious he hadn't changed since work. He had a smudge on his cheek, and his expression was weary. There was something so defeated in the big guy's stance that my heart skipped a beat before I'd had the chance to be relieved he was okay.

Rose darted out of the room she'd ducked into with Imogen, a smile springing to her face. It fell as she took in Seth's expression.

"What happened?" Ky said. He had to be able to read

his twin's demeanor even better than the rest of us could. "Where've you been?"

Seth swiped a hand over his short hair, only managing to rumple it more. "I'm sorry," he said. "I was going to call when I realized I'd be late, but the battery died on my phone, and I was already on my way... I was at the hospital in Burns. They had to take Dad there."

We all stiffened. Ky's hand twitched as if he'd almost dropped the phone he was still clutching. "Dad? Is he—"

"He's okay. At least he's going to be. They think." Seth cleared his throat. "The addition we were working on—the frame collapsed on him. He took a pretty bad blow to the head, and his shoulder is messed up... They had him sedated for most of the time, but when he came to he was talking okay. If I'd thought there was any chance he wouldn't make it I'd have called you to come."

"You should have called me anyway," Ky said. "Jesus. What the hell— How did that even happen?"

Seth's gaze slid to Rose. Her mouth tensed into a flat line.

"Magical interference," she said. "Like the fire."

"I looked at the boards," Seth said. "I know how my dad works. I was there with him for most of the construction. There's no way it should have collapsed like that under any normal circumstances."

"Those *bastards*," she spat out. "They could have killed him. They could have killed *you*. They were probably hoping they would. They're just not going to be satisfied, are they? Not until they destroy everything— No. If they dare set foot anywhere near here again—"

She halted, her hands clenching at her sides and a

light so fierce it unnerved me coming into her eyes. "There is someone here we can get answers from, isn't there?" she said. "Let's take everything he can give us."

She swiveled toward the door.

"What are you talking about, Rose?" I said. "What are you going to do?"

"My father thinks it's worthwhile consulting with Master Courtland," she said. Fury radiated from her taut voice. "I think it's time I had a talk with him too."

I wasn't letting her go there alone, not in that state. "Let me drive," I said quickly. "You can concentrate on what you're going to ask him, the best approach to take."

"Oh, I know what approach I'm taking," she muttered, but she nodded before she stalked out.

"If he knows something about what happened to my dad, I want to be there," Seth said.

"Same," Kyler put in, even though his eyes were nervously wide.

Damon cracked his knuckles. "I'm not missing this."

Jin gave the rest of us a tightly bemused smile. "Rather than squeeze myself into the party, maybe I'd better stay here. Hold down the house. So I can let you know if they launch some kind of direct attack."

Rose was already halfway to the garage. I squeezed Jin's shoulder. "Good thinking. Tell Rose's guests to stay in the house too, all right?"

He gave me a quick salute.

I hurried across the front yard to get the Buick that was Rose's favorite ride. She dropped into the passenger seat next to me, and the other guys piled into the back. "Are you sure he's even home right now?" I said. If she had time to cool off a little before this confrontation, maybe it'd go better.

"If he's not, we'll just come back later," she said, leaning back in the seat with her arms crossed tight in front of her. "But he'll probably be there."

I wished the drive to Courtland's house took more than a few minutes. Far too soon, I had to pull up outside the little country house that was much less imposing than Rose's manor.

Rose was pushing open the car door in an instant, striding past the wooden gate and up to the front door. By the time the rest of us had clambered out, she was already knocking on it a second time.

Courtland's thick voice carried from the other side. "All right, all right, I'm com—" He froze the second he opened the door wide enough to see Rose.

Rose didn't even try to talk. With a jerk of her elbow and a twist of her hand, she shoved him backward into his house with a burst of magical energy. My throat closed up. I dashed after her.

When we reached the front hall, she had Courtland on the floor in the kitchen. "You can talk to my dad, you can talk to me," she said, looming over him, her hand braced at her side ready to cast another spell. Power crackled through the air, so potent it raised the hairs on my arms. "I think you owe me plenty. What are the Frankfords and the rest of them planning? Who are they going to come after next?"

"I don't know," Courtland said, his voice wavering. He'd flung his arm across his face protectively. What did *he* think she was going to do? "They don't discuss those plans with me. I'm not officially aligned with anyone."

"You were aligned enough with my father to help him figure out how to turn me into a slave," Rose snapped.

"I'm telling you, I don't—"

She wrenched her hand to the side, and his voice cut off with a flinch and a choked sound. My stomach lurched. She'd hurt him.

Rose's hair lifted from her shoulders as if stirred by a private wind. "I'm done hearing excuses," she said. "Their people come after mine, I come after theirs. And you're theirs enough to count. What do you know about the security on the Frankford properties? Who else has evidence of what you all have been doing?"

"Nothing," Courtland said around a gasp. "And I don't know."

She flicked her fingers again, and he groaned, but that didn't change his answer.

"Rose," I said, and her other hand shot up in a gesture that clearly said to back off. Next to me, Damon was grinning sharply, but the twins were staring. Seth looked almost as sick as I felt.

"I should drag you into the Assembly," Rose said, leaning closer to Courtland. "*Force* you to tell them everything you'd seen, everything you've heard."

He lowered his hand enough to glare defiantly back at her. "They'd arrest you for illegal mind magic before you got one word out of me that would count as testimony."

Rose's jaw set. She obviously knew that was true. She

spoke as if through gritted teeth. "You *will* tell me something I can use against the Frankfords. And you'll want to tell me quick. Because no one will be able to tell that I did this to you. Now you know what it's been like, knowing someone hurt you and not being able to prove it. I can think of all *sorts* of 'accidents' I could make happen in an instant."

Her arm whirled, and her hand balled into a fist. Courtland knifed over, his arm dropping to hug his belly. Rose's hand squeezed tighter. Her knuckles whitened, and Courtland gasped.

"Rose," I murmured again. An ache ran through me from throat to gut. I wanted to grab her, to pull her into my arms and away from here—but I was afraid to find out what she might do if I tried. Maybe she'd end up hurting him even more badly if I distracted her.

"I don't know anything," Courtland sputtered.

"I don't believe you," Rose said flatly.

I took a step forward, my heart thudding. Before I could figure out how to intervene without making this worse, Courtland shuddered, and his mouth flew open again.

"There's one thing. Charles has gotten more paranoid. He doesn't want to discuss anything confidential in the Assembly building since one of your boys breached it. He's got a code, when he sets up an important meeting somewhere private. He always mentions the place where he met you last, so you know for sure it's him. Doesn't trust his phone and computer not to get broken into either. I only know *that* because your father was complaining about it."

Rose dropped her hand. Courtland sagged against the floor with a grateful sigh. His arm was still clamped around his abdomen. A smile stretched across my consort's face, so bright and satisfied it brought acid up my throat.

"Thank you," she said. "That's something."

Oh, Lord, that was not the woman I loved. That was not the Rose I'd lived and breathed for so long as kids and so much of the last two months.

As she turned toward us, still smiling, a horrible understanding crept up through my body. *I'd* done this. I'd drawn her into our group way back when, even though I'd known the lonely-looking girl sitting on the manor's front steps was a Hallowell, even though I'd been aware even at seven that the owners of the estate didn't get friendly with anyone not their kind.

If Rose had stayed the obedient girl her father had wanted, one who'd never mixed with unsparked guys like us, would he even have sacrificed her the way he had? Or had that first transgression made all the difference?

I couldn't answer that. There was no way to know. The only thing I could say for sure was that I couldn't let it go on.

Whatever it took, wherever it took me—I couldn't let her fall any further into that darkness she'd once been so afraid of.

CHAPTER FIFTEEN

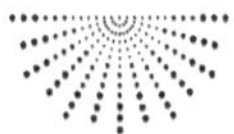

Rose

For the first few minutes after Master Courtland had talked, a victorious energy hummed through my veins. By the time the Buick's engine rumbled to life as we set off for the estate, that exhilaration had dulled. What had we learned, really? How much could we even use it?

I snatched after that sense of accomplishment, holding onto it as tightly as I could to ward off the helpless feeling that had been gripping me for far too long.

"We can do something with that information, right, Ky?" I said. "You could figure out how to hack into Frankford's phone, and then we can send a message pretending to be him."

"I should be able to manage it, if I had his number for whatever phone he uses to set up the meetings," Ky said.

"But we'd have to get that first. And who would we be messaging? What would we be telling them?"

I bit my lip. "I'm not sure. We might be able to trick someone into admitting more than they should over the phone. Or… we could have people from his faction bring something incriminating to the same place as legitimate people from the Assembly and expose them like that." Of course, we'd have to figure out what that incriminating "something" would be and which people in the Assembly were definitely legitimate.

"If we do use it, we'll want to make sure we've got the best possible plan," Seth said. "We're probably not going to get away with that ploy more than once before Frankford realizes. It'll be hard enough making sure he doesn't find out about the fake meeting in the first place."

"Yeah. And we'd need to know where he's seen whoever we're inviting to that meet-up most recently beforehand." It didn't seem likely Frankford would leave that information around where someone could find it.

"Once I'm in his phone, I'd be able to see the old messages," Ky said. "But anything he wants to keep secret, he'll be deleting after he sends it."

"Oh, come on," Damon said. "We've got something we can use. We'll figure out the rest. And that Courtland guy is shitting his pants right now at the thought of getting on Rose's bad side even more. I doubt he'll be cozying up with her old man again any time soon."

Gabriel hadn't said anything. When I glanced over at him, he was watching the road, his hands tight around the wheel, his expression difficult to read. Normally he would have pitched in an idea or two of his own. Did he figure our trip out there had been a total failure?

"The witch who joined us a couple days ago," I said, thinking out loud. "Thalia. When she's feeling up to it, I'll talk about the Assembly families with her. She might not be able to talk openly about what she's been through, but she can tell me if there's anyone not in Frankford's files who was involved in any way. Who she's sure wasn't involved. If we cross-check that with what my Aunt Ginny and Naomi have found out and what I know from my dad, we'll have a decent idea of who we could bring this to."

"You could do that trick you did on Courtland with one of the people closer to Frankford," Damon suggested. "Hell, even on your dad. They'd have more sensitive info they could cough up."

I paused. I hadn't really thought through what I'd done to Courtland. My anger and my fear for the people I needed to protect had propelled me onward. It was hard to imagine *planning* to go up to someone and torment them into revealing what we needed.

"I don't know," I said. "I guess if we found the right person, the right time—"

The car jolted to a halt with a screech of the tires. I jerked against my seatbelt and turned to stare at Gabriel. He was already unbuckling his seatbelt and shoving the car door open. By the Spark, what was he doing?

"Gabriel," I said. When he kept moving, I scrambled out on my side, my pulse rattling in my chest. We were just a few feet down the road from the gate to the estate, the big stone wall looming over me from the other side of the ditch. I spun to face him. "Gabriel, what's going on? Where are you *going*?"

"I can't do this," he said, his voice raw. His bright blue eyes caught mine, stark with pain. "I can't just sit there and listen to you talk that way. I can't watch you *torture* people like you're having fun doing it. I can't."

With a wave of dizziness, the ground seemed to tip beneath my feet. I grasped the still-open door to keep my balance. "I was trying to make sure the Frankfords don't hurt anyone else. They came after Seth and his dad, they burned Jin's house—they didn't know he wouldn't be in it—"

"It doesn't matter," Gabriel said. "The Rose I used to know would have found another way. She wouldn't have given in and sunk to their level. They were attacking us the whole way to New York and back, and you never did more than you had to."

The other guys had pushed out of the car too. "You can't talk to Rose like that," Damon said. "Who the fuck do you think you are? She's kicking their asses, and they deserve it."

"Damon," I said, motioning him quiet. Having him butt in wasn't going to resolve anything. I kept my gaze on Gabriel.

"They might have deserved it," he said. "But it used to bother you anyway."

"It still does," I protested. But I couldn't help remembering that moment when Master Courtland had cried out, when I'd been able to sense that if I pushed him just a little farther his control would break... and a rush had shot through me with that surge of power that had been almost gleeful.

"Maybe," Gabriel said. "Not enough."

"What do you want me to do?"

"I don't know," he said. "I..." He raked his hand through his dark red hair, the thick strands scattering around his ears. "I've tried talking you down. I've tried reminding you of how you used to think, but it hasn't worked. And I can't keep helping you if this is how you're going to fight this war."

My stomach dropped. Beside me, Seth stiffened. All three of the guys still standing with me were gaping at Gabriel.

"What are *you* going to do, then?" I said, the question wrenching through me.

"I'm going," he said. "Maybe sometime later, when all this is over... I don't know. But I can't stay with you like this."

For a second, I couldn't speak. Then my legs were moving, running, around the car. Gabriel backed up, holding up his hands to stop me. The bond between us, the one we'd only committed to weeks ago, throbbed inside me.

"Don't do this," I said. Tears were welling up in my eyes. No amount of blinking could hold them back. "You can't really mean this. You promised—you swore yourself to me, Gabriel."

"I swore myself to the Rose I knew," he said. "You're not her. I'm starting to think they were right to try to cage your magic, if you're going to enjoy hurting people with it."

He turned on his heel and started to stalk down the road. My arm flew up on instinct with a tearing sensation in my chest. No. He couldn't. There had to be some way we could work through this, some way I could convince him.

My fingers closed against my palm, and Gabriel's legs locked. Without even thinking, I'd whipped my magic around him.

I yanked my hand back, a cold wave of nausea rolling over me. I'd thrown magic at my consort. I'd tried to restrain him, to trap him.

The tendrils of energy shrank back from Gabriel's ankles. He looked down at them and then at me, his face blank with shock. He hadn't really thought I'd go that far.

Neither had I. Spark help me, what was I even doing?

"I'm sorry," I said. My voice came out ragged and small. I swiped at my tears, and Gabriel's mouth twisted. For a second, I thought maybe he'd waver. "I won't force you to stay. Can we please just... talk a little more?"

"I don't think any amount of talking is going to be enough at this point," he said. "I'm sorry too, Rose. But I can't stand by and watch you destroy the woman I loved."

My chin trembled. I braced one hand against the hood of the car. "Your motorcycle. Your things in the apartment. You're just going to walk off with nothing?"

His gaze slid to the estate wall and back to me. "They've been on your property. You stopped yourself just now, but how do I know whether you could reach me through them, what you might do to me later? No, I think I'm safer like this."

He turned and set off again, walking down the road

with strong brisk strides. My hand, my traitor hand, itched to reel him back to me. How could he leave?

It only took a minute before he disappeared over the top of the first low hill on the way into town. My legs gave. I collapsed against the car, my head dropping into my hands, a sob hitching from my throat.

The three consorts still with me surrounded me in an instant. Seth tipped my head against his shoulder and Kyler slung his arm around me from the other side in a tight hug. Damon spat on the ground in Gabriel's general direction.

"Good riddance then," he said. "He ran away once, and he's running away again. You don't need a guy like that."

"We should get into the estate," Seth said, his voice rough. "We're vulnerable out here."

Right. The estate. The protections there. The protections Gabriel no longer had. Would it matter to the Frankfords that he'd declared he didn't stand with me anymore?

Another sob worked its way up from my chest. I let Kyler draw me into the car. Damon scooted in on the other side and looped his arm around mine. Seth got into the driver's seat. Gabriel had left the key in the ignition.

Seth pulled up to the gate and tapped the control on the dash to open it. I buried my face in Ky's chest, clutching Damon's hand tight, as the car eased up the drive and over to the garage.

What if Gabriel was right? Had I gone too far with Master Courtland? With the decisions I'd made before?

I'd just wanted to strike back, to hit them where they weren't expecting it...

To make them pay. Yes. That was part of the impulse too—the impulse I'd given in to, like he'd said.

"We're still here, angel," Damon said. "None of us is going anywhere. We've been here since the beginning and we'll be here until the end. You never have to worry about us."

"That's right," Ky said, kissing my forehead. "I know all you want to do is protect us."

"What if I *did* want to hurt them too?" I said. "Has it bothered you, any of the things I've done or said?"

He hesitated—not for long, but for long enough that I wouldn't have believed him if he'd said no.

"I've never seen you this angry before," he said. "I understand why you are, but that doesn't mean I like seeing it."

The engine shut off. Time to get out, but I couldn't quite bring myself to move. The shock and the loss were still reverberating through me.

"Come here, angel," Damon said, kicking open the door. "We're going straight to that bedroom of yours, and you're going to forget you ever had a fifth consort."

A pained laugh escaped me, but I followed him. Seth got out, his movements stiff. He exchanged a glance with Damon, and he tipped his head as if in acknowledgment. "I've got to get my charger so I'll have my phone ready if there's any news about my dad. But I'll be back soon."

He went to his truck as Damon and Ky walked with me to the manor. Jin appeared in the living room doorway as we came in.

"What the heck happened out there?" he asked, taking us in.

"We're not talking about it right now," Damon said fiercely.

Jin backed up a step, holding up his hands. "Hey, okay. I'll be here if you need me."

The thought of telling him about Gabriel made me feel twice as wretched. Tomorrow, I could go to him for comfort too. Today... Today Damon clearly wanted me to himself, and I didn't have it in me to argue.

Damon led me into the master bedroom. He shot a wary glance at Ky following us in, but Ky raised an eyebrow as if in challenge, and Damon must have decided we didn't need another fight. He shut the door and locked it. Then he pulled off his protective token and his shirt, revealing ripples of muscle from shoulders to six pack. Something stirred inside me beneath the vicious aching.

"I'm yours," he said, a slight rasp creeping into his voice. "Do whatever the hell you want with me, Rose. Bring your magic out. Push me around. Test my limits. I'll take it all. I want you to know there's nothing you can't do with me. Nothing you can't show me."

Just for an instant, desire flared over the hurt. Yes. I wanted to push him, to hold him like I hadn't let myself hold Gabriel. To let out all that power that had been crying out for me to stop my consort from walking away.

I swiveled my wrist, splaying my fingers with a pulse of my spark, and my magic shoved Damon toward the bed. He caught his balance and grinned, so eagerly any guilt I might have felt about manhandling him melted away. The sense of control leached away at the pain coursing through me.

With another twitch of my fingers, I opened his belt and his jeans at the same time. The second he'd kicked them off, I shoved him again, hard enough to toss him right onto the bed. He landed on the mattress with a chuckle.

"Come and get me."

Oh, fuck, yes, I was going to. I marched up to him and climbed up, straddling his hips. Then I stopped, looking down at him. My breath came in ragged bursts. Damon gazed up at me with those dark blue eyes, like he could see right inside me. But even I wasn't sure exactly what I wanted here.

Hands came to rest on my sides. Kyler's. He hitched up my dress to my waist and paused there. I nodded, raising my arms, and he tugged it off me.

"I'm here for you too," he said, soft but sure. "Always. Whatever you need."

A shiver ran through me. "Touch me," I said. "Push me. Make me forget. Just for now. Make me *feel* something that doesn't hurt."

He undid my bra and slid his hands around to cup my breasts with a confidence he hadn't had a couple months ago when we'd first come together like this. I leaned over Damon and trailed my fingers over his chest. He watched me with languid eyes, his gaze hot enough to burn. Then Kyler pinched my nipples—not too hard, like he was testing my reaction—and I gasped as a much more pleasurable sort of pain shot through me to my core.

"Yes," I managed to say. "Just like that."

I stroked my hands back up to Damon's shoulders and farther to pin his arms in place. Ky kept working over my breasts, kneading and pinching a little harder each time, as I leaned down to kiss my other consort. Damon kissed me back hungrily. His arms flexed as if to reach for me, and I pinned them to the mattress with an extra jolt of magic. My body tingled with the thrill. He must have enjoyed it too, because he groaned against my mouth.

Ky bent to press a kiss to my back with a scrape of teeth that sent an even sharper tingling through me. Sandwiched between the two guys, flooded with heat, I rocked my sex against Damon's hard-as-steel erection. He let out another groan and bucked up to catch my lips again.

I fumbled with his boxers to free his cock. The feel of it, so silky smooth and rigid at the same time, had my panties soaking with arousal. I yanked their thin fabric to the side and lowered myself onto Damon with a stuttered sigh.

It felt so good, being filled by him. So good, the way he thrust up to meet the pace I set. So good, the way Kyler's hands moved with us, finding every sensitive spot on my upper body and teasing it to the limits between pleasure and pain.

But not good enough. Every time I thought my peak was in sight, it faded away into the distance again. I couldn't quite let go. Couldn't quite rock fast enough, absorb enough sensation, to completely drown out the deepening agony echoing through me.

One of my consorts was gone. Really gone, because

he'd *wanted* to leave. Because I'd made him stop loving me.

A lump filled my throat. I tried to ride it out, but my eyes went hot. My inner battle must have shown on my face, because Damon slowed. He shifted his arm, and I let him go so he could touch my cheek.

"Angel..."

I crumpled over him, and he stopped thrusting altogether. His strong arms came around my shoulders while Ky's softened to hug me around my waist. My breath shook as I fought the tears.

"It's okay," Damon said hoarsely. "It's okay. You don't have to— I just thought—"

I nodded to show I understood, my forehead brushing his chest. Kyler hugged me tighter and planted a gentle kiss on my spine.

Damon eased to the side, rolling us so we were lying next to each other. Ky snuggled close against my back. I tugged them both closer, wanting to be enveloped by their warmth. Wanting to drown in it so I didn't have to remember those moments after Gabriel had stopped the car yet again.

"I don't know what to do," I whispered into the space between us. A few tears leaked out with that admission.

"You just keep doing what you were doing," Damon said. "He's the one who had a problem."

"And if you want to try something else, we'll try something else," Ky added. "We're here for you. All of us."

As if on cue, there came a light rap on the door. Seth's voice carried through tentatively. "Hey?"

My heart squeezed. There wasn't any cure for the pain I was feeling, but I knew what I wanted while I rode out this first wave of it.

"Can you tell Jin to come up too?" I called. "I need all of you." All of them that I could have now.

Damon didn't protest, just ran his hand over my hair in a soothing gesture. Did he even realize how tender he could be when he wasn't trying to show how tough he was? I hugged Ky's arm where it was slung across my chest and nuzzled Damon's shoulder. One thought pierced through the pain.

"I don't know what I'm going to do," I said, a little more steadily, "but there are too many people depending on me now. Too many people who don't even know they're depending on me. I can't back down now."

CHAPTER SIXTEEN

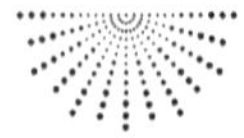

Rose

I woke up foggily, the way you do when you're fighting off a cold. My eyelids were heavy and a bit sore; there was an ache in my throat and my chest. It took a moment before the memory surged up: Gabriel's accusations, our argument, the way he'd stormed off.

The bed around me felt empty. A splinter of sharper pain shot through the ache. I rolled over, opening my eyes, and found I wasn't alone after all.

Kyler scooted closer to me. When I reached for him, he pulled me into his arms. I nestled against him, skin to bare skin, wrapped in his warmth and his faintly minty smell.

"You slept late," he said. "The other guys got up to grab something to eat. But we didn't think you should wake up alone."

"So you volunteered to go hungry?" I said.

He chuckled. "I traded off with Damon. It was hard enough convincing him he wasn't going to be much comfort if he was starving. How are you doing?"

"You know. Pretty awful." I swallowed thickly. "But I can't mope around in bed all day. Not with the Frankfords attacking us like this. Have you heard any news about your dad?"

Ky nodded. "They had to bandage him up pretty good, but he's coming home with my mom this afternoon. Seth and I will go see them, but we'll come back here to sleep. All of us want to be here any way you need us."

They'd said as much last night, but it loosened a fragment of the tension in my chest hearing it again.

"I don't know what to do," I said. "I don't know how to protect everyone. We can't just move all your parents and everything that matters to you on to the estate. I don't even know how well I can protect all of the estate grounds... I can lay down spells over the main roads into town that should detect if anyone with magic crosses over. At least that would give us more warning that they're up to something."

"But really what we need is to shut the Frankfords and their people down," Ky said.

"Yeah." A brief flare of anger seared through me. If I could have just raced into Portland or wherever they were right now and burned *them* to the ground... But even as I pictured it, my fury faltered with an uneasy twist of my stomach.

I didn't think I could have gotten away with doing that kind of violence anyway. The Frankfords would be protecting themselves as well as they could. Even making the attempt would probably get me arrested, and who knew what would happen to my consorts and the estate then?

But even if I could have gotten away with it, murdered them without consequence, it was thinking like that, acting like that, that had driven Gabriel away. Could I really blame him for not wanting to be with someone who'd contemplate cold-blooded murder? The real wonder was that the other guys were still here.

I squeezed my eyes shut tight against a fresh flood of tears. "Hey," Ky murmured. He caressed my hair and kissed my temple. "Any moment I can spare, I'll be working on this. I'll go through all the files again. I'll talk to the witches who came to you and see if they've thought of anything else they saw or heard that might help. I know I have to be missing something. Normally I'd have put together some kind of an idea by now."

"I know how much time you've put into this," I said. "If there's anything you can figure out, you'll get there. I'm sure of it."

"But I want to be sure you're okay too." He stroked his hand over my hair to the crook of my jaw. I tipped back my head to seek out his lips.

We kissed long and slow, a tingle of pleasure spreading over my skin. My nipples pebbled where they brushed Ky's bare chest. My spark fluttered, spreading warmth through my insides in turn.

"You know," Ky murmured against my mouth, "it was fun playing a little rough last night. But that's not the kind of lover I prefer to be."

"Good," I said softly. "Because I don't think that's the

kind of lover I need right now anyway."

He smiled and kissed me again, sure and gentle, his thumb grazing my cheek as if he were mapping the planes of my face. He eased down to mouth the tender skin of my throat, and my breath hitched. I tangled my fingers in his tawny curls as he dipped even lower, nibbling across my collarbone, following the curve of my breast until he could flick his tongue over the tip. I quivered, a whimper working itself from my throat.

He eased me onto my back as he suckled and fondled one side of my chest and then the other, until my nipples were stiff with delight and the rest of me squirming with desire. With a sly grin that suggested great plans, Ky drew farther back, kneeling over me. He kissed my stomach, my belly button, the hollow of my belly just beneath it. His hands slid down my panties and then traced up and down my thighs. I gave a murmur of encouragement and then a gasp as his mouth settled over my core.

My hips arched instinctively, seeking more of the hot sweet pressure of his lips. He swiveled his tongue around my clit until I was panting with the waves of pleasure that rolled through me. My fingers curled into the sheets. My eyelids fluttered, and my gaze caught on Ky's erection jutting against the fabric of his boxers. Ready at attention with no one attending to him.

That wouldn't do. I hooked one finger around his boxers and tugged. He moved his hips toward me, closer when I pulled again. I yanked his boxers down. He groaned with a hot rush of breath over my sex as I sucked the head of his cock into my mouth from below.

At my encouragement, he rocked over me, his lips and tongue having their way with me while his cock bobbed up and down, as deep into the back of my throat as I could take him. I lapped the salty musk from him and moaned as he suckled me harder. My hips started to buck in time with the movement of his mouth.

He dipped a finger inside me as he licked my clit, and that pressure tipped me over the edge. Bliss raced through me with a shudder. My lips clamped around his cock, and Ky came too, a flood of thick salty fluid shooting into my mouth. I swallowed it, coasting on my own quivers of pleasure as he groaned with his.

He kissed my sex one more time and then eased around to cuddle with me. The ache of loss still gripped my chest, but I could offer him a dreamily pleased smile.

"I don't know why we've never tried *that* before."

His gray-green eyes gleamed. "Oh, I'm sure there are all sorts of experiments still ahead of us."

As I nestled against him, an even sharper pang dug between my ribs. An uncertainty I couldn't shake, even though I'd tried to reassure myself yesterday. I pushed myself back to look Ky in the eyes again.

"Tell me the truth," I said. "Do you think I've gone too far? Was I too hard on Master Courtland yesterday?"

Ky wet his lips. "Rose... I don't understand why Gabriel left, but I understand why he was worried. You have seemed angrier, and more ruthless, than I'm used to. Than I like seeing you have to be. But I'm not sure that you *don't* have to be that way right now. If you see other ways to fight these people, then I'd be happier, but if that's the only way, then you have to fight. I'm not going to blame you for that. I promise. We've all talked—we all feel the same way." His tone turned wry. "Well, other than Damon, who thinks it's about time you got ruthless."

I had to laugh even as a lump rose in my throat. It wasn't as comforting an answer as I could have hoped for, but it was fair. I didn't think I could stand to lose another of my consorts.

Maybe Gabriel had just been overwhelmed. Maybe he'd come back—today, even—and we could talk it out properly. He couldn't have really meant what he'd said about Frankfords' group being right to want to control my magic, could he?

I shouldn't dwell on that question. Like I'd said to Ky earlier, there wasn't time for moping around. After a brief cuddle longer, I got up to shower and get dressed.

I was halfway to the stairs to rejoin the others when my ringtone went off. My heart skipped a beat at the thought that it might be Gabriel. But the number was a Portland one I didn't recognize. My spine stiffened as I answered it.

"Hello?"

"Hi, Lady Hallowell?" the woman at the other end said. "This is Investigator Ruiz from the Assembly's Justice Division. We spoke a few days ago."

The tension in me relaxed but only a little. "I remember," I said. "I told you everything I could then."

"I'm sure you did. But there's another matter I need to discuss with you. Have you had any contact with a witch by the name of Thalia Ainsworth?"

My back went rigid all over again. Thalia had never said it in so many words, but from her anxiety at the thought of being tracked here and the precautions she'd taken, I could be pretty sure she didn't want anyone knowing where she'd gone. I couldn't promise I could protect her if the Assembly and her husband knew she was here.

I hadn't told any outright lies to Ruiz last time, but if that was what I had to do now, so be it.

"Ainsworth?" I said. "No. I don't think I've ever met her. Why?"

There was a skeptical note in Ruiz's voice. "I gather she left her house rather suddenly... Her husband says she's been having some episodes of confusion—he's worried about her and wants her home. I only wondered since you have been collecting stray witches lately."

"Well, if she does show up here, I'll be sure to let you know," I said.

"Uh huh." She wasn't even trying to hide her skepticism now. "Lady Hallowell... I do want to help, you know."

I swallowed hard. *I believe you*, I thought. *I just don't believe you* can.

"I've seen things, heard things," she went on in my brief hesitation. "I know not to trust the official take on everything. I *asked* to be assigned to your case because I feel there's more here we need to understand. If you have another side to the story—to *any* story—I'll listen and give it due consideration."

"I'll keep that in mind," I said, but she'd sounded sincere enough that I had to add, "and I appreciate that."

"Are you sure there's nothing else you can tell me?"

My hand tightened around the phone. "I'm trying," I

said. "If I've got a story I can properly tell, you'll be the first one I call."

"All right. I can't ask for much more than that. You've got my card. Stay well and may your spark glow brightly, Lady Hallowell."

It was an old formal farewell, the kind recorded in witching fairy tales, not really used much these days. Hearing it, I really wished I could have told her something more.

When I hung up, the soft clearing of a throat behind me made me jerk around. Thalia was standing in the doorway to the bedroom she'd been hiding away in for most of the last two days.

I took her in with a whisper of relief, seeing the steadiness of her stance. For the first time since she'd arrived, there was an energy in her eyes that fit the forty-something years old she was, not the aged weariness she'd shown before. I'd been starting to worry that our newest arrival might have had her nerves permanently fractured.

"Hi," I said. "How are you? Did you want me to bring up some breakfast—or to come down?"

Those questions seemed to slide right by her. "That was the Assembly," she said, nodding to the phone I'd just lowered.

I tucked it into my pocket. "It's no problem. No one's realized you're here."

"You lied to them for me."

The words held more weight than I would have expected. I paused. "I did. I thought that's what you'd want me to do."

"It is. But I—" Her mouth twitched. I couldn't tell if it

was moving toward a smile or a frown. "I wouldn't have asked that of you. They could arrest you just for that if they find out. You hardly know me."

Was that all she was worried about? "It's nothing," I said. "Really. You came here because you thought it'd be a safe place, and that's what I'm trying to make it, as much as I can."

She studied me. "Why?" she asked simply.

It took me a moment to find an answer that felt true enough. "I wish I'd had someone in the witching community I could turn to when I needed them," I said. "Everyone should have that. At least I can give it to other people, so they can feel a little less scared than I did." My stomach twisted even without thinking too hard about all the trouble I'd been through with no one who fully understood to turn to.

Something about the answer must have sat right with Thalia, because her grip on the doorframe eased. She tipped her head toward her bedroom. "Come in? I feel there's more we should talk about."

Inside the bedroom, she sank onto the edge of the bed, and I sat on the stool at the cherry-wood vanity.

"It is good to see you up," I said, not sure how else to start.

Thalia let out a sharp breath. "It's good to *be* up. I'm sorry for being such a lay-about the last few days—I didn't even know I was that worn out until my head hit that pillow..."

"The kind of magic you've been doing, it took a lot out of you?" I ventured.

Her gaze held mine with a knowing expression.

"Yes," she said. "You could say that. I was hoping... You're *not* entirely safe here, are you? There've been difficulties. If there's anything I can do, anything I can offer, I'll do whatever I can for you."

"Thank you," I said. "It's— We're safe here on the estate. But it has been an increasingly tense situation. People who have reason to be afraid of what I know— they've been attacking us in roundabout ways. Ways I can't really prepare for. If there's anything you can say from what you've been through, anywhere you can point me to that we could find proof to expose what's going on or take them down some other way...?"

She looked down at her hands. "It's hard," she said. "They were afraid of what I could say too. I'm so bound up. The power they have... It's much stronger in the source, but it still gives them something they shouldn't."

The demons had a strong magic that didn't totally transfer to the men who borrowed it, I suspected she meant. But it was still power. Tainted power. We had to fear not just the witches but the witching men as well, in more ways than I was used to.

"Maybe we can get somewhere talking about the things and the people who *aren't* the problem," I suggested. "If I knew who I definitely didn't have to worry about, who you can freely talk about because there's nothing bad you could say about them, that would let me know who to turn to for more help."

Thalia raised her head again, her face brightening. "Yes," she said. "Yes, that could work. Do you have some paper? This might take a little while."

CHAPTER SEVENTEEN

Kyler

"I don't know how else to explain it," Imogen said, twisting one of her red curls around her finger as she frowned in thought. "It was just a feeling I got. The way the guys they brought around looked at me. The way they talked more to my aunt and uncle than they did to me, as if they were deciding whether to marry *them*... Nothing more obvious than that. That's why it's so hard to talk about it. It's not like I can say, 'See, of course I was scared when they said this horrible thing.'"

I looked up from my tablet where I'd been poised to take notes. The open document was blank, because Imogen hadn't been able to offer any data that would get me anywhere. "That still sounds awful," I said. "Regardless of why they were doing it. I might not have been part of this world for very long, but I know you deserve a consort who's interested in *you*."

She shrugged, her mouth twisting. "We were a small enough family to begin with, and my parents weren't around to make any kind of name for themselves. It's not like there's a lot to gain from marrying me."

"I didn't gain anything from—" My voice cut off before I could say *marrying Rose*, the magical vise of the oath clamping around my vocal chords. I coughed. Imogen should be able to fill in the blanks after the amount of time she'd spent in our company. "From marrying who I married. Except for getting to be with a woman I think is amazing. That's what marriage is supposed to be."

"For some people. You don't know what it's like. Anyway, I'm sorry I can't help more." She paused. "You know how worried I have to be, don't you? You know something about what my aunt and uncle are mixed up in. That's part of what you're not allowed to talk about."

My tongue went heavy as lead in my mouth. What could I say to that without bumping up against the magical restrictions laid on me? Normally I was a pretty even-tempered guy, but right then, the frustration that had been growing in me over the last several days seared through my stomach. My hand clenched around the tablet.

For fuck's sake, I should be able to tell this one girl her family had been ready to sell her into virtual slavery.

"I think you're right to have come here," I managed finally. "I think you're safer away from them."

"Yeah. That's all Rose will say about it too." Imogen grimaced and flopped back in the armchair.

"I'm sorry."

"It's okay. I know it's not your fault. If I think of anything specific, I'll tell Rose, okay?"

I nodded, tension still churning in my gut. "Thanks."

I got up and walked into the front hall, but then I didn't know where to go. I'd already talked to Lesley, who hadn't been able to give me any details I hadn't heard the first time I'd talked to her, and Rose had related everything she'd learned from Thalia, the older witch who'd only just arrived. We had a list now of several high-ranking Assembly members who we could be decently sure had no loyalty to the Frankfords—a couple who might even be actively antagonistic to them.

We just didn't have anything to give them that would let us take that demon-feeding faction down.

I'd been working through the files and pursuing leads for more than a month now with nothing useful to show for it. And the Frankfords were closing in. They'd almost killed my dad—they could have killed my brother. They'd burned down Jin's home. Who would they hurt next?

Jin was working on paintings to bring to each of our parents' houses, but that wasn't going to do them much good when the enemy witches were attacking them in the most convoluted ways to get around the oath anyway. And there was nothing I could do to help.

I couldn't even bring Gabriel back. I'd tried texting him and then calling him yesterday, but I'd gotten no answer and then a "not in service" recording. Where the hell had he gone? *Why* the hell had he gone, and like that? I'd known he was worried about Rose, but how could he have lost faith in her that quickly? How could he have abandoned her?

It didn't seem like him at all. Maybe the Frankfords had gotten to him in some other underhanded way, but I hadn't been able to determine that either.

In short, I was useless all around.

I was still standing there when Rose came down the stairs. She smiled, seeing me, but the gesture didn't remove the sadness from her eyes. I had the feeling that emotion was going to linger in her face for a long, long time. What even happened if someone a witch was consorted to just left? I hadn't wanted to break her heart more by asking, and that wasn't a question I could ask an internet search engine.

"Hey," she said. "Finished with your interviews?"

"Yep," I said, putting on my best optimistic expression even if it didn't reflect how I was feeling.

"Do you want to run through some of the practice forms—the dual ones? I was thinking we should keep that up. I mean, especially now..." She let herself trail off, her jaw tightening.

After one of her consorts had proven so thoroughly he didn't trust her. I opened my mouth, knowing the right thing to say was yes. That was what she needed from me. But my body balked, with a ribbon of resistance that constricted around my ribs.

I was too wound up, too overwhelmed. I'd probably screw up the forms too and just make her even more unsettled.

"I don't think that's a good idea right now," I said cautiously. "I'm all..." I made a spinning gesture with my hand by my head. "Trying to put all the pieces together, to find a connection we can use. I don't know. I don't think I can concentrate on much else right now."

Part of me, the part that had cringed watching her torture Courtland, braced itself for her to be upset with me. But all that happened was her smile slanted and she took my hand to squeeze it.

"You've been running around working on that for weeks," she said. "Maybe what you need is a break. Take a little time for yourself, get away from all the craziness here for a bit. Just... be careful if you leave the estate, all right?"

Love swelled in my chest in answer to the love she'd just shown me. My smile came a little easier. I tapped the token I was wearing under my shirt. "I've got you protecting me wherever I go. You might be right. Just a quick walk to see if I can clear my head and get somewhere."

I headed out thinking maybe I'd swing by my parents' place again. Dad had seemed to be recovering fine when Seth and I had visited yesterday, but it was hard not to worry. Of course, visiting Dad also meant visiting Mom, and she'd pulled the two of us aside yesterday to rant for a few minutes about where we'd been and who we might have been with until Seth had managed to extricate us.

No, I didn't want to be harped on about my choice in lovers today. I'd already chatted with Dad a bit on the phone this morning.

Instead I ambled down the main road and onto the main street through town. The water was burbling from the fountain in the square. I walked up to it and stood by the base, enjoying the cool flecks that dabbled my skin while the sun glared down. Damn, it'd be nice to just soak myself in that pool.

There was that pond on Rose's property—the one where we'd used to go swimming when we were kids. It'd always been the perfect temperature in the summer. I should revive that tradition... if her protections could extend that far. It was a bit of a hike into the woods.

That thought dampened my enjoyment of the moment. I wandered on through the square, playing a game with myself of identifying the tourists and guessing where they'd come from. A few of the locals tipped their heads to me. A couple others watched me warily. Wondering if I'd brought oddness cooties with me from the Hallowell manor? I didn't roll my eyes at them, but it was a near thing.

The summer heat wafted off the cobblestones too. Sweat started to bead on my forehead and beneath my shirt. I ducked into the little bookstore just off the square with a wave to Marsha at the front counter. She made a hesitant gesture with her hand, her eyes going a little round beneath her bun of white hair.

Oh, good Lord, don't tell me *she* was hearing—and listening to—rumors too. I'd been coming in here for reading material for two decades, whenever there was a topic the internet wasn't supplying me quite enough info on.

I walked down the aisle, skimming my fingers over the spines of the books. The chill of the air conditioner drove away the heat that had soaked into my skin. Other than a few new popular novels that weren't really my thing, there was nothing here I hadn't seen before. I was going to turn around and head out again when my gaze caught on the guy at the far end of the shop.

He was standing in the corner where Marsha wouldn't have been able to see him, taking books off the shelf, paging through them, and sticking them back in their spots. But there was a twitchiness to his movements, the way he scanned the aisle periodically, that rubbed me the wrong way. And who the hell would wear a vest, even a thin one, over their shirt on a day this hot?

I meandered around to the other aisle and peeked at him through the gap in the bookcase between the rows of books. He glanced at a couple more volumes and then reached for one he'd already put back. With one more jerk of his head to check for witnesses, he slipped the book into an inner pocket on his vest.

My eyebrows shot up. What a jerk. I didn't know him —he was either a tourist or a newcomer in town. Maybe a local from a neighboring town who went elsewhere for his criminal activities.

I leaned on the counter on my way out and murmured to Marsha, "You might want to check that guy's vest. Just saying."

She blinked at me, startled, and then the guy came around the corner. I gave her another wave and went out.

The blast of heat didn't diminish my sense of accomplishment, minor as it might be. I might not be able to take on any real villains, but I'd protected our neighborhood bookstore from a little petty theft.

My feet stalled halfway down the street. The idea beamed through my head as if it'd been a literal light bulb.

I'd been thinking about my other problems all wrong. Or not wrong, just forgetting a whole huge aspect of them. Our enemies were magical, so I'd been trying to find something within their world to take them down: a crime of the witching sort. But everyone in Rose's society still lived in the real world with all us unsparked people—and our unsparked law enforcement—too. They had to follow the laws of this nation as well as their own.

And I'd bet the clothes off my back that if the Frankfords' allies had been breaking their own people's rules, they'd been finding ways to cheat the unsparked systems too. They'd have just as much trouble enslaving witches like Imogen to demons from the inside of a regular prison cell. The business dealings Frankford had mentioned in his files would give me the perfect jumping off point to investigate.

A grin stretched across my face. I set off again, back toward the Hallowell estate, with more sense of purpose than I'd had since I'd stolen that hard drive in the first place.

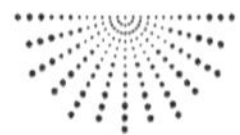

CHAPTER EIGHTEEN

Rose

I'd thought I wanted a little time alone after dinner, but the manor's kitchen felt far too big and empty when I was the only one in it. When the door swung open and Lesley peeked inside, my spirits lifted.

"Need a little help with that?" she said.

I'd just started filling the sink with soapy water, the tang of lemon in my nose. The dirty dishes were stacked on the counter beside me. "You could dry, if you really want to," I said. "I think there's a dish towel around here somewhere... Over there, hanging from that cupboard handle."

Lesley plucked it off and came to stand beside the dish rack. I set the first few bowls into the water, and she cocked her head, watching me through her rectangular glasses.

"How are you doing?" she asked.

It was a simple question, but somehow so unexpected that my throat closed up. "Oh," I said. "Okay. I mean, as well as I can be with everything that's going on."

"I don't mean to pry. It's just hard not to notice... Gabriel went off somewhere. And you didn't want him to go."

For a second, I couldn't talk at all. "Yeah," I managed.

"If you don't want to talk about it, it's okay," she said, holding up her hands. "I thought maybe... I don't know if I can give any advice, really. But I know what it's like to lose a consort. So, if you need to let anything out with someone who's got the general idea, I'm here."

The offer was so kind that my eyes welled up despite my best attempts at self-control. "Thanks," I said. "I don't know if I can compare our situations. He's still alive. He could come back. I have no idea what it's like, what you've been through."

She shrugged, but her gaze had gone distant. "It's like a piece of yourself has been hollowed out, and nothing you can do will fill it. I don't know if it ever gets completely better. But that hole does start to feel less hollow over time. The good memories fill it in. Finding other people you can count on."

"I can't say I don't have those. But it's good to hear that the painful part gets better." I paused. "Do you still think about him a lot? Your consort?"

"Not as much as I used to right after he passed," she said, tucking her mousy hair behind her ear. "But every day, definitely. On the harder days, every hour." She shook her head. "That's how I knew something was wrong, the way my parents were acting. It's been less than a year. I'm not ready to form that kind of attachment with anyone else yet. I don't know why they were so insistent… I couldn't stand it anymore, the way they were trying to rush me."

My pulse stuttered as I remembered my recent conversation with Imogen. "Have you had any contact with your parents? Are they hassling you at all about staying here?"

"I blocked them," she said with uncharacteristic firmness. Her mouth set in something that was almost a smile. "It's been a relief not having to deal with them going at me day in and day out."

I had to smile back. "You can keep them at a distance as long as you want. And remember what I promised you —I'm going to make it safe for you to go back and reclaim your estate if I possibly can. I got this property from my dad because of the way he treated me. We can do the same for you."

"I know," she said quietly, but her smile grew a little. She picked up one of the bowls I'd gotten around to washing and rubbed the towel over it, considering it as she turned it in her hands. "You know, I was thinking… A lot of the trouble you've been having is focused on the guys, isn't it? There are ways you could be more sure they could defend themselves if they needed to. The batons the male enforcers use—one of my grandmothers worked for the Assembly for a while magicking those. She's talked about the process. I'm sure I could help you make something similar."

An actual magical weapon the guys could use to defend themselves? It might not have helped against the attacks on their families, but at least I could feel a little more secure when they were off the estate. "That would be amazing," I said.

The door murmured open, and I caught a glimpse of a matching set of tawny hair, curly here and short-cropped there.

"There she is!" Kyler said. He ambled over, kissed my cheek with a hand on my waist, and then hopped up to sit on the counter on the other side of the stack of dishes, his legs dangling in a boyish pose.

Seth followed behind his slimmer twin, looking more serious, as usual. "Thalia mentioned you sent the staff home early," he said, stopping next to Ky with his arms folded over his broad chest.

Lesley glanced at them and then me, looking amused. "We'll talk more tomorrow morning?" she suggested, setting down her towel.

"Definitely," I said. She slipped out of the kitchen, leaving me to my consorts.

"Why are you hiding away in here?" Ky asked.

I shoved my hands deeper into the hot sudsy water to grab a plate. "I just wanted to do something definite," I said. "Something I can feel with my hands. I don't know. It's kind of grounding, washing stuff."

"You still don't have a dishwasher in this place, huh?" He craned his neck as he scanned the length of the kitchen. It'd been built to accommodate the parties that I guessed had been thrown a lot more often in earlier times when the Hallowell family had been larger. For most of the time I'd lived here, it'd been just me and my father. The house might have seen more activity after he'd married my stepmother, but we'd moved to Portland not long after that.

Ky and Seth had been more familiar with this kitchen than most of the rest of the house. Their mom had worked in here when we'd employed a full kitchen staff, baking our bread and breakfast muffins and desserts.

"Oh, there is," I said, nodding to the stainless steel appliance on the other side of the room, next to the massive double-doored fridge. "But *that* wouldn't be hands-on, letting a machine do all the work."

"Well, I've got good news about other things working," Ky said with a grin. "The police took in two of the Frankfords' allies this evening. I just saw the reports."

My heart leapt. I set the plate in the rack and turned to him. "They were able to use the evidence you arranged for them to find. Do you think the charges will stick?"

"The one woman will have a pretty hard time getting out of everything. I think they'll probably take her husband in too when they dig deeper. There was a ton of fraud and tax evasion and more with their business. The other guy's case isn't quite as egregious, but the fact that they arrested him at all is a good sign."

"What do witches usually do if they tangle with the unsparked law enforcement?" Seth asked me. "Can they magic their way free?"

I shook my head. "Sometimes, maybe. But that usually depends on covering up the evidence so they're not found out in the first place. Once there are computer records of the crime and the arrest, and all kinds of people are aware of the issue... Unless they're vital to some mandate of the Assembly's, the usual policy would be to see it as their own just punishment for their carelessness."

"Perfect." Ky kicked his feet playfully. He was obviously enjoying his new role as anonymous avenger. "I've got a third couple I'm digging up some shady stuff on right now. If the trails lead me where I think they're going, I'll have them locked up in a few days. Actually, let me check my progress on that."

As he pulled out his tablet from the little satchel he had slung from his shoulder, Seth stepped closer. He rubbed my back as I set the last of the plates in the rack. "It's coming together," he said. "We're really making progress now. If Ky can put enough of the people involved behind bars, they won't be able to conspire anymore."

The remaining witches could still attack us, though. And after our first two strikes, I suspected any other of the Frankfords' colleagues who'd been engaging in questionable practices were scrambling to erase any proof right now. It seemed unlikely that people as high up as the Frankfords themselves would have left proof in the first place. But it *was* a start. It was real ground gained. I smiled at him, drying my hands on a towel, and leaned in for a quick kiss. "It feels good to be getting somewhere."

Kyler's feet went still with a thump against the cabinets. When I glanced up, he'd stiffened, his gaze glued to the tablet's screen. The small piece of happiness I'd found vanished under a wave of panic.

"What?" I said.

His head jerked up. The color had drained from his

face. He blinked at me, his lips parting and then pressing together again.

Seth moved to his side and poked at the tablet. His expression darkened a few moments later. "Is that…?"

Ky nodded.

"*What?*" I said again. "Tell me what's going on, or at least show me."

I held out my hand. The twins exchanged a glance. "Whatever it is, you're going to have to tell me eventually, aren't you?" I said.

Ky hesitantly extended the tablet to me. "There could be other explanations than what it looks like," he said. "There's no way of knowing what's definitely going on."

The screen was paused at the beginning of a video. I recognized it immediately: it was the traffic cam Ky had hacked into on the intersection near the Frankfords' Portland house. We'd been checking the footage periodically to see who he might be meeting with at home. So far it hadn't turned up much. What could they be so upset about now?

I hit play, my gut clenching. A couple of cars cruised by. Then a taxi arrived, pulling up to the curb at the corner of the screen where you could see just the corner of the fence outside the Frankfords' house.

The back door of the cab opened. A head of dark red hair came into view, a familiar set of well-muscled shoulders, a stride I would have known anywhere. Gabriel crossed the sidewalk and out of view of the camera, heading toward the Frankfords' house.

My stomach plummeted. The tablet shook in my hands. I set it down on the counter before I could drop it.

"He went to them. He went right to them." I swallowed hard, nausea bubbling inside me. "When is that footage from?"

"Yesterday afternoon," Ky said quietly. "It could be— We don't know for sure that he even went to their house."

"Who else's house would he have been going to there?" I said.

He didn't have an answer for that. I dropped my face into my hands. Seth put his arm around me, steadying me with his embrace, but part of me wanted to cringe away.

Did I deserve that comfort? I didn't want to believe that Gabriel had not just left me but gone to my greatest enemy, but there he'd been. I'd seen it with my own eyes.

The way he'd talked right before he'd left... Did he really think I was so dangerous he'd go to those lengths to make sure I didn't do anything worse? That I was more dangerous than the Frankfords' faction and that monster we'd seen in the cave?

I couldn't wrap my head around it, but I'd heard the horror in his voice when he'd accused me of becoming someone he couldn't love anymore. That had been real.

"The Frankfords could be using some kind of magic on him," Seth put in. "Especially if he's taken off his protective token. I didn't see it on him in the video."

Ky skimmed back through the recording to check. He squinted at the screen. "It's hard to tell with the limited resolution," he said. "But I don't see the string around his neck where I'd expect to."

"So either he's gone to the Frankfords of his own free

will or they've used the doubt he was feeling to control him," I said. Both of those possibilities were awful.

"We'll get him back," Seth said firmly. "No matter what's going on. We'll end this, and we'll find him, and—"

"He doesn't *want* to come back," I said. "I can't force him to still act as my consort." My hands dropped to my sides and balled into fists. My stomach was churning, but a sense of resolve rose through the nausea. "We have to be better than them. No more hurting any of them. No more lashing back just because I can. Everything through official channels, witching or unsparked—like those arrests." I couldn't be a woman one of the guys I loved saw as a monster. I couldn't let our enemies change me like that.

Ky nodded. Seth's arm tightened around me. "Where does that leave us, then?" he asked.

I paused. "Maybe we've been trying too hard to find a loophole, a way to work *around* the conditions of the oath. It's gotten us thinking the wrong ways. If we focus on what we can talk about, what we can tell people, completely openly, then the oath doesn't even matter."

"What have we got that it doesn't cover?" Seth said.

Ky piped up. "Anything we knew from before we saw those records. All the things that Rose's dad was doing around her consorting. The fact that Frankford helped him with that scheme. The way they arrested us and then pursued us across the country."

"That part won't get us anywhere," I said. "They arrested us because of the illegal magic I used on my father, and they can say they were trying to apprehend us after we escaped. But there's also the Cliff and the demon and the little bit my father explained about that. The problem is just how we convince anyone we're not crazy, that those things actually happened. I'd have trouble believing it if I hadn't been there!"

"Yeah," Seth said. "I didn't see it, and even though I trust you completely, it's hard for me to wrap my head around the idea of demons."

Something in his words set off a spark of an idea in my mind. I gripped his arm where it was wrapped around my waist. "Say that again."

He frowned. "I just mean the whole story sounds crazy unless you've seen it with your own eyes."

A smile started to curl my lips. "That's it. We don't need to get out to the Cliff to gather proof, or even to try to destroy it. We need to *use* it as the proof. If we can call the right people in the Assembly for a 'meeting' with the Frankfords there..."

"Then *they'll* see what they've been up to with their own eyes," Ky filled in. "But we still need enough access to be able to clone his business phone and the right code word."

"If he's even still using the same code," Seth said. "Gabriel knew we'd found that out."

And he might pass that information on to the Frankfords. They might change their tactics. I bit my lip.

"Let's not worry about that yet," Ky said quickly. "We need to know how Frankford is setting up meetings with them. We'll need a way to contact them as him either way. We start from there and figure out the rest once we have that information."

Seth nodded. His phone pinged with an alert. He

fished it out and glanced at the screen, and his jaw set. He shoved it back in his pocket without answering the text.

"What was that?" I asked.

"Nothing important," he said. "Ordinary life stuff. I can deal with it later."

"Are you sure?"

"Hey," he said, pulling me to him again and kissing my temple. "Everything's fine. I just want to focus on you right now."

Ky clapped his hands and hopped off the counter. "I'll get back to work on hacking my way to that phone number."

Seth looked abruptly uncertain. There wasn't a whole lot I'd thought of that either of us could do to help that effort. He dropped his arm to take my hand in his. "Do you want to do some more of that form practice?" he asked. "Strengthen our connection even more?"

He didn't say it, but I had a feeling we were all thinking it—I might need those solid bonds even more now that one of them was gone. Now that the whole balance of our group had been thrown off again. But I balked.

"It's getting late. If you're getting tired..."

When we'd been on the road before, he'd worn himself out trying to keep my spark brightly lit. The intimacy between us had become painful for him. The thought of him pushing himself too hard again brought a lump into my throat.

He shook his head. "I'm good. You don't have to

worry about that, Rose. I promised you I'd tell you if I ever felt overwhelmed again, and I meant that."

The honesty in his voice reassured me. "All right," I said. "Maybe I'll come up with another plan, a better one, with that to clear my head."

"Rose," Ky said, cocking his head as he looked at us. "Do you remember a little while back I asked you about the deeper consorting? The permanent one, that allows the strongest bond?"

My heart hiccupped. "Yes," I said cautiously. "And I said I didn't think it was a good idea. Not when you're all so new to the witching world." The lifebond consorting was rarely performed these days. A normal consort bond could be severed after a few years on the wishes of either party. But a lifebond... It really was permanent. It only ended if one of the consorts died—and when they died, their partner died too.

"We know more now," Ky said. "If it would give you more power to fight the Frankfords and their faction—"

"No," I said firmly before he could go on. My chest had constricted. "Not right now. Not with so much uncertain."

I was not tying any of the guys to me permanently when I'd already driven one to separate from me. I couldn't do that to them, couldn't let them take that risk.

Who knew who I might be by the time this was over—and whether the rest of them would still want to stand by my side then?

CHAPTER NINETEEN

Rose

I hefted another box to the side and sneezed at the puff of dust that rose up. Naomi's laugh carried from my phone I'd left on top of one of the trunks, on speaker mode.

"Sounds like that attic really needs to be cleaned more often."

"No kidding," I said. "I don't think anyone's been up here since before we moved, and that was almost twelve years ago now."

"But you think you'll find something useful up there?"

"If I'm going to rattle my dad and get him to rattle Frankford, I'll be better off with old projects where they might not remember all the details." I opened the next box, found it stuffed with suits, and pushed it to the side too. "We know they've been skirting the rules in a lot of ways, so chances are they've done some shady stuff here and there along the way. I just need to make them think I might have uncovered something incriminating. With the arrests Kyler has been prompting, they'll already be on their toes."

"And then you hope Frankford will set up a meeting with the Assembly people who are above board."

"Exactly. I've already found some notes from a real estate deal they worked on together twenty years ago, one that involved negotiating with some unsparked company heads. That would be under the domain of Unsparked Relations. Now I just need a good one to get them worried about International Affairs investigating." Justin Brimsey and Gwen Remington, the heads of those two divisions, were two of the Assembly officials both Thalia and my aunt Ginny had felt confident were no friends of the Frankfords.

"You know if I hear anything useful on this end, I'll get in touch ASAP. I wish I could stay down there and really pitch in." Naomi sighed.

"It's good just being able to bounce ideas off you," I said.

My hand stilled on the flap of the box I'd just opened. This one was full of fancy dresses: silk and satin with ornate embroidery in rich jewel tones. My mother's old dresses. Even as I thought that, a smell I couldn't attach to any conscious memory but that struck a chord in me all the same wafted from them over me. She must have used to wear that perfume, a mix of peach and amber notes. It closed around my heart.

"Rose?" my cousin said, and I realized she'd started talking again without me even hearing her.

"Sorry," I said. "I just— I found a box with some of my mother's stuff. It's still hard to think about her, with everything I know now."

"Oh, Spark help me, I can only imagine." Naomi paused. I ran my hand over the delicate fabric, listening to the soft hiss of its movement. I didn't quite dare to pull one of those dresses out. I wasn't here for that, and I was already distracted enough just looking at them.

"Do you think it really was cancer that killed your mom?" Naomi went on in a low voice. "I mean, it does seem strange that she died so soon after she was getting suspicious of your dad."

I'd wondered that so many times since I'd talked to my aunts and heard their side of my mother's story. The whirlwind courtship and romance with my father, the way he'd isolated her, the letter she'd sent while she was sick claiming he was trying to steal her power.

"I don't know," I said. "Your mom said mine was already sick when she wrote that letter. There's no way to know what she'd found out. Dad always seemed to really care about her." But then, I'd thought I'd been able to tell that he cared about me too. "I'm not sure there's any way to find out at this point. Any evidence of *that* would be long gone."

"Yeah. And it's not like you can expect your dad to tell you the truth about it."

I forced myself to close the box of Mom's dresses and moved to another. This one was full of file folders. "Oh, I might have something useful here," I said. "This looks like work stuff."

Naomi was silent for a moment as I started flipping through each of the folders. Then she said, "You're hanging in okay, right? With Gabriel... and everything...? If you want to talk about any of *that* stuff with someone who's not one of the guys, you know you've got me."

My mouth twisted with a bittersweet smile. "I know," I said. "I— Mostly I'm trying not to think about it. It still hurts a lot. And obviously if he was going to come back, he would have by now." I just had to show him he hadn't really lost me. That I could tackle the Frankfords without stooping to anywhere near their level.

I'd rather take them on that way anyway.

I hesitated over the folder I'd just opened. "Hey, I think I've got something useable here. My father and the Frankfords did some project together in Brazil in the late '80s." Just a year or two before Dad would have met my mother.

"Sounds promising," Naomi said. "Does that mean you've got everything you need?"

"I think so." I paged farther through the documents. It'd been a big business endeavor, taking six months to complete. One of the first deals they must have worked on together. My father would have been in his early twenties, the Frankfords about ten years older. Taking him under their wing like a sort of apprentice. My hackles rose at the thought.

Had the Hallowells already been tied to the Frankfords and their schemes before that? Or was that when Charles Frankford had roped Dad into this horrible conspiracy? If there were files that went back before Dad's time, they hadn't been on that hard drive, so I could only speculate.

I couldn't put all the guilt on the Frankfords, not when my father had made his own decisions, but that didn't stop me from gritting my teeth when I pictured them cajoling him into going along with their schemes. Just promise your first-born daughter to tame a few demons. No big deal.

Oh, I was still furious with Dad too, no doubt about that.

I pushed that anger aside with a few deep breaths and jotted down some notes about the project on a piece of paper. I couldn't let my emotions get in the way. To get the reaction I wanted, I'd need to play Dad just right.

He'd used me, and now I was going to use him in return. It'd be perfect as long as he didn't realize that was the point of my call. After the way I'd reacted to the Frankfords' previous attacks, I didn't think he'd have trouble seeing me as vengeful.

"I'd better let you go now so I can make this call," I said to Naomi. "Thanks for keeping me company up here."

"Any time!" she said cheerfully. "And if you need more than that, you know I'm just a few hours' plane ride away."

After I'd hung up with her, I took the phone and my notes, and sat with my back against the wooden chest. My pulse had kicked up a notch. I closed my eyes and willed the surge of adrenaline away. Calm and collected, on the inside at least. That was what I needed to be.

My hand still shook a little as I tapped on Dad's name in my contacts list. My fingers curled against my palm where I was resting my free hand on the floor. I held my breath as the phone rang, and rang, and—

"Rose?" Dad's voice on the other end was startled. I couldn't tell if it was a happy surprise or a wary one.

"Hi, Dad," I said evenly.

He didn't seem to know what to say after that. "I— It's good to hear from you. How are you?"

"I've been better." I rustled the paper purposefully. "This isn't going to be a long call. I just wanted to give you a chance to make amends, since I know everything that's happened was more Charles Frankford's idea than yours. I've been doing some digging. I think International Affairs and Unsparked Relations would be very interested to hear about a couple of the projects you two worked on together."

Any warmth that had been in my father's voice fell away under a nervous edge. "What are you talking about?"

Good. He wouldn't be nervous unless he knew there were things I could have uncovered.

"Oh, it seems like some of your choices in Brazil way back when were pretty questionable." I glanced at my notes. "I'm not sure any amount of land or profits in coffee farming will make up for it. And that San Francisco real estate deal in '98..." I tsked my tongue. "You didn't even respect unsparked people who had the savvy to do business with you, did you?"

"I don't think dragging up all that history is going to help you get what you want," Dad said.

"Well, I don't think you understand what I really want, so you can't really make that decision. But here's the thing. If you come with me to the Assembly and tell them about all the recent crimes the Frankfords and the rest of their faction have gotten up to, then I'll leave out your part in the business deals. It was Frankford who took the lead on those early ones anyway. I just wanted to give you the chance to do the right thing."

I hadn't even for a second expected him to take that offer. The whole point of this ploy was to send him running to Frankford to warn him. But a pinching sensation jabbed through my heart anyway when Dad said, without hesitation, "I can't do that. There's too much at stake. *You* don't understand, Rose."

I did. Better than he could probably have imagined, after what I'd heard from Thalia Ainsworth. But he didn't know I'd even spoken to her.

The witching men didn't want to give up the power the demons were lending them. Not even when they'd put the whole world at risk by making their deals in the first place, if Dad's warnings were to be believed. Not even when they were sacrificing the sanity of their wives and daughters to get it.

"Fine," I said. "If you change your mind, you know how to contact me."

I'd meant to hang up there, but one thing I still didn't understand, fresh from my perusal of the attic boxes, stopped me. Before I could stop myself, I was saying, "What really happened to my mother, Dad?"

Dad hesitated a beat longer than was comfortable. "What do you mean? She had an aggressive cancer spread from her liver. We did everything we could, but it moved so quickly…"

"I know that's the story you've always told me," I said. "I also know that she was writing letters about you, about how she was afraid of you, to her family before she died. I know what tends to happen to people who mess with the Frankfords' schemes."

He swallowed audibly. "I don't want to talk about this with you right now, Rose. But you have to know that I had nothing to do with the sickness or her death. I wouldn't have made that call."

Something about his wording made me abruptly sure that even if he hadn't, someone else had. And he knew that. He knew her death hadn't been just a random tragedy.

But he'd stayed loyal to those people, more loyal than he was to his own daughter, anyway.

"Sure, Dad," I said, allowing a sliver of sarcasm to creep into my voice. Then I hung up before I could screw up whatever progress I'd made by letting my tongue fly with my temper.

I sat there for a few minutes longer, my shoulders shivering and stilling, shivering and stilling, until the lingering discomfort of the conversation had faded. Then I headed down into the main body of the house.

At least I'd put that plan into motion. Ky would keep watching the Frankfords, following their movements as well as he could. If they reached out to Charles's colleagues at the Assembly for any sort of secret meeting, Ky would be watching to catch them.

The front door was just opening as I came down into

the second-floor hall. Damon stepped inside. Like my other consorts, he had the code to the gate—a new one after I'd reluctantly changed it after Gabriel's departure.

He looked around the foyer with his shoulders slightly hunched in a wary stance, as if even after the last few weeks of dropping by regularly, he half expected my father or the staff to show up and chase him off.

I waved to him and hurried down to meet him. "Hey," I said, stepping into the arms he opened and hugging him back. "I wasn't expecting you."

"I just heard from my 'friends' who went to scope out the Cliff property," Damon murmured by my ear. "Are we okay to talk?"

None of the staff was around right now, but I was trying to limit how much they saw me being affectionate with the guys. I tugged him into the sitting room and closed the door. "What did you find out?" I asked eagerly.

His grimace dulled my excitement. "There are a ton of guards patrolling the property, plus a squad staked out around the gate. My contact said something along the lines of, 'They'd have to have the queen's jewels stashed in there for us to risk that attempt.'"

"Oh." I tried not to let my disappointment show, but I must have visibly deflated, because Damon caught my hand again.

"We'll find a way to get those Assembly pricks out there without the Frankfords stopping us," he said. "You might even manage to convince me not all of the Assembly people are pricks. I've got all the details on the patrols for us to go over. The guys from the gang—they wouldn't have counted on having magic on their side."

No. There was that. But as he pulled a sheaf of paper out of his pocket to go over those details, my heart had already sunk.

What good did it do us to know how to reach the right Assembly members if we couldn't show them what we needed to?

Jin

"Well," I said, toeing a charred chunk of plaster that had fallen from the even more charred gallery ceiling—or what was left of its ceiling. There didn't seem to be a whole lot else I could say.

Seth's mouth twisted as he rotated on his feet, taking in the whole space. The foundation of the building was still standing, but that was about it. The fire had gutted the rest, from the roof to the once-gleaming hardwood floor that was now a scorched mess of cinders. It'd eaten away at the white walls and the paintings that'd been hung on them, exposing the brick exterior from the inside out. All that was left of the second floor were some blackened stumps of joists protruding from the edges of the space like jagged fingernails.

The smell of burnt wood and plaster hung heavy in

the air. I rubbed my nose. With each breath, the stink coated my throat too.

"Yeah," Seth said, coming to a stop facing me again. "I don't think there's much we can preserve here. We'll need to strip it completely and rebuild from scratch."

I nodded. I'd figured as much after seeing the reports, but I'd wanted to get an educated second opinion. Even if hearing that opinion made me feel a little sick.

It was hard not to picture the gallery the way it had been the last time I'd set foot in it—hard not to remember the works I'd been proud of creating or acquiring that were now simply gone. Their absence resonated through me twice as strong as before, standing here where they'd used to be. My whole chest ached with it.

"You lost a lot," Seth said quietly.

"Things," I said with a dismissive gesture that wasn't really honest. "At least no one was hurt."

I should have known he wouldn't buy that. We all knew each other too well at this point, and Seth had never been one to shy away from tough conversations.

"I'm pretty sure your art was more than just 'things' to you," he said with a hint of dryness. "You don't have to pretend it doesn't matter, Jin. I can't say I know exactly how you feel, but I know how awful it is, looking at the way those people have destroyed things or nearly managed to and not knowing how to properly fight back."

A lump rose in my throat. My voice was a little hoarse when I answered. "It sucks. That about sums it up, right? But... we knew we were messing with something dangerous from the moment we got involved with Rose again. We knew there could be trouble. I can't imagine going back and making some other decision about whether to be with her. I lost a bunch of artwork—I can make more. If we let that faction get away with what they're doing, they'll keep ruining who knows how many lives."

"We're doing something good," Seth agreed. "It'd just be easier if we knew we'd all come out of it okay. All of us, including Rose." He paused. "I don't want to think what she might have done if they'd actually managed to kill my dad. She was so angry even after what did happen…"

I hadn't been there when Rose had tortured her former teacher for answers, but I'd heard enough of the other guys' talk about it to know it'd been brutal to watch. I loved Rose when she was fierce and filled with power, but it'd pained me a little just seeing the rage tear through her when she'd heard the news before they'd headed out.

"She's sorting herself out," I said. And we'd keep bracing ourselves for the next potential attack we couldn't really predict. So far no other witches had come into town, but that didn't mean the Frankfords weren't making new plans. My lips curved into a slanted smile. "I guess if I really want to be safe, I'll have to have the new studio and gallery built on Rose's property."

I meant it as a joke, but Seth's expression turned thoughtful. "She'd let you, you know. We could clear a spot—even add a new gate and a road in."

I laughed. "Like that wouldn't get tongues wagging ten times as fast. No, I think I'll stick to creating rather than displaying until this is all over." I'd ended up taking over one of the brighter rooms in the manor for my work, since I'd ended up doing an awful lot of art incorporating Rose's magical glyphs. The temporary apartment I'd found over one of the shops in town was a good enough sleeping spot for now, for the nights I didn't spend with her.

Seth gave me a knowing look. "Have people gotten on your case?"

Had they gotten on his? I shrugged. "Nothing major. A few odd looks here and there, but I'm pretty used to those already." I didn't want to talk about the one person who'd really spoken up, whose comments had niggled at me. The other guys didn't need to know that my mom had decided Rose was ruining my life. I'd rather *I* didn't know it.

"Well, when you're ready to start planning, just give me a shout," Seth said. We headed out onto the street together. "For a project that big, you'll need to bring an architect on, but I can help you find a good team."

"Thanks," I said. "I appreciate it."

"Do you want a ride over to your mother's place?"

"Nah, I can walk that." I hefted the bag I'd brought with me out of the back of Seth's pick-up truck. I wasn't exactly looking forward to this visit either. It'd be even worse if she started complaining in front of him.

But even if I was frustrated with Mom, I wanted her safe. The painting I had in this bag should be one step toward that. Not enough, but I knew Rose was doing everything she could.

The muscles in my arms were starting to ache by the time I'd carried the heavy painting through the streets to my mother's house. After my conversation with Seth, I was even more aware of the occasional figure by a drawn curtain, noting my passing. Although maybe any gossip about me now would be more along the lines of, "The poor Lyang boy, did you hear about his art gallery?" with plenty of hand-wringing on the side.

I'd rather that than them discussing my love life.

I knocked on the screen door of my parents' house and then walked right in. I'd texted Mom, so she knew to expect me. "I'm here," I said. "And I brought something for you."

Mom emerged from the living room. Her smile looked a bit strained. "Jin," she said, "I don't need presents."

"I think you'll appreciate this," I said in my breeziest tone. "You were worried about my creative growth being stunted. Well, now you have definitive proof that I'm still making art."

I carried the bagged painting into the living room and glanced around. Rose had said the magic would work best where it could draw on the energy of sunlight as well. She'd adjusted the spell to try to increase its protective power that way. I'd already known the perfect spot for it.

"Can I take that down?" I said, motioning to the impressionist landscape she had hanging over the couch. "If you decide you don't like mine, we can switch them back."

"All right," Mom said, but she fidgeted with her hands as I stepped onto the couch to unhook the painting from where it was mounted. "You know, producing one painting doesn't change the point I was trying to make. It's about the whole artistic spirit, the creative drive. I think there's a reason so many artists are pretty much married to their work. That's what's best for the art. If you turn all that devotion onto a person instead, you just don't have the emotional energy you need."

Oh Lord, I'd hoped she wouldn't start in on this right away. "Mom," I said. "Can we not talk about that right now? I'm trying to do something nice for you here. And I *am* still devoted to my art. You really don't have to worry."

"I have to say something. You don't think it's awfully strange that while she's distracting you from your work, your gallery mysteriously catches fire? Do you think she really wants to compete with a passion like—"

I set the painting down with a louder thump than I'd intended and spun around. "Are you seriously suggesting that *Rose* might have arranged for my gallery to be burned down because she's jealous of my art?"

"Well, I..." Mom faltered a little at the sharpness of my voice, but I could tell from the flash of her eyes that she had meant exactly that. "How well do you really know her, Jin?"

"More than well enough," I said. "And you should know her better than that too. Just stop, okay. Let me get this up." And then I'd probably be leaving again, because I sure as hell wasn't sitting through more of this conversation. For fuck's sake, didn't she remember how Rose had come here just a couple months ago offering everything she could to make up for how her dad had abruptly fired Mom?

I tugged the bag off my painting and lifted it to set it in place on the wall.

"I know you don't want to hear it, but it's not about what you want," Mom started in again. "It's about—"

The painting tapped against the wall and settled into place. My mother's voice faded. She looked at it, and at the sun streaming through the window, and rubbed her forehead. Her expression clouded. "What was I saying?" she said. "There was something important, but it just escaped me."

I stepped down from the couch and studied her. "Are you okay, Mom? You were talking about my art, and Rose."

"Oh. Yes." She paused, still looking bewildered. Her gaze went back to the painting. A smile crossed her face. "That's lovely, Jin. Thank you. Are you sure you don't want it for when you get a new gallery set up?"

Her sudden change in demeanor was unnerving. I kept watching her warily. "No, I made this specially for you. Actually, Rose helped a little." In magical rather than artistic ways.

Mom's face brightened more. "Did she? I'm so glad you've found someone as supportive as she obviously is."

What the hell was going on? Had someone just replaced my mother's brain?

I looked around the room, and it hit me. Maybe someone had—but not right now. This was how I'd have expected Mom to talk before she'd started getting all strange about Rose.

What if those thoughts hadn't really come from her head? What if some magic had been stirring up paranoia and distrust? A magic the protective spell on the painting had just disrupted.

My heart started to thud faster. The Frankfords had been acting against us in ways so subtle I hadn't even realized. What might they have been doing to the other guys and their families? To the whole town, for all we knew?

I had to get back to the manor. Rose needed to know this—everyone needed to know.

But first I had to say one more thing to Mom, for the parts of her that paranoia had fed on.

"Sit down for a second," I said. "I've got to go, but there's something I want to talk about with you first."

She frowned as we sat on the couch together. "Is something the matter?"

"No, Mom. It's just..." I dragged in a breath. "I know you care a lot about seeing me pursue my passion for art, just like Dad has always been wrapped up in his music. You want me to find someone who's going to be my support, like you've been for him."

"Of course," Mom said.

"And that's fine. But I think—" My mind drifted to the forms I'd done with Rose, that dance of magic where we'd seemed to move in perfect harmony with each other, and a rush of warmth filled my chest. "I think maybe I'll be happy sometimes being the supportive one for someone else. I want that kind of relationship in my life, one where I'm helping someone else achieve what they need to, too. So I don't want you to worry that just because I'm not setting off to indulge my creativity all around the world every other month that it means I'm losing my art. I'm always going to have that passion. I don't want to chase it quite the way Dad does; that's all. Okay?"

Mom looked at me for a long moment. Then she clasped my hand with a quick squeeze. "You're a good boy, Jin," she said. "No, I should say a good man. You know what you need in your life. You go chase that, and as long as I can see that joy in you, I'll be happy for you."

The tension in my chest loosened. For a moment, even with everything I'd just learned, the battle ahead of us didn't feel quite so hopeless.

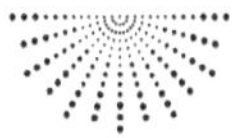

CHAPTER TWENTY-ONE

Rose

"Is it okay if everyone stays?" I asked Jin. "I want the other witches to start feeling like more a part of what we're doing."

My artist glanced across the family room to where my guests had gathered. Lesley was perched at the edge of one of the sofas, her hands clasped on her lap. Imogen sat at the other end, her arm dangling over the side. Thalia hovered behind them. Every minute or so she paced a few steps, as if she didn't feel comfortable staying totally still.

"I guess we're a little past the point of total secrecy," Jin said with half a smile. He dropped his voice so they couldn't hear. "I don't think anything I want to talk about should conflict with the oath. And maybe they'll have some insight that'll help us."

He'd called my remaining consorts together here in

the manor too. The twins were sitting on the other sofa, Seth's forehead furrowed and Kyler's foot tapping against the floor nervously. Damon was slouched in one of the armchairs. His dark blue eyes looked even more shadowed than usual. Jin hadn't said yet what he wanted to talk about, but it was clear he thought it was important. And when the most carefree spirit of our group got serious, it was hard not to worry.

The manor's cook had baked fresh tarts for this get-together, but even with the crisp lemon-sugar smell drifting off their plate on the coffee table, no one had moved to take one. I guessed we were all too tense.

Everyone's eyes followed Jin and me as we moved from the doorway to join the group. I sank onto the sofa between Seth and Ky, taking comfort in their presence, and Jin dropped into an armchair.

"I might as well get right to the point," he said. "In the last week or so, my mother has been making comments about Rose—the time that I'm spending with her, how committed I might be to her... Comments trying to convince me that I shouldn't be seeing her."

My back stiffened. "Jin," I started, but he held up his hand.

"You need to hear all of this," he said. "It's not as bad as it sounds—and, well, maybe it's worse too. I thought there must just be a lot of gossip going around town, and that must be provoking a side of her I hadn't really seen before... But I brought a painting with protective magic to her house this afternoon. As soon as I got it up on the wall, she couldn't even remember what she'd been upset about. She went back to sounding like herself."

Not as bad and also worse, he'd said. I could see what he'd meant now. "She wasn't really upset," I said. "There must have been magic acting on her that the protective spell interfered with."

Imogen's eyes widened. Thalia had stopped in the middle of another pacing moment, leaning her arms on the back of the sofa. On either side of me, the twins exchanged a glance.

"That's what I have to think," Jin said. "And I have to think if our adversaries were trying to stir up her paranoias, they probably went after all of our families."

That wouldn't have applied to Gabriel, since his dad was dead and he had no contact with his mother. But the other guys...

Ky shifted on the sofa, his head ducking awkwardly. "I didn't want to talk about it, because it didn't change anything about how I felt," he said. "But my mom started hassling me about how much time I've been spending up here a couple weeks ago."

Seth grimaced. "She's laid into me too. My dad even made a few harsher comments the last time I saw him... If the spells are directed at the house, that makes sense, since she's home a lot more than he is."

My heart squeezed. "You didn't tell me they were giving you a hard time."

"Like Ky says, there wasn't any point," Seth said. "You'd have felt bad about it. We knew it wasn't going to be possible to avoid rumors altogether. We were prepared to get some comments."

"I've heard my grandmother talk about a spell like that," Lesley put in, her voice quiet but steady. "She told this story about how when the Assembly wanted to help a lot of unsparked people during an approaching emergency, one quick way was to make them feel more fearful, so they'd react to the earlier smaller signs of danger and get out of there faster. But sometimes that could backfire and they'd end up freaking out over totally unrelated things."

Thalia was nodding, her mouth tight. As if she knew of those spells but couldn't talk about them. Because she'd seen or heard her husband and his associates using that strategy?

I gritted my teeth. I couldn't talk about the oath in front of the other witches, but that explained how the Frankfords' people could have gotten around it. A general spell to increase apprehension could be framed as something helpful, not harmful. But they could easily have guessed that the guys' parents would be sensitive to rumors of a strange relationship with a woman who wasn't really part of the town.

It wasn't just paranoia. If that was the sort of spell that'd been used on the guys' parents, then it was feeding off concerns they really did have about me, deep down. How much were those concerns exaggerated and how much had their comments been truths they simply wouldn't have said otherwise?

"I was working on the tokens to lay around the property," Jin said, "but I'm thinking I'll put that on hold to get a bunch more paintings done for you all to bring to your parents' houses. Maybe their workplaces too? We'll just need to talk about what they'd be willing to display, or if I need to make smaller ones that you could just tuck away somewhere, that sort of thing. I can get a bunch done tonight and tomorrow if I don't get too ambitious in size."

Damon hadn't said anything during the entire exchange. "Have you visited your mom recently?" I asked him. "How's she doing?"

He shrugged, his gaze flicking away from me for a second. "Pretty much the same. Can't hurt to make sure her apartment is protected too, though."

From the tension in his shoulders, I had the feeling there was something more on his mind. But Damon wasn't always a fan of group sharing. I'd have to nudge him about it the next time we were alone.

"I don't understand," Imogen burst out. "Why won't these people just leave you alone? You're not *doing* anything."

My mouth slanted at a pained angle as I looked at the younger witch. "They're worried about what we could do. What we wanted to do. We know things they don't want anyone outside their circle knowing, and that means we're a threat as long as we're around at all."

She shuddered, her curls rustling. "It seems like there's nothing you can even do."

"We can do this," I said. "Construct as many protections as possible, ward them off in every direction we can. And—"

My phone chimed with an incoming text. I pulled it out, expecting to see a message from Naomi, who was the only person who even had the number for the burner phone I used for my more confidential conversations other than my consorts.

It came up as an unknown number. *Is this Rose Hallowell?*

Ky leaned over to peer at the screen. "They've cloaked their number."

"Can you get around that, figure out who it is?" I asked.

"Maybe. Depends on what method they're using." He grabbed his tablet, which he never let get very far from his side. "The more texts you can get them to send, the better. More activity I can try to trace."

I nodded. "It could be a witch who needs help. Naomi might have passed the number on." Even as I said that, though, I didn't really believe it. Naomi might like to joke around about our situation, but she took it very seriously underneath. She hadn't compromised the security of this number with anyone before.

It is, I wrote back. *Who is this?*

We waited in silence for the reply. Jin scooted closer on his chair to watch. A long text popped up on the screen a minute later.

That doesn't matter. All you need to think about is that it's more than time for you to back down from this ridiculous fight. You know how outnumbered and outclassed you are. The longer you stretch this out, the worse things will get for you and everyone around you.

My stomach flipped over. Definitely not someone asking for help. "Wonderful," I said. "Now they're sending anonymous threats. How did they even—"

Oh. I knew how they'd gotten this number. Gabriel must have told them. The sharp retort I'd been forming faltered.

He really had gone over to them if he was giving them information like this.

Ky tucked his arm around my back with a reassuring squeeze that suggested he'd connected the same dots. "I'll pick you up another burner they won't know the number to," he said.

"Should I answer this? Keep them talking?" I asked.

He nodded. "As long as you can stomach it. Maybe they'll let something useful slip in the conversation too. Act like you don't believe them."

"Yeah," Damon said with a vicious grin. "Provoke them and see what you get."

"If you want me to do the talking," Seth started to offer.

I shook my head even though my throat had clenched. "I can handle this." I should be able to do at least this much.

We've dealt with everything you've thrown at us so far, I typed back. *Somehow I'm not so worried.*

This reply came back faster. *And yet your own consorts are no longer so devoted. Even they think you need to be stopped. Look who I have right here with me.*

A photo came through in crisp color: Gabriel, sitting to the side of what looked like a dining table. He was looking at something off camera, not toward me, but my heart lurched anyway. I almost dropped the phone.

Ky took it from me, gently extricating it from my tensed fingers. "Do you recognize the place?" he asked, his voice gentle too. "Do you know where he is?"

I forced myself to check the photograph again. The phone was zoomed in enough that there wasn't much to see around Gabriel except the end of the table and a cabinet with a glazed clay pot and a brass pendulum clock. The wall above the cabinet was painted a plain beige. Nothing about it looked familiar.

"If I've ever been there, I don't remember it."

Thalia skirted the other sofa and came up beside ours. Ky offered her the phone. She studied the photo, and her eyes widened.

"I know it," she said. "In the basement. Their house in Portland. The..." She stumbled around something—whatever spells they'd laid on her prevented her from saying. "Meetings," she managed finally. "So many meetings."

"The Frankfords' house?" I said, watching her expression.

Her jaw tightened. She couldn't quite nod, but her unwavering gaze was answer enough.

"Wait," Lesley said, sitting up straighter. "Charles and Helen Frankford?"

"It could be one of them sending these texts," Ky said. "We've got a location, at least." He tapped away at his tablet.

"Yes," I said to Lesley, because I could at least confirm that. I took the phone back from Ky and typed quickly, trying not to look at the photo.

Or you drew him in with magic. You've sent enough of that our way.

I resent that implication. Mind-altering magic is against Assembly law, even if you've gotten away with it. Your dear fellow came of his own free will. And I'm sure the others will follow soon.

"Rose," Seth said, his voice low. "He's just saying garbage to upset you. Let me."

"No," I said. "I've got to—"

But whoever I was talking to had already sent another message. *You've heard what I have to say. Think carefully before you make any more moves. It's a shame to live with regrets.*

Sounds like a lot of bluster to me, I shot back, but no further reply came. "I think they're done," I said. "Did you get enough?"

"I don't know yet," Ky said, his gaze intent on his tablet. "If I can find the right cross-reference..."

I let out a shaky breath. Seth took my hand, pulling me closer to him.

"They're just trying to rattle you like the assholes they are," Damon said. "Don't let them get to you. Don't let *him* get to you."

Gabriel, he meant. I wouldn't have been rattled anything like this if they hadn't used him.

Which was why they had, of course. They wanted to distract me from what mattered the most—taking them down.

"Right," I said. "Just the same thing they've been doing all along. Try to get at me through the people I care about." I rubbed my temple. I couldn't let that strategy work, not again.

A fierce gleam lit in Damon's eyes. "Any way we could turn that around on them? Or do they not care about anyone except themselves?"

I paused. The idea sent a sliver of nausea through my gut, but at the same time, he might have a point. "They have a daughter," I said, "in her thirties, already consorted... I don't know what the situation is there. They never talked about her all that warmly. Other than..."

"What?" Jin said when I hesitated again.

"There is someone they always talked about a certain way," I said. "I never heard them talk about anyone else like that... They have a grandson. He's seven. Their 'little treasure.'"

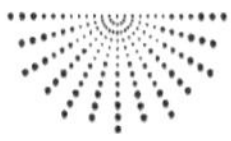

CHAPTER TWENTY-TWO

Damon

When I arrived at the Hallowell estate in the hot mid-day sun to pick up Jin, he was waiting in the front hall. The paintings he'd done for my mom's apartment were already packaged up.

"I can unwrap them to show you them, so you can make sure you think she'll like them," he offered. "I went by what you said, but the way artistic tastes go, it can be hard to tell..."

I waved him off. Like he wanted to spend any more time than he needed to on my troubles. It'd been embarrassing enough going to him after last evening's little meeting and telling him I was pretty sure my mom had been affected, maybe a lot, so I definitely wanted a few of those enchanted artworks to hang around her apartment.

I should have realized something was up with her in

the first place, the way she was talking. How could I have believed she'd really think that way about Rose?

Kyler loped out of the house while we were loading the paintings into the trunk, looking annoyingly chipper as ever. I'd gotten the impression he was spending more nights at the manor than in his apartment in town, what with all the digging he was doing through the Frankfords' files. From what he'd said, he was worried that if he brought any device with the files away from the property, the Frankfords' might figure out we'd copied them and come after us even harder. I figured he didn't mind the excuse to keep Rose company at night.

I guessed I couldn't really fault him for that. The brainiac did have some catching up to do when it came to that kind of experience.

"Hey," he said. "Hope you don't mind me tagging along. We did my parents' house this morning. I'd like to look around and see if I notice any common patterns that might tell us how the spell was set down or working or whatever."

"You never know how to turn off research mode, do you?" I said.

He grinned. "It's worked out well for us so far."

I couldn't deny that. "Sure," I said, even though I could already picture the faces the two of them were going to make when they saw Mom's shabby place. She wasn't going to be picky about the art. She'd be thrilled to have anything decent up at all. The best she had right now was a couple of faded poster prints tacked to the living room wall.

Well, let them see how people who'd been a little less

fortunate lived. I didn't need to be embarrassed about that. If they wanted to look down their noses at my family like most people in town did, then let them.

"How was your mother the last time you saw her?" Ky asked as we got in the car, already diving into the information-gathering part of the trip apparently.

"I haven't stopped by since she freaked out about me seeing Rose," I said. "I figured she needed some cooling off time." And I hadn't wanted to risk hearing another rant like that one. I wanted to still *like* my mother when all this was over. "She's been fine when I've checked in by text, but it's pretty normal for us not to talk much except when I go see her. She's busy with work."

"She's cleaning for what's-his-name, the guy who bought up all those properties on the south side, right?" Jin said.

"Yeah. He expects long hours." And he expected his employees to put up with a whole heap of nasty comments. I'd overheard him verbally leering at my mother once and the only reason the guy still had his dick attached was because she'd pleaded with me not to go off on him. She needed that job, she said. I was pretty sure she could have found something better. If she'd tried some longshots, something would have panned out, but she was afraid of people scoffing at her for even trying. She found leers easier to take than sneers.

Thankfully, Jin didn't make any comment about what other jobs Mom maybe could have gotten or what a step down it was to go from cleaning some majestic manor house to people's apartments that weren't really that much nicer than her own. I hit the gas and turned us toward town.

In the middle of a weekday, the streets were particularly quiet. It didn't take long to reach the house my mom lived on the second floor of. I parked in the driveway, and we each grabbed one of the paintings to bring up. Jin had done a large one for the living room and a couple of smaller ones for wherever we could reasonably put them.

"She didn't reply to my text saying we were coming by," I said as we started up the rickety stairs along the side of the house. "Might have her phone turned off on the job. I've got a key anyway. Better that we get this stuff up as soon as possible. If she's not here, I'll stick around to show off her 'present'."

I didn't look back at the other guys as I talked, not really wanting to see their expressions as they took in the place. They were probably already looking forward to when they could get out of here.

No one answered when I knocked on the door. I knocked again and then fished my keys out of my back pocket. The door squeaked as I opened it. A sour smell immediately filled my nose, so gross I winced.

Normally Mom kept the apartment at least *clean*. What the hell was that?

"Mom?" I called, heading in and setting down the packaged painting in the short front hall. "Are you home?"

No answer, but the smell thickened. My pulse started to thump harder. I peeked into the living room and then turned to the kitchen.

A leg was protruding, sprawled, from the other side of the table. My heart just about burst out of my chest. I threw myself around the table.

Mom was slumped there on her stomach, her arms splayed, a pool of half-dried vomit on the floor near her face. Her skin was clammy when I touched her cheek. Her eyelids fluttered at the contact but stayed closed.

Fuck. *Fuck.* What the hell did I do now?

As panic blared through my body, Kyler dropped down next to my mom. His eyes widened, but he managed to keep his voice even. "We have to check for a pulse and make sure she's breathing," he said. "If she's not, I know CPR."

"You *know*, or you internet-know?" I couldn't help muttering automatically.

Ky gave a choked laugh. "Internet-know, but let's hope that's good enough, right?"

As he pressed his fingers to the side of her neck, Jin's voice carried from the doorway. "Yes, the second floor. She's unconscious. I don't know for how long, but it looks serious. Ten minutes? Okay. What should we do until then?"

He had emergency services on the line. I held my hand by my mother's nose and felt a wisp of breath at the same moment as Ky announced, "Got a pulse! It's pretty erratic, though."

"They say to cover her up with a blanket or something," Jin said. "To make sure she doesn't go into shock."

I leapt up and ran into her bedroom. Oh, God, she wouldn't want me to use her usual duvet, risk getting puke on it—she'd saved up to buy that one special. I snatched a spare wool blanket out of the closet and dashed back.

Ky helped me roll Mom onto her side. Her head lolled so limply that my chest clenched like a vice. "The ambulance will be here soon?" I said to Jin, even though I'd heard what he'd said on the phone with my own ears.

He nodded. "I'll get the paintings up while we're waiting. If this was another magical attack, maybe they'll help her until the paramedics get here."

Right. They might even help *more* than any doctor could, depending on what those witching assholes had done to her. I checked Mom over one more time and, seeing no change, scrambled up. "I'll help you. You take the living room and I'll put one in the bedroom."

"This one would be good for that," he said, shoving one of the paintings toward me. He handed me a couple of nails and braces. I grabbed a hammer from a drawer. One of the few tools Mom kept on hand.

In the bedroom, I tore the plastic wrapping off the painting as quickly as I could—and froze for a second staring at the image. It was a spray of lilies, so perfectly painted you could almost believe they were leaning out of the canvas. I couldn't see where the enchanted glyphs were woven in even though I knew to look for them.

Mom was going to cry when she saw this, it was so nice. It must have taken Jin a while to pull that off.

I shook myself out of the momentary daze and picked a spot to mount the painting. When I came out, I found Jin hanging the other small one in the hall. That one matched the bedroom picture, but with orange lilies instead of purple.

I went around to the living room to check out the larger one and had to stop and stare again. It was a landscape, a meadow dotted with all kinds of flowers, the sun rising over treed hills in the distance.

Jin came to stand beside me. "You said she liked flowers, especially lilies, and peaceful landscapes," he said. "I tried to hit that as dead on as I could."

"You did an amazing job," I said with bald honesty. I wasn't any kind of an art connoisseur, but I knew a fantastic painting when I saw one. "She's no critic, you know. She'd have been happy with something a lot more basic."

Jin shrugged. "If you're going to do a thing, might as well do it well. My signature is on these, you know."

He winked at me, but there was a kindness in his smile that made me waver on my feet. I'd figured it was just a job to him, just busy work to make Rose happy since I mattered to her. But Jin looked honestly pleased that I appreciated the pictures. Hell, he and Ky had jumped in there the second they'd seen my mom was in trouble, as if she meant almost as much to them as she did to me.

"Her pulse is feeling steadier!" Ky hollered from the kitchen. "I think the protections must be helping."

I hustled over to wait with Mom for the last couple minutes until the ambulance got here. My heart wrenched again, seeing her on the floor, but a weird sort of warmth had settled over me too.

Whatever had happened to her, it was awful. I

wanted to tear those pricks like the Frankfords limb from limb. But if I had to, I wouldn't be alone. The other guys would be right there with me. I was suddenly sure of that.

"Thanks," I said as I brushed her hair back from her forehead. "For, well, everything."

"Of course," Ky said. "Do you want us to stick with you going to the hospital? I don't mind. I don't have any plans I can't delay."

I looked from him to Jin, who nodded to show the offer included him.

Fifteen minutes ago, I wouldn't have thought I'd want any of the other guys' company for something like this. But now... there was actually a little comfort in the idea. I didn't have to wait it out alone.

For the first time since my dad had taken off all those years ago, I had more family than just Mom.

"Yeah," I said, the words sticking in my throat before I forced them out. "If you could... I'd like that."

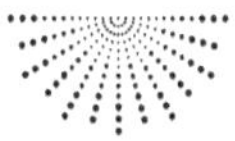

CHAPTER TWENTY-THREE

Rose

My hands gripped the steering wheel so tightly my knuckles ached. I flexed my fingers, urging them to relax, but within a minute they'd clenched again.

We had a new moon tonight, the sky dim except for a smattering of stars. The country roads were so quiet it almost felt as if the two of us in the car were the last people in the world. Damon, hunched over in the seat next to me with his head resting on the window, let out a soft rasp of sleeping breath. Even asleep, the muscles in his arms looked coiled tight.

He'd tried to convince me that he should drive back, even though he'd run himself ragged pacing the halls while the doctors had worked on his mom and running around grabbing everything he could think of that would make her more comfortable once she was awake and in recovery. Despite himself, he'd nodded off within a few minutes of us leaving the hospital. I'd have to wake him up once we got back to the estate, but he deserved this rest.

It was those memories—of his mom, wan and trembling, and Damon, his face stark with fear—that kept tearing through me, jarring against my nerves. The Frankfords or their lackeys had been responsible for this. That was the only explanation that made sense. The doctors hadn't found anything wrong with Mrs. Scarsi that would have caused her to collapse like that. They'd dismissed it as food poisoning, but she couldn't think of anything she'd eaten that would have caused that.

And anyway, how huge of a coincidence would that be?

I had no idea how they'd twisted their magic around the oath this time, but they'd managed it before. They'd shown they could be creative.

After a while at the hospital, the other guys had left to find a pretense for hanging out with their parents for a while. Jin wanted to set up some sort of protections around his mother's yard, and Lesley had offered to do the magicking while I was away. Jin was going to make more art for the twins' dad's hardware store and the café where their mom worked. But that still wasn't enough.

I didn't think the Frankfords would be satisfied unless we were all dead. And right now every inch of me was burning to pay them back in kind.

How would they feel if it was their grandson unconscious in a pool of his own vomit? Or buried under a fallen building? Would that make them realize what monsters they were?

But I'd have to turn myself into a monster to show them that. I wouldn't ever have put a kid's life at risk, but part of me was willing to make a bluff of it, to push right up to the line between momentary fear and pain and actual trauma... and could I say for sure whatever I set up wouldn't accidentally tip over?

I could try to blaze through whatever protections the Frankfords had in place around their own home, their car, probably anywhere they spent any time these days... There was a chance I could manage it, and fast enough to be done before the Assembly came after me. If *they* were dead, this would all be over, wouldn't it?

No, there'd still be the demons on the other side of that portal. What if the Frankfords were the only ones who knew how to control them?

But they couldn't just *get away* with this.

My mind bounced back and forth in an exhausted circle. My rage had been simmering from the moment Kyler had called me to the hospital, and being angry was tiring. I just wanted to let the emotions out, to let them burn right through me and onto the people who deserved that rage.

The walls of the estate loomed by the right side of the road. I stopped at the gate and waited while it whirred open. Damon stirred as I parked by the garage.

"Hey," I said softly. "We're back. I thought you'd rather stay here for the night."

He sat up and rubbed his eyes blearily. His jaw clenched as he restrained a yawn. "Sounds good."

I undid my seatbelt, but then I stayed where I was. The shell of the car contained everything I was feeling right now. I had the sense that if I stepped out while my emotions were still churning like this, they'd somehow explode out into the open air.

"What do *you* think I should do?" I said.

Damon glanced over at me. "Probably get out and go to bed," he said, but his eyes were serious. He knew I meant more than that.

"You thought I was right to go after Master Courtland like I did. To fight back. 'Burn them all down,' isn't that what you said when we first found out what the Frankfords were doing?"

"Sounds like me," he agreed. "Why? Do you have a plan for burning them down? Can I be there to strike the match?"

"If I did, of course you could," I said. "I just... I want to hurt them for what they did to you. For what they did to all of you. But I know it's not because I think it's a good strategy or that it'll really fix anything in the bigger picture. It'll just make me feel like the world's a little more fair." Make me feel a little less helpless.

"Are you asking me for permission to go ballistic on their asses?" Damon asked. "I'm not sure I'm the person you should be checking with when it comes to moderation."

"That's why I'm asking you." I dropped my hands into my lap, but they squeezed into fists there. "It was your mom this time. It's my fault—"

"It's not your fault," he broke in sharply. "None of this is your fault. They're the fucking villains."

"Okay," I said, although his words didn't quite make the guilt go away. "We've got some fucking villains. Is that what you'd want to see me do—'go ballistic' on them? Would it make you feel better?"

Damon opened his mouth and hesitated. He wet his lips. "Rose... I'd gladly see those fuckers dead. You know that. Do I want you to be the one who does it? Not, like, defending yourself, but planning it out, calculated murder?" He groaned. "I don't know. I want them to come at you and give you a reason to blast them to smithereens. I want a proper fight like when we were on the road, not this sneaking around."

"We don't have that," I said. "We have this. But I can still fight."

"You are fighting," he said. "You have been fighting." He was silent for a moment. "I don't for one second think you've done anything wrong since this whole thing started, angel. I love the fire you get when you're angry—I love you fierce. But I love the part of you that stopped to ask me this instead of burning them all down to begin with too."

He stopped for a moment, his head bowing. "You're a good person, Rose. You're the kind of person who goes out of her way to see the good in other people. I'm damned lucky you are, or I probably wouldn't be here with you right now."

His words yanked at my heart. "Damon..."

"You know it's true," he said, meeting my eyes again. "I was a bastard to you when you first came back, but you've never held that against me. I don't want you to lose that side of who you are. You do what you feel you have to do. I'd never stand in your way. I'm never going to leave, not unless you tell me to. But maybe one person aiming to burn everyone to the ground is enough? Maybe you should leave that approach to me, and you be you."

I swallowed hard. He was right. I wouldn't have asked him in the first place if I'd really been sure I should give in to that rage.

He leaned in to kiss me, and I melted into his embrace. There was a tenderness I wasn't used to under his usual intensity. He kept his head close when our lips parted, his hand cupping my face.

"Thank you," he said. "For asking me. For caring enough to be that angry. For letting me be a part of this crazy, fucked up, incredible life with you."

A different sort of lump filled my throat. I kissed him again, hard. "I wouldn't want to be doing this without you."

"You've got me, angel. All the way to the end."

We finally got out of the car and walked up to the house. Damon slung his arm around my waist, knowing there'd be no staff around at this hour to notice. I didn't expect anyone at all to be up, but when I opened the door I found the hall light on. A murmur of laughter carried from the sitting room.

Lesley, Imogen, and Thalia were sitting around the card table there, playing rummy from the look of the table, glasses of wine interspersed with the cards. My assorted witch guests glanced up at us with smiles that were a little tipsy, probably both from the alcohol and the late hour.

"You're back!" Imogen said. "We waited up for you. To make sure you were okay and all."

"We were prepared to rush to your rescue if need be," Lesley informed us in an over-serious tone, and then giggled.

Thalia's gaze was a little more solemn. "Nothing's changed since you called? She's still recovering?"

"It looks like she should be fine in a few days," Damon said.

"And if you all want to be fine, I think you should get to bed after this hand," I added, raising my eyebrows. But nothing could have stopped a grin from crossing my face. They looked like they belonged here. Like they were happy here. I'd accomplished something if I'd been able to give them that. Maybe I should remember to count my victories as often as my failures.

Damon trailed after me upstairs. He waited for his turn to wash up, leaning against the counter in the en-suite bathroom while I used the sink.

"I don't know how you can be so sexy even when you're brushing your teeth," he said.

I waggled the toothbrush at him. "This is turning you on, is it?"

"I'll turn *you* on," he muttered, tugging me to him. I turned to face him—and my gaze caught on a dark shape darting around the sink.

A spider. Black with long spindly legs. The shape of it triggered a reflexive flinch before I'd consciously identified it. What in all that was lit and warm was a black widow doing in my *bathroom*?

I jerked back, pulling Damon with me, and more of

those black bodies raced across the floor, along the walls. A yelp burst from my throat.

They were everywhere. Dozens of them, everywhere I looked.

As I fled to the bedroom, a shriek carried from downstairs. It was the whole house. Spiders were scrambling all over the bedroom, not just on the walls and floor but across my mirror, over the sheets on the bed. A shudder rippled down my back.

As I spun around, trying to decide where to go, one dropped from the ceiling onto my arm. Before I could swat it off, its fangs dug into my skin with a jabbing pain.

Damon swore and kicked at the ones on the floor. Another scrambled up my pantleg. The bite on my arm burned. How long did I have before the major symptoms started?

Downstairs someone was babbling frantically, and someone else cried out. I sucked in a breath and threw all my focus into a spell.

A stomp of my feet. A whirl of my arms. The spark inside me sputtered and flared. I slammed my arms out straight from my sides with a force that rattled my bones and radiated through the entire house.

The spiders shot away from us as quickly as they'd appeared. Another jab seared through my calf where I must have been bitten without even noticing. Damon was clutching his shoulder where one had gotten him. A few more spiders skittered across the walls, and I hurled myself into the magicking one more time for good measure. Gone. We needed them all gone. Before—

Before they hurt anyone else? From the sobbing

filtering through the floor below, I didn't think I could hope for that anymore.

"Come on," I said, grabbing Damon's hand. "The others might need help."

"*You* need help," he protested, nodding to my arm.

"Not yet. I have to look after them first." They'd come to me for shelter... and they'd gotten this instead. With a ragged breath, I ran for the stairs.

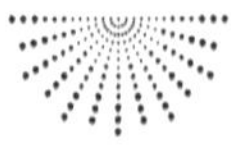

CHAPTER TWENTY-FOUR

Rose

It killed me to let this latest attack slow me down, but the next afternoon my muscles were still throbbing, my head still aching dully, as I spun out one more piece of the protective spell around the front yard and the back gardens. The magicking that had normally taken me about an hour each morning had stretched almost to dinner time as I'd had to stop and rest after every few minutes of casting.

It didn't help that I was adding another piece to dissuade any potentially dangerous creatures I could imagine the Frankfords sending toward us next. I wouldn't put it past them to encourage a herd of rattlesnakes onto the property. Maybe some imported fire ants?

Under that grim humor, my anger continued to smolder. I had no idea how they'd gotten around the oath not to harm us this time, but they were getting closer and closer to me and the people I cared about most with each loophole they opened. The Hallowell estate was *mine* now. And they'd dared to break even that boundary, to attack me and my guests in the one place I should have felt secure.

Thalia had managed to escape being bitten before I'd sent the black widows off, so she'd used whatever magic reserves she had left to stem the poison and ease its effects in those of us who hadn't been so lucky. There'd only been so much she could do, though. Even more spiders had come through downstairs. Lesley had suffered two bites and Imogen three. They'd spent most of the day in bed, sleeping the effects off.

Damon's one bite hadn't hurt him too badly. It'd made me nervous seeing him off to bring his mother home from the hospital, but he'd looked steady enough on his feet.

"I'll convince her she needs to take a few days off to rest," he'd said. "To stay in her apartment. They shouldn't be able to get at her again while she's there, right?"

"I don't think so," I'd said, but it'd been with an uncomfortable pang in my gut. I didn't actually know, because I didn't know what our enemies might try next. I hadn't been ready for a flood of poisonous spiders.

I was just coming back into view of the front gate when it swung open. Kyler ducked in, his face brightening when he saw me. He hurried over, his hands slung in the pockets of his khakis.

"How are you doing?" he asked. He, Seth, and Jin had already checked in a dozen times today. Seth had swung by earlier bringing fresh scones his mom had baked, and Jin to collect a couple of canvases. I knew they were torn between staying to look after me however they could and keeping an eye on their parents, but really it was their parents who needed more protection. I'd been able to defend myself at least partly.

"About the same," I said. "I've finally got the protections all reinforced."

I wiped my hands together, and his gaze dropped to the reddened mark on my arm where I'd taken one of the bites. He winced. "They're really pulling out every dirty trick in the book, aren't they?"

"I just wish I had the same book so I knew what to ward off next," I said with a crooked smile.

"No kidding." He dragged in a breath. "Are we okay to talk here? Should we go in the house?"

I motioned him closer to the manor. "We should be good here. What's up?"

He grinned. "I've got his number. Frankford's. Literally, I mean, although I guess it applies in the figurative sense too."

It took a few seconds for his words to sink in. "*The* number?" I said, my eyes widening. "The private one he'd use to call meetings with his colleagues? Are you sure it's the right one?"

"About as sure as I can be. I got into that account last night and started recording the texts in- and out-going. Earlier today he texted your dad reminding him of some restaurant where they talked last and then asking him to come to a different café. As soon as your dad replied,

Frankford deleted both of the messages. The whole account is pretty much blank."

My pulse kicked up a notch. "It sounds like he's still using it then. The number and the code. Even though Gabriel knew we were looking for it."

"Frankford might figure there's no way I could ever ferret it out in the first place," Ky said. "Arrogance tends to be the downfall of a lot of villains. Or they *are* working magic on Gabriel somehow, and they haven't managed to get that information out of him."

"Or Frankford knows and he switched codes, and he's just periodically sending dummy messages as a trap," I said.

Ky hesitated. "Yeah. That's possible too."

"And there isn't really any way to know, is there?"

"Well, I can check whether your dad really does go to that café, or at least near it, at the right time," Ky said. "Portland has lots of traffic cams. Although I wish they had a few more. It looked like Frankford and that Gwen Remington from the Assembly who we're hoping will be on our side headed out around the same times the other day, but I couldn't narrow down where they might have met up or if they definitely did."

"And we'd still need a plan for getting through all that security around the Cliff before we could use that information anyway."

"Hey." Ky stepped closer and wrapped his arms around me. "It's a start. We're getting there. These people have been doing what they do for decades. It's amazing how scared you have them after just a few months."

I hugged him back, ignoring the throbbing that spread

through my muscles as they flexed. "I know. But amazing doesn't really matter if it's not amazing enough to protect all of you."

"We're making it through. We're building up our defenses. It'll be easier to launch some kind offensive when we're not scrambling to stop their next attack so often."

"Right." I made myself inhale and exhale slowly, sinking into his embrace even more. Something he'd said tickled deeper into my head. I'd *scared* them. The Frankfords were doing some pretty crazy things trying to destroy us or at least convince us to leave them alone, and they'd started before I'd ever retaliated. "If I unnerve them enough, they might slip up more."

Ky rubbed my back. "What are you thinking, Rose?"

"I'm not completely sure yet. But can you give me a list of all the businesses and other buildings the Frankfords own? And their allies who seem the highest up too?"

"Of course." He gave me one last squeeze and stepped back. "I can go through the files and then the internet databases right now. It shouldn't take me more than an hour to get a pretty thorough list."

"Perfect."

When we came into the house, Imogen was standing in the hall. From her unusually meek posture, my first guess was that her aunt and uncle had been on her case again. Or maybe it was just the lingering effects of the spider bites dampening her energy.

Ky gave me a peck and headed upstairs. I waved the young witch over to the sitting room. "You look like you need to talk. Are your symptoms getting worse? I can try to help with that."

Imogen shook her head. She came into the room, but she didn't sit even after I'd closed the door behind us. She looked down at her hands and then at me.

"I'm going home," she said.

I blinked at her. "What? You don't mean—not to your aunt and uncle's house."

Imogen dropped her gaze again. Her red curls hung limply on either side of her wan face. An angry red blotch marked the side of her neck where she'd gotten one of the spider bites.

"I don't know everything that's going on," she said. "But there's obviously a lot going on, and you can't tell me, but someone is very, very angry with you, and... It seems like I'm in more danger here than I was back home. I can say no to my aunt and uncle. I can turn down suitors. I can't defend myself from massive spider attacks." She rubbed her elbow, where one of the other bites was.

"I've just laid down fresh protections," I said. "They've only managed to breach the spells I put in place here that once."

"But whoever's against you, they've hurt other people. I know from hearing you talk with your consorts. They're going to keep trying." She bit her lip. "And, I don't mean this as an insult, but I don't really know you. I don't know what you're messed up in. You've been really kind to me, and I'm grateful for that, but it just doesn't seem smart to completely throw myself in here when I don't even know..."

She trailed off as if hoping I'd take that cue to fill her in. I even opened my mouth, willing the words to come out. But the full truth of it, the nitty gritty details that would make her believe, were locked in my throat.

"They want to use you," I said. "They want to…" Spark help me, the specifics wouldn't dislodge from my throat. "I wish I could show you everything I know."

"But you can't. I get it." She let out a huff of breath and raised her chin. "I've got to look out for me just like you're looking out for you. As long as I don't take a consort I can't trust, I've got no magic for anyone to exploit anyway, right? I can hold my own back home."

A faint tremble ran through her voice. She didn't sound completely sure. How could she be, when her family's pressure had gotten so bad that she'd come running out here in the first place?

I groped for something more I could tell her, something that would convince her, keep her here safe. Once she was back with her aunt and uncle, who knew how they might persuade her to go along with their plans? How they might threaten her?

"We're getting closer to shutting them down," I said. "If you just wait a little longer…"

"They're going to fight you harder if you're getting closer, won't they?" She bit her lip. "I already made up my mind, Rose. Thank you so much for letting me stay here as long as I have. But I can't—I can't look anywhere without seeing those spiders, how they were crawling everywhere. I can't relax in this place anymore. It doesn't feel safe. So I have to go. I promise I won't tell anyone anything I overheard here, not that I think I know much that could hurt you anyway."

I hadn't even thought of that, I'd been so focused on how those people might hurt her. My lungs constricted. I didn't know how much of our planning she might have overheard. She couldn't know what details the Frankfords or their allies could use.

My fingers closed into my palm. I could have forced her to stay, said that was for the safety of everyone else here. Locked her in a room. Set a magical barricade tuned to her at the gate.

Like my stepmother had done to me once when she'd wanted to ensure I did what *she* wanted.

I forced my hand to relax, willing the tension clamped around my chest to loosen. I was not going to be that kind of witch. I was not going to trap Imogen like her family meant to.

"All right," I said. "I'll say one more time that I think you're still safer here, but I'm not going to stop you. Just... If you go back, please be careful. And you'll always be welcome here if you change your mind."

Imogen swallowed audibly. She gave me a quick squeeze of a hug. "Thank you," she said again. Then she was hustling out of the room. I watched her go, an even tighter hopeless feeling winding through me.

Every time I thought I'd gained a little ground, I lost more.

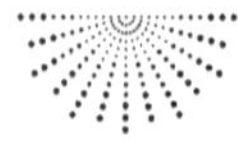

CHAPTER TWENTY-FIVE

Seth

"This stretch of land hasn't been used in almost twenty years," I said, nodding to the overgrown field on the outskirts of town as Rose and I drove past. "I looked up who the owner is, and they're open to selling. They just haven't had the motivation to really look into it."

Rose gazed out the window of the pick-up truck, her brow knitting, but she didn't say anything. She hadn't said much since I'd told her there were a few things around town I wanted to show her. I knew she was waiting for me to finish this little tour so she'd have all the pieces, but I could also see the stress weighing on her movements. It was more than the after effects of the bites she'd gotten.

My brother had told me one of the witches she'd taken in had gone back home yesterday. And Rose had already been beating herself up about the Frankfords piercing her home defenses.

Seeing her deflated like this made me ache from head to toe. I didn't think she was beaten, not for a second, but this constant conflict was wearing her down. I had to hope that the plan I was going to lay out for her would boost her spirits.

I turned the wheel, bringing us back around to the side of town where we'd started. I pointed to a for-sale sign standing near the road at the start of a long gravel driveaway. The house at the end of that drive wasn't much more than a shack. "And this one," I said. "It's going cheap. You want to take a look? The house is vacant at the moment."

"Okay," Rose said, sounding confused.

I parked partway up the drive, and we stepped out onto the gravel. It rattled under our footsteps as we walked a little closer to the house. The blue sky overhead was dotted with puffs of cloud, and a hot summer breeze wafted over us, not offering a whole lot of relief.

Rose considered the house for a minute and then glanced at me. "If I'm supposed to have figured out where you're going with all this, I'm lost," she said. "You've got something you're thinking of doing with all these properties? Isn't the one house we can't even use that much enough?"

I'd shown her seven spots at various points around the town. Closer than the farmhouse I'd renovated a couple months ago before everything had gone to hell.

I ran my hand over my hair. "Well, you can tell me if this sounds crazy."

"Crazy? You?" She raised an eyebrow with more of her usual good humor. "You're the last person I'd expect that from."

I chuckled. "Me too. But I was sitting with my dad this morning, looking at the painting Jin did for their living room, just being impressed by how well he worked in the glyphs you used for your magic—you'd never know it was anything other than a work of art. And my dad started talking about the addition we were building, the one that collapsed. Saying how we must have gotten too ambitious. We'd have to tell the clients we needed to cut back on the plans."

"And?" Rose said when I paused. "I guess you couldn't tell him there wasn't any problem with the plans to begin with."

"No. So I guess we'll just build a smaller addition there. But it got me thinking—maybe that's looking at things the wrong way. That's how *I'd* usually look at things: if something goes wrong, scale back until you get it right. The cautious approach. But maybe what we need right now, with as big a threat as that faction of witches is posing... Maybe we need to go big too. To do something that does sound crazy. I mean, magic is kind of crazy in general, to me anyway. So, who cares if it'd look bizarre to anyone who doesn't understand, as long as it works?"

Rose nodded, her expression thoughtful. "What's your big crazy idea, then?"

I held out the notepad of graph paper I'd been sketching on to show her the rough plans I'd been making. "We'd need to hire on someone professional to make sure the engineering side is all up to snuff, but the general idea is... build a little house on each of these properties using the shape of one of your protective glyphs in its structure and layout. Like seven huge protective symbols you can fill with magic, spaced all around town."

"Seven houses," Rose said, blinking.

I hurried on. "The witches like Lesley and Thalia who have nowhere else to go could stay there, and maybe they'd like to have that independence. More people like them could end up joining us too. And Damon might be able to convince his mom to move into one. Maybe he'd want to take one for himself. Jin too. I'm not sure how the magical side works, but if you could string a spell between them, maybe you could protect the whole town? At least more than you already can."

Rose's lips had parted. "Oh, wow. That's—that's amazing, Seth. I never would have come up with that on my own. But you know... with a glyph construction that big... I might be able to get the effect to radiate pretty far."

A rush of relief and joy swept through me. "That's great. I'd help as much as I can. Obviously I don't have the funds to buy up all the properties myself—"

Rose waved her hand dismissively. She was beaming now, her whole face lighting up as she considered the possibilities. "I've got the Hallowell accounts now. Our pockets run pretty deep. I can fund the properties and the building materials and whoever you need to hire on." She paused. "We wouldn't be able to get these up all that quickly, though, would we?"

"No," I said with a grimace. "The real estate side alone will take at least a few days, and then getting the permits, and construction... It isn't going to fix things right now. But it's something we can move toward. Something to offer any witches who need your help, so they know they're not going to be dependent on your estate forever. If we end up in a standstill instead of immediate victory, we'll be able to fight back harder next time once we have that infrastructure in place. If I could have come up with something that'd help us sooner..."

"This is wonderful," Rose said, touching my arm. She pulled me into a kiss, her light floral scent wisping around us. "Very ambitious, but not crazy at all."

Her gaze slipped past me for a second, and her body tensed. She eased away from me, turning as if to get something from the truck. I glanced behind me and saw a couple I recognized from town ambling along the country road. Just out taking a walk, it looked like. Of course they'd had to come along this lonely stretch while Rose and I were here.

Resolve tightened around my stomach. It felt *wrong* to stand here pretending there was nothing between me and the woman I'd just been kissing.

"Rose," I said, quietly so my voice wouldn't carry, "who are we protecting with that rule about not letting anyone know about our relationship?"

Rose looked at me with a frown. "What do you mean?"

"I mean, we don't have to *hide* it because of the oath. That just stops you from talking about it. Are you at all worried about what people would think about *you* if they found out?"

She hesitated. I could almost see her weighing the

truth against what she thought I'd do it if she told me to. But this was Rose. She'd never been anything but honest with me.

"No," she said. "They already think I'm weird. It doesn't matter to me if they think I'm weirder. I just—you guys still have to deal with your parents, your friends—you live there in town..."

I stepped closer to her, setting my hand on her waist. Her eyes darted toward the approaching couple and back to me.

"It's okay," I said, bowing my head toward her. "They can say whatever they want. The other guys can decide how they prefer to handle it, but I'm proud of what I have with you, and I don't give a shit what anyone else thinks. I'm in this with you until the end, in every way I can be."

"Seth..." A shimmer that looked like tears had come into Rose's eyes, but she was smiling. I cupped her face and pressed my lips to hers.

She kissed me back cautiously at first and then with growing heat. The movement of her mouth against mine sent an eager shiver through me. I nudged her back against the side of the truck, leaning into her. More heat flooded me where her breasts brushed my chest.

"I want you," I murmured against her mouth. "I love you. So goddamned much. I don't care who knows it."

She let out a shaky breath and then she was kissing me again, her arm slung around my neck as she bobbed up on her toes. I teased one hand into her hair as the other gripped her waist. If my neighbors were watching, they were getting quite an eyeful, but I didn't feel the slightest regret at that. This was what I'd signed up for—

to have this spectacular woman at my side. Why the hell would I hide that?

All that heat shot straight to my groin. My cock hardened against the fly of my jeans. It took all my self-control not to grind up against Rose right there and then. But we were still in view of that passing couple, and I didn't want to embarrass Rose with too huge a PDA.

The thought of hiding *that*, of pleasuring Rose without them realizing how far I was taking it, sent an unexpected thrill through me. I tipped my head back from hers. At the same moment I let my hand slide up from her waist. My body would block it from the view of anyone on the road.

"I want you, right here, right now."

"Seth!" She clamped her lips to muffle a gasp as my fingers traced over the tip of her breast. Her nipple hardened beneath the fabric of her thin dress and bra. I flicked my thumb over it, and she couldn't quite swallow a whimper. Her eyes had hazed with desire.

I lowered my head to claim her lips again as I fondled that breast. The little noises Rose made against my mouth turned me on even more. Her hips moved against mine in a stuttered rocking motion as she tried to hold them still. Damn, this woman set me on fire without even trying.

My hand trailed back down to the hem of her dress. It nudged the silky fabric up inch by inch to bare her thigh while mine shielded her. My fingers came to rest on the dampness at the base of her panties, and she nicked my lip with her teeth as she bit back a moan. Her eyelids fluttered. I dipped my head even farther to kiss her neck, and she peeked over my shoulder.

"They're gone," she gasped out, arching into my touch more fully. "I can't see them any—"

I didn't need to hear the rest of that sentence. With a heft of my arms, I'd scooped her up and swept her around to the back of the truck. The tailgate dropped with a clang. I sat her on the edge, her dress shoved up to her hips. Her legs splayed around my thighs.

"Is this okay?" I managed to ask. "Please." I was burning to be inside her. Burning with the exhilaration of letting all this affection free.

Rose licked her lips, and my cock strained even harder as I followed that movement. "If someone else comes by..."

"They probably won't. It's a quiet road. And if they do we'll hear them coming before they can see much."

I stroked my hand between her legs again, and she let out her whimper. Then she was dragging my mouth to hers in the clearest answer she could have given me.

I wrenched her panties down as she unsnapped my jeans. Her fingers closed around my cock, and I groaned. With each pump of her hand, another wave of bliss rushed through me. I crushed my lips against hers and guided myself to the deepest slickness at her core.

Rose gasped as I thrust inside her. She hooked her legs behind me to pull me even deeper. Her fingers clung to the back of my neck, tangled in my rumpled shirt, as I plunged again and again into the beautiful bliss that was my lover.

My consort. My wife, in every way that mattered.

"I love you too," she murmured, and moaned as I thrust faster. Her breath turned shaky. I kissed her, a crash of lips. My hand slid down so I could circle her nub with my thumb, drawing every bit of ecstasy into her that I could.

Rose arched into me over and over with those ragged breaths, and then she clenched around me. The bliss of her release sang through the quiver of her muscles, the cry that broke from her throat. My balls squeezed, and I spilled myself into her, riding my own wave of pleasure.

I held her to me as we both came down from our peaks, my cheek resting against hers. "No matter what happens," I said, "I'm here with you. And I couldn't be more honored to be here."

CHAPTER TWENTY-SIX

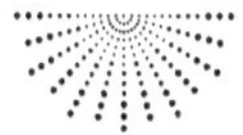

Rose

I swiveled on the smooth hardwood of the private magicking room that was now mine, channeling heat and energy from my spark through my body and out into the world. Every shred of my attention was focused on the images I'd been able to dig up of a little cottage near the Canadian border that belonged to one of the Frankfords' regular associates.

We'd checked to make sure no one was there right now. And I wasn't going to burn the whole thing down anyway. Just set up one of the outbuildings, a shed or a garage, in flames. Make them think I was on the attack in some erratic fashion.

I couldn't deny it was kind of satisfying even destroying a few minor pieces of their lives.

A flare from my spark seared through me. I hurled it across all those miles with the strength of my will and my concentration. As it left me, my legs sagged. I let myself sink to the floor.

I'd only managed a few of these castings since I'd gotten the idea a couple days ago, and not just because the black widow venom was still wearing off. Throwing even a small spell that far took a lot of effort.

After a few minutes catching my breath, I pushed myself to my feet and headed out to shower and change. As I scooped up my handbag, a phone chimed from inside it. My legs locked.

That wasn't the chime I had set on the new burner Ky had picked up for me after Frankford's taunting. It was the old one, the one our greatest enemy had reached us at, which I was still carrying in case he texted me again. As much as his threats had pricked at me, I couldn't lose the chance to get any information he might let slip.

Had he heard about the fire already? It seemed unlikely anyone would have noticed and contacted anyone that quickly.

I fished out the phone and braced myself before looking at the screen. But the message there made me frown in confusion rather than bristle. It was an unfamiliar number, but not an unlisted one like Frankford had used.

Follow the page that called me to you.

Follow the— My pulse stuttered. My gaze rose to the door to the larger magicking room down the hall where I'd practiced those dual forms with Gabriel—where I'd asked him if he still had that page from *The Lion, The*

Witch, and The Wardrobe that I'd given him all that time ago.

It's tucked away in my wallet right now, he'd said. *It brought me back to you. I'd like to know it always could again.*

My throat squeezed tight. Who else could it be? What else could he be talking about?

My hand shook as I fumbled for my new phone. I typed a quick text to the group conversation with the rest of my consorts.

I just got a message. I think it's from Gabriel.

I couldn't stand there waiting to see how they'd answer. I ducked back into the magicking room and set down my purse. With a slow breath, I summoned the energy of my spark again. I didn't need to light any fires this time. Just to touch the essence of a piece of paper that had meant so much to me in so many ways both before I'd given it to Gabriel and afterward.

My arms drifted through the air. My tongue moved, forming the syllables of words I'd read so often I knew them by heart. I pictured that day those months ago when all my longing for my former friend had welled up inside me and I'd gone into the forest to the old witching ruins to try to summon him here through that page.

A faintly sweet flavor trembled across my tongue. A tickle of energy shot down my throat. It formed into a tiny bead of sensation in my chest—a bead that gave me a faint tug to the west, as if I were being drawn by a tiny glowing thread.

That way. That was where the page was. And maybe my missing consort too.

* * *

"Are you sure this is a good idea?" Damon said, peering out the window from where he was sitting next to me in the back of the car. The Portland suburbs slipped by us. "What if it's a trap Frankford got him to set up?"

I closed my eyes, focusing for a moment on the tug of magic that had brought us this far. The magic that was tracing the path between me and the page I'd given Gabriel. "If the Frankfords wanted me to show up somewhere, having him say where he needed to meet me would make more sense. I'm the only person who could have understood that message—well, except the four of you. Why would he do that unless he was sending something he didn't want them to understand if they saw it? Something he was hiding from them?"

"Why would he send us on this scavenger hunt at all?" Damon said.

At my other side, Jin slipped his hand around mine. "That's what we're here to find out, isn't it?"

"The Frankfords can't come right out and hurt us directly," Kyler said from the front passenger seat. "The oath stops them. They've had tons of chances to attack us a lot more effectively otherwise."

"That doesn't mean it couldn't be a trap to hurt us *in*directly," Seth put in. He checked the street signs as he hit the brake at a stop sign. "Still straight here?"

"Keep going," I said. "And we'll be cautious. I'm not going running in anywhere assuming it's all good. But we have to see. Do any of you really think we should have ignored that message?"

The silence that followed that question gave me my answer. I shut my eyes to tune back into that thread of connection.

Gabriel wasn't with the page anymore. We were close enough to the spot that I'd have sensed his presence through our consort bond now if he had been. When I'd stretched my awareness out to search for him as we approached, I'd gotten a vague impression from the opposite edge of the city, where the Frankfords' house here was. He *was* still with them, I had to assume.

So, what was it he could have wanted me to see?

The lawns and more distantly spaced houses gave way to packed city streets. The thread of magic tugged me. "Take the next right turn," I said. We cruised by a few blocks, and the tug shifted again. "Now left. Wait. Stop here."

Seth found a spot to park by the curb. It was mid-afternoon now, but a cooler breeze broke the summer air as I climbed out of the car. I paused for a second on the sidewalk, getting my bearings. Focusing on that tug inside me.

It reeled me back down the street until I reached what looked like a posh nightclub, tidy brick exterior with a sleek black sign, the name of the place written there in graceful white lettering. *Den of Spades*. I shifted my hands in a quick casting, searching for any signs of magicking in or around the building, but there didn't appear to be any spells laid in the area.

I started up the front steps tentatively, expecting to send another testing spell before I entered, but the tug stilled as I reached the black doormat. Okay. I was here. Where was the page?

I prodded the thread of connection delicately, and my hand lifted to a plaque mounted to the side of the door, proclaiming the building's historical legacy. The barest tip of a piece of paper protruded from behind it. My heart skipped a beat.

No unsparked person could have fished that paper out. I summoned it with a twitch of my fingers over the plaque, and it leapt from between the brass and brick with a soft rasp. I clutched it against my palm.

Two men in business suits were coming up the steps now, one of them giving me an odd look. I slipped past them down to the sidewalk.

"That's it?" Ky said, glancing at the club. "You found it?"

I nodded. "Let's get back in the car to look at it. It's safe enough. No magic on it." Except the tinge my love had imbued it with.

We piled back into the car in the same positions. Seth and Ky twisted around to watch as I unfolded the paper. My pulse thumped on at a frantic rhythm. There had to be some reason Gabriel had left it there, had told me to come for it. None of this made sense yet.

It still didn't make sense in the first instant my eyes fell on the open page. Gabriel had scrawled seven pairs of words—seven names, I realized after a moment—in the margins, his handwriting so messy I almost couldn't decipher the letters. As if he'd been writing without even being able to look at what he was doing, I thought, a lump rising in my throat.

Dorothy Meyer

Vincent Wilder

Justin Brimsey

My breath stopped. The head of Unsparked Relations. One of the people in the Assembly we'd been hoping to reach.

My gaze darted to the next name. Another I didn't recognize. But the fifth was Gwen Remington of International Affairs. And the sixth Miriam Travers, a witch who was second in command in the Finances division who we'd also considered approaching.

"What?" Damon demanded. "Can you even tell what he was trying to say?"

"It's the names of people from the Assembly," I said. "Including three of the people we thought we could trust to go against the Frankfords if they knew the truth."

Jin's eyebrows arched. "What do you think that means?"

"I don't know. I—"

My gaze drifted back to the club. The men in their business suits who'd passed me going in—Charles Frankford would have fit right in with them, wouldn't he? A sudden certainty closed around my chest.

"Frankford met with these people here," I said, shaking the paper. "Recently."

Ky's eyes lit up. "Gabriel knew we needed a meeting spot to use Frankford's code."

"Hold on," Seth said. "Did Gabriel know we specifically wanted to talk to *these* people?"

I shook my head. "We hadn't come up with our list of

trustworthy people until after he left. I don't even know half the people he mentioned here."

"He was at the meeting," Ky suggested. "He could tell they weren't huge fans of Frankford, so they seemed like good names for us to know."

"We can't just assume he was doing this in good faith," Damon said. "He was brutal to Rose and then he took off. He went straight to those assholes. I don't trust him for a second."

The memory of my last conversation with Gabriel made me wince. That pain ran deep, so deep I didn't know if I'd ever quite heal completely. But Gabriel hadn't been all wrong. I had been changing; I'd been acting in ways I never would have wanted to if I'd been able to think some of those situations through calmly.

And I knew him. I knew the boy who'd drawn me into this circle of love when we were only kids. I knew the man he'd grown up into, who'd crossed the country at my call, who'd bound his heart to mine even after he'd seen the danger a loyalty like that had brought down on the other guys.

For the first time since he'd stalked down the road away from me, a glow of hope covered the wound inside me like a salve.

I hadn't lost him. Not completely.

"No," I said. "Everything about this feels genuine to me. He's trying to help. I don't know why he did everything else he's done, but this—we have to listen to this. He's given us the key we needed."

Now we had to make sure we used it well.

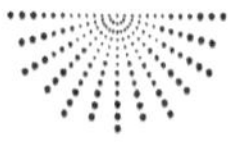

CHAPTER TWENTY-SEVEN

Rose

"Are you ready?" I asked Naomi.

She nodded where she was leaning against the van she'd rented when she'd flown into the state. We'd set up a little base of operations in this field, far enough into the middle of nowhere that no one would notice our little group but close enough to the Frankfords' seaside property that we could get there in under an hour. The tall grass rustled with the warm summer breeze, carrying the scent of freshly reaped hay from a nearby farm.

"Does this look good?" My cousin showed her phone to me. She'd already composed the text to send to her mother, my Aunt Ginny. *I don't know what to do! Rose is getting ready to make some kind of attack on the Frankfords' grandson, and I don't think I can stop her.*

"Perfect," I said. "Go ahead and send it."

Aunt Ginny was in on the ploy. She'd invited my other aunt, Irene, over for lunch. She'd get the text, act distressed, and "accidentally" leave it where Aunt Irene could see the message. We were pretty sure Irene would pass on a warning about this latest crazy behavior of mine like she had before.

We weren't counting on a frantic message from Aunt Irene doing all the work for us, of course. I stepped away from the van to join Lesley where she'd been meditating in preparation for our casting. She could feel her spark wearing thinner, she'd told me, but she still had some power left. And the last thing she'd wanted to do was sit this effort out, even if she didn't have the full picture of what we were fighting against.

There were two-person and larger forms that witches could perform with each other too. I started to turn in a slow circle, fanning the flame of my spark with flicks of my fingers, and Lesley swayed through a larger circle around me. The tingle of her magic wafted over me, joining with mine to send it sparking even higher.

With her help, I'd cast my illusion all the way to Seattle. All the way to the house the Frankfords' daughter and husband lived in, where we expected the family to be home right now. I'd conjure a small real fire on the tree at the back of the yard to add a smoky realism —and the illusion of larger flames flaring around the house's windows. Enough to scare them, I hoped. Enough to make them think I was trying to hurt them without putting them at the slightest real risk.

The Frankfords and their faction believed I was dangerous? I could skew that assumption in my favor. A crazed witch might attack a child associated with her enemies. The Frankfords would have to respond to the threat.

And while they were distracted by our bluff, we could put our real plan into motion.

Heat whirled faster and hotter in my chest. I pressed my toes into the ground as I spun faster. My arms wove out through the air and up. Then I stopped, my hands clapping together with fingers splayed, every ounce of my will hurling the energy inside me across the state line.

Even with Lesley's support, the casting left me briefly exhausted. I stumbled, and Damon was right there to catch me. "Careful, angel," he murmured.

I turned in his arms, seeking out his mouth. He met my kiss without hesitation. I drank in both the sizzle of energy that generated between us and the warm glow of love that radiated from him.

"Are you all right?" Naomi asked when I eased back from my consort. "I could have pitched in too if it was going to take a lot out of you."

I shook my head. "I want you fresh for when we're out there at the Cliff. I'll be pretty much recovered by the time we make it there." I glanced past her to Kyler, who was sitting in the front passenger seat of the van, turned toward the open door. "Any word from Seth yet?"

"They haven't seen any movement," Kyler reported. His brother and Jin were staked out closer to the Frankfords' property, watching the security there. He rubbed his mouth. "How long do you think we should wait before we— Hold on."

He peered at the phone. The rest of us hustled over. A smile stretched across Ky's face.

"It worked," he said. "The Frankfords must have called some of their lackeys onto other duty—to check things out in Seattle, probably. Six cars just left the estate. They couldn't see exactly how many guards were in each of them, but that means the numbers there are down at least a little."

"There'll still be at least a couple dozen on the property," Damon said. He cracked his knuckles. "But we'll make sure they wish they'd left too, right?"

"We're not going to hurt anyone we don't have to," I reminded him with a nudge of my elbow. "We want it to be totally clear that *they're* the bad guys here."

"Yeah, yeah," he said, but he grinned at me.

"Ready to call the Assembly in?" Ky asked me. "I've got the phone simulation running."

I nodded. "If the Frankfords are reaching out to their security, they're already distracted. We've got to get this moving before they decide there's no real threat in Seattle."

I came up beside him to type out the message I'd prepared. It'd appear on the phones of our contacts as if it'd come from the number they'd connect with Frankford. *A lot has changed since the Den of Spades. I need your presence urgently at the coordinates I'm sending. We're on the verge of catastrophe here.*

Ky shot off the messages and the location. We waited, my heart thumping, to see how Gwen Remington and the others would respond.

What's the emergency? Justin Brimsey wrote back. *How does it involve my department?*

You really need to see this to fully understand, I replied. *Hurry, please.*

All right. I'll make my excuses. It'll take an hour to get out there. This had better be as serious as you're saying, Charles.

Similar responses were coming in from the other contacts. They didn't sound all that happy with Frankford, but that was a good sign for us. All that mattered was that they'd believed it.

"They're coming," I said, and Damon let out a whoop of victory. Lesley bobbed excitedly on her feet. "The next part of the plan, then?"

"We'll head over and get in position," I said. "We won't want to start the next phase until our, er, guests are pretty close."

Naomi hopped back into the front to drive. Damon, Lesley, and I climbed into the back of the van. I ducked all the way into the third row of seats where Thalia was sitting in quiet meditation. She opened her eyes when I sat down beside her. The van's engine rumbled.

"We're heading over there now?" she said. Her voice was tight. I couldn't even imagine how many horrible memories she must have of that place. How many times she might have faced those demons down, been forced to pit her magic against their unnatural energy.

"We'll be there soon," I said. "Are you sure you're up to this?" Her powers weren't the strongest after the way her experiences had rattled her nerves, but she was a wild card none of the Frankfords' allies could have been prepared for. The people from the Assembly would know her—they'd respect her more than they might respect me with my now highly checkered past.

"I'll manage," she said. "Just as long as I don't have to go right into that place." She shuddered.

"You can hang back when we head to the cave," I said. "I don't want you having to face those things again."

She gave me a sharp but grateful smile.

As the van pulled onto the main road, I took out my own phone and tapped in the number for Investigator Ruiz. This last bit of the plan might have been the riskiest, but I'd gotten a good feeling about that witch—and the more pieces we had in play that ended up being on our side, the more likely we were to come out ahead in what I hoped was going to be our final gambit.

This is Rose Hallowell. You asked me to contact you if I could tell you more. Come out to this address as soon as you can make it, and you'll find out why those witches were no longer safe at home. Bringing back-up might not be a bad idea of you have people there you trust.

After I'd sent the address, I turned off the phone. She'd either come or she wouldn't. The mystery would hook her more if I refused to say anything else.

We turned off the paved road onto a bumpier dirt one. A few minutes later, we pulled up beside Jin's Nissan. He used the car so little we'd figured none of Frankfords' people was going to recognize it on sight.

We got out for a quick conference. "Okay," I said. "We should get moving. Do you all have everything you need?"

Damon waggled the stick he was carrying, about the

length of his forearm and half as thick. With Lesley's guidance, I'd cast a spell on it with enough energy that it should be able to stun several people on contact, a lot like the batons the male enforcers carried. He patted his hip too. "And the pistol for back-up. Only if I absolutely have to, I know."

The other guys held up their own makeshift batons. Both excitement and apprehension shimmered in all their eyes. I dragged in a breath. "Good. Just like we planned, then. Seth and Lesley, you go around the south side in the van. Jin and Naomi, you go north with the car. Start your magicking to draw the guards away in fifteen minutes. The Assembly people should be here not too long after that."

The rest of us—Thalia, Damon, Ky, and I—were going to head right to the front entrance on foot.

Naomi gave me a quick salute and a determined smile. Seth and Jin kissed me in turn. I wanted to linger in the warmth of their embraces, to hold on to them as if I could hold them away from the danger, but there wasn't the time, and I couldn't completely protect them. If this effort was going to work, it needed all of us.

The two pairs drove off in their respective directions. The remaining four of us started toward the front of the property. I checked my watch every few minutes as we ambled along the road. Eight since we'd parted ways with the others. Twelve. Fourteen.

I motioned us to a stop below the last low rise before the driveway would come into view. We didn't want to be seen too early.

Reddish light flashed toward the south. An

unnerving screeching sound carried from the north. I'd left it up to the other witches what spells they cast, but both of those looked like they'd catch a lot of notice. Then they just had to ambush and knock out the guards who came investigating.

We waited a minute, and then I sent out a testing brush of magic. The quivers that returned to me suggested there were still eight guards waiting near the property's entrance.

I could handle that many in one go.

Thalia and the guys stepped back as I moved into the form I'd first used in a haze of panic when we'd escaped from the Assembly prison. It was my own construction, melded from bits of other spells I'd learned and the readings I'd done on magic to affect the mind. A whip of my arms, a spin of my feet, gathering all the power I could summon to me—and heaving it forward.

The air crackled with that power. I hadn't needed to throw it quite this far ever before. My heart lurched for a second as I wondered if it wouldn't be enough, if it would just irritate the guards but not topple them. Even as the worry passed through my head, the questing spell I'd sent out ahead of time wavered. Those conscious presences I'd felt turned blank.

"Come on!" I said, waving the others forward with me. We jogged over the slope and down toward the packed dirt driveway that ran through the Frankfords' seaside property.

Bodies were slumped beside the sparsely scattered trees on either side of the driveway. "Over there," I said quickly, pointing to a small wooden building not too deep into the property. "We can shut them up in there. Take any phones or radios off them first."

Damon and I grabbed the nearest guard and hefted her over to the building. The locked door opened at a twist of my fingers and a flash of my spark. We set her on the floor inside. I was just stepping out when a holler carried from the direction of the old farmhouse closer to the coast.

"Return to position. Boundary breached. I repeat, all units return—"

Snuff my spark. There'd been more guards farther afield than I'd been able to sense who hadn't gone after either of the diversions.

I didn't have time to think. I launched myself into the magicking again, putting every bit of force I could into the spell, and flung it toward the house.

The voice cut off. There was a thump somewhere closer by as I'd hit an approaching guard I hadn't heard at all. I froze, reaching my magic out toward the house and the row of trees beyond it that hid the Cliff.

"That's all of them," I said. As long as the others had dealt with the ones who'd come their way.

We hurried to drag the other guards into the building. I sealed the door with a locking spell and a blanket of silence that should last at least a few hours. By then we'd be long gone or it wouldn't matter anyway.

Even with the intermittent shade of the trees, I'd started to sweat. I wiped at my damp brow. Kyler checked his phone. "The Assembly people could get here in the next few minutes if they left as soon as they said they would. Where do you want to meet them?"

"Let's wait by the farmhouse," I said. "The closer they already are to the Cliff, the easier it'll be for us to convince them to go look."

We sat ourselves on the chipped paint of the house's porch steps. The Frankfords really didn't keep this place up at all. How much time had they even spent in this house, rather than just leaving it up to hide the fact that their real use for the property was something very different?

An engine growled in the distance, but it was Jin's car that turned down the drive. I watched him and Naomi join us with a mix of relief and nerves. The longer we waited for the Assembly officials, the more chances the Frankfords would have to uncover our real plan and act against us.

"Seth says they've handled all the guards who came their way," Ky reported, looking up from his phone. "We're good there."

The show was ready. We just needed our main audience.

The sound of another engine reached my ears—and another. My pulse sped up. Three sleek sedans turned onto the drive. They purred toward us and stopped several feet from the house.

Gwen Remington got out of the car at the head of the bunch, a man I guessed was her assistant following. She looked us over with a frown as I stood up. "What the hell is going on here? Where is Charles Frankford?"

Justin Brimsey was getting out of the second car, Miriam Travers from the third. They were really here. We'd done it.

I'd gotten them to cross tens of miles. Now I just needed them to walk another quarter of one, and the Frankfords' faction would never get away with their awful scheme again.

"Charles and Helen Frankford aren't who you think," I said. "I asked you to come here so we could show you the horrifying things they've been keeping on their property."

"*You* asked us to come," Brimsey said. He took a step back toward his car. "You're Rose Hallowell. I don't think—"

"You know me, too, don't you?" Thalia said, joining me. "Or at least you used to, before my consort..." She grappled with the words she couldn't say for a moment before giving up. "You *need* to see what's been happening here. I swear to you, we're not the villains in this scenario."

Honesty hummed through her voice. The Assembly officials exchanged a glance.

"Just come with me past those trees to the path down the cliff," I said, pointing. "Or go by yourselves if you'd rather. You can arrest me first if you want to. But you have to at least look. You'll see why this is so important. There's a cave there, where there's a spell giving dangerous beings access to our world."

Another car pulled down the drive. I tensed for a second before I recognized the tan compact as the one Investigator Ruiz had arrived at my estate in. She parked behind the sedans and got out with another woman, both of them in enforcer sweats.

"What are you doing here?" Travers demanded.

"Lady Hallowell said she had information about a crime," Ruiz said, nodding to me.

"Apparently we have to take a walk down a cliff to some cave with 'dangerous beings'," Brimsey said. "It all sounds like a lot of bluster to me. You lied to us to bring us out here, and—"

"It was the only way we could bring you to a place where we could prove what we need to," Thalia interrupted. "By the Spark, *I* will lead you down there if that's what you want."

A shiver ran through her body as she spoke, so obvious Remington's eyes widened.

"Please," I said. "Why do you think we went to all this trouble? We've been fighting for our *lives* to make sure you see this."

Ruiz stepped forward. "I want to have a look at whatever the hell this is. Whether the rest of you join me is up to you." She jabbed her finger at me. "*You* stay here."

I nodded, swallowing through my tightened throat. "After you've seen... it... I can explain some of what I know about it."

She nodded sharply and walked on toward the trees. Remington wavered on her feet and then hurried after the investigator, motioning for her assistant to follow. Brimsey grimaced, but he shifted forward too.

And at the same moment, tires screeched as a gleaming SUV raced onto the driveway. Charles Frankford's thin face leaned out the open window, the wind rippling through his slate gray hair.

"Stop right there! Stop this, all of you!"

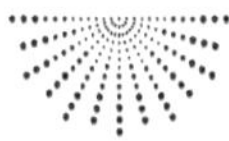

CHAPTER TWENTY-EIGHT

Gabriel

*P*ebbles rattled against the SUV's undercarriage. I couldn't see the speedometer from where I'd been shooed into the back seat between two of Charles Frankford's guards-on-staff, but I could tell he had his driver racing us down the country roads way faster than the legal limit.

I didn't know what he'd heard when he'd gotten that call. He'd been pacing in the stately living room of his Portland house, alternating between glaring at his phone waiting for updates from Seattle and glaring at me while he barked questions about what I thought Rose might do next, and the second he'd answered that last ring, his face had gone white with rage. He'd stepped out of the room with a slam of the door and returned a few minutes later.

"You," he'd said with a snap of his fingers. "Come." Like I was a dog.

But that was essentially what I was pretending to be here, what I wanted him to see me as: a poor stupid mutt who'd gotten so scared I'd run off with my tail between my legs, only realizing hours later that I had nothing left but the clothes on my back. Nowhere to turn but to the one person I knew for sure stood against the woman I was supposedly terrified by. So I'd followed him to the car.

It wasn't that hard to act as if I were terrified when it came to Rose. The Frankfords didn't know me or her well enough to realize I was terrified *for* her, not of her.

She wouldn't really have tried to hurt this kid, his grandson, would she? I hadn't gotten a clear picture from what Frankford had said of what exactly he'd heard or she'd done, but it'd sounded like the boy was still fine. If Rose had actually wanted to attack him, I was pretty sure she'd have succeeded before the Frankfords ever got wind of it.

It was a diversion. A ploy. Please, dear Lord, let it be a ploy.

I'd managed to get those names to her, to point to that meeting place where the Frankfords had hauled me and had me retell my story about how unstable and aggressive Rose was becoming, how I was worried about what she might do next in her vendetta against her father and his colleagues. A story I *could* tell where the Frankfords couldn't speak against her because of the oath. I'd made myself useful enough to get what I needed.

I hoped I hadn't done too good a job of convincing the other Assembly people. They hadn't looked as if they thought much of what some unsparked former employee had to say. Honestly, they'd seemed a little fed up with the Frankfords' dramatics. And the Frankfords had been nervous. They saw that bunch of witching people as a threat. So I'd taken the opening I'd seen. I'd been waiting too long already.

The landscape outside the window started to look familiar. I caught a glimpse of the blue stretch of the ocean, and my stomach lurched.

We weren't heading to Seattle to see some horror Rose had visited on a seven-year-old boy. We were heading to the Cliff, to something even more horrible.

Had she come out here to try to destroy the cave after all? Had his guards caught her and whoever she'd brought with her? Why had Frankford wanted *me* here?

He might have suspected Rose was about to strike here. I'd heard him and his wife talking about a trip he'd made out here just last night. Helen Frankford had left for Seattle as soon as they'd heard of the threat. I guessed I should be glad for that. Of the two of them, she was the one with the magic. But there was an unnerving energy that radiated off of Charles sometimes, when he was angry or particularly happy, that took me back to that moment in the cave when the demonic face had loomed through the glowing portal and I'd been a hair's breadth from pissing my pants.

Frankford muttered something to the driver. The engine thrummed with an erratic rhythm that meant it was being pushed to its limits. Somehow I didn't think the witching man was going to appreciate me piping up with mechanical advice.

I leaned back in the seat, keeping my breath as steady as I could, considering my options. It was difficult to prepare when I didn't know what was waiting for us or what Frankford planned to do with me. All I knew for sure was that I had to be ready to make a move in an instant. If he tried to hurt Rose, I had to stop him. That was all there was to it.

"There, there, let's go!" Frankford snapped. The driver hauled on the wheel. As the SUV swayed around a bend, Frankford sent his window whirring down. Warm salty air flooded into the air-conditioned space. Frankford leaned out the window, his shoulders so tense you'd have thought a stiff wind like that could snap them.

"Stop right there! Stop this, all of you!"

The middle seat, where two more guards were sitting, blocked my view of the windshield. Who was he shouting at like that? I braced myself in my seat. I couldn't do much with the guards on either side of me, but they'd get up as soon as the car stopped, right? Then I might have a chance, if there was anything at all I could do.

The SUV jolted to a halt. Frankford was throwing open his door before the engine had even fallen silent. He motioned for the guards with a jerking motion of his arm. The women on either side of me did get up—but not before the one at my right had clamped her well-muscled hand around my forearm. She yanked me up with her.

I scrambled after her, the metallic taste of adrenaline sharp in my mouth. What the hell was going on? The guards up front heaved open the back door and spilled out ahead of us. My guard dragged me out into the hot mid-day sun to face a cluster of startled-looking figures.

My gaze went straight to Rose. God, it wasn't much

more than a week since I'd last been in her presence, but every part of me ached at the sight of her, as if I'd been deprived of a substance as vital as water that was now in reach. Her dark hair lifted in the breeze as her head jerked around. When our eyes met, pain flashed across her face. An echo of it jabbed into me like a knife.

I'd been afraid from the first moment I'd come back into town that I'd cause her pain like that, but I'd never thought I'd end up doing it purposely.

I opened my mouth—and the guard who'd dragged me out shoved her hand against my throat. She wasn't carrying a weapon, but she didn't need to. I'd watched witches call forth incredible forces with just a twitch of their fingers. The threat couldn't be more clear.

This was why Frankford had brought me. I wasn't a resource to him anymore. I was a hostage. My life for Rose's compliance.

Rose's mouth tightened further as she caught the gesture and the guard's glower. I tried to move, and the woman's hand clamped down harder. She might crush my windpipe without any help from her magic at all.

"What by the Spark is going on here, Charles?" a woman I'd met briefly at the Den of Spades—Gwen Remington—was saying. "This young woman is saying—"

"I'm sure she's making up all kinds of stories," Frankford said. His voice came out smooth, only a hint of a tremor in it. I hoped the others would hear it. "Clearly Lady Hallowell's animosity has carried even farther than I imagined."

"I haven't made up anything," Rose said. "They can see for their own eyes what I saw here a month ago. If there's nothing there, you shouldn't care if they take a look."

Another woman stepped forward, the middle-aged witch I'd met briefly when she'd arrived at Rose's estate just before I'd left it. Frankford's stance tensed at the sight of her. "Lady Ainsworth," he said quickly, before she could speak. "Has she roped you into her delusions too? My colleagues, you really must—"

"You can't dismiss me just like that," the older witch said in a taut voice. "Don't you dare stop this. Your time is up. Maybe I can't talk, but I can fight."

"Now, then, this doesn't need to come to blows," one of the other Assembly officials—Justin Brimsey—said, holding up his hands.

"It won't if these criminal intruders are removed from my home." Frankford turned to Rose and shook his head with a disbelieving laugh. "You threaten my grandson, break onto my property, and you're still making demands? You belong tied up in a cell where you can't hurt anyone else. Keep in mind what's at stake here for you too."

He made a subtle gesture, and the guard holding me shifted her other hand in what must have been a threatening gesture, the beginnings of a spell. Rose's whole body stiffened. He was counting on her still caring about me, regardless of how I'd betrayed her, and she did. Fucking hell, I didn't deserve all the anguish that was etched on her face.

She'd fought so hard to get this far. Given so much of herself. I'd thrown myself into the fray to save her, not to be the one who brought her down.

"Do whatever you have to do," I said. "I don't matter."

The guard's hand jammed on my throat. But even as I choked, I caught a glimpse of the only thing I needed to see if I was going to die. Rose's eyes held pain and fear, but a shimmer of understanding had crept into them.

She knew. She knew even though I'd hurt her that I'd been doing this for her all along.

She whipped out her arm so fast I wasn't prepared. The guard wasn't either. A spell slammed into the woman's head from the side, and her grip loosened. One of the other guards leapt in to grab me, but Ky was already lunging at her with a stick he brandished like a club. I didn't have time to wonder what he figured he'd accomplish with that. I hurled myself forward.

A magical grip caught my legs. Another spell smacked against the first. I stumbled as the strands of magic wrestled with each other.

"That's enough!" one of the Assembly witches shouted, just as Rose made a slicing motion with her hand.

The pressure around my ankles shattered. I staggered toward her, and Jin tugged me into their midst between him and Rose.

My throat was still throbbing, but I had to use this moment of freedom, however short it might be.

I spun toward the Assembly officials. "I lied to you before. Frankford is the one who's the real threat. You need to see what's down the cliff."

CHAPTER TWENTY-NINE

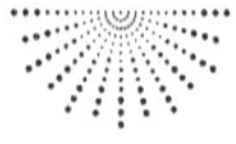

Rose

The other Assembly members looked bewildered, but Frankford's face twisted into a mask of anger. "You," he snarled. His gaze jerked from Gabriel to me, his eyes blazing. He smacked one hand against his chest and thrust both upward in a stiff mockery of a witching form. Three guttural syllables I didn't understand burst from his lips, and then, "I forsake the oath I took."

The air shivered between us. I had only a split-second to register what that declaration might mean, that he'd somehow been able to make it on his own without my agreement to dissolve the oath, when he was thrusting his arms toward me, sending a bolt of searing energy straight at my heart.

My hands leapt up to cast a shielding spell, but I couldn't have spun it out fast enough. I would have died if Gabriel hadn't realized what was happening. Even as Frankford sputtered out his words, my consort was reaching for me. The heat of that spear of magic singed my skin, and I was stumbling out of the way at my consort's yank as he threw himself in front of me.

Gabriel buckled an instant later, a pained breath hissing through his teeth. His side was blackened and seeping blood where Frankford's spell had hit him. Frankford growled and lifted his arms again—and Investigator Ruiz charged up to him, snatching his wrists and hauling them behind his back.

I dropped to the ground as Gabriel sank to his knees. My fingers fluttered over his wound, summoning the energy to seal it, to dull the pain, anything I could do. From the raggedness of his breath, I wasn't sure it hadn't hurt internal organs I didn't have the slightest idea how to start mending.

"He needs a medic," I shouted to anyone who'd listen, clutching my consort's shoulder. "Fast! Please."

"Don't worry about me," Gabriel mumbled. He managed to raise his head. Pain had tensed his features, but his gaze found mine and held it. "I'm so sorry, Rose. I love you. I always loved you. I always will."

My eyes welled up. Around me, the meeting I'd set up had erupted into chaos. Voices clashed and hands waved. Kyler knelt next to me. He'd torn off his shirt and pressed it to the wound on Gabriel's side.

"What do you need me to do?" he said. "Who should I call?"

I didn't know who the nearest medic was. There were a couple names I knew from Portland, but they wouldn't come at some unsparked man's request. I didn't even know if they'd come at mine.

"Let me *go*," Frankford was snapping at Ruiz.

She glared at him. "I witnessed an unauthorized use of hostile magic against an unprepared victim. This is my job."

"How did you even do that?" Gwen Remington broke in. Her gaze twitched between us. This was the first time I'd ever seen a witching man cast magic of his own, so I'd bet it was a first for her too.

Not magic of his own. Magic he'd borrowed from those demons. My heart skipped a beat. He'd broken the oath. I could say anything I wanted about him now.

"He's made a deal with the things in the cave down the cliff," I said. "Him and a bunch of the other families—my father and the Almeidas and—I have a whole list of them, I have their records. They summoned monsters and they force them to give over power. They trick witches into unbalanced consortings and then force them to control the things."

Frankford let out a scoffing laugh. "Listen to her. She's completely delusional. An unprepared victim? I was defending my property and myself from this witch who's determined to tear me down. I have a right to do that."

"How many people have *you* torn down?" Damon retorted from where he was standing over me, his enchanted stick still gripped in his fist. "I've seen the files. I saw the creature down there. You're as much a monster as it is."

Frankford rolled his eyes toward the other Assembly

officials. "And this is who she brings into her side. Unsparked men she's dallying with. Impressionable young witches who don't have the experience to know better. Jilted wives out for vengeance." He nodded to Thalia.

Whatever spell he'd cast on her wasn't broken. Her lips curled back as she tried to find words she could speak. "He's lying," she said. "He's had a lot of practice at it, so he does it well. You can't listen to him."

"Oh, and they should listen to you? The Justice Division will definitely hear about this. High ranking Assembly members tramping around one of their colleagues' homes searching for monsters on the word of a known degenerate? How long do you think your careers will last after this gets out?"

"If there's nothing to see, what does it matter to you if we look?" Remington asked. The question would have reassured me if her stance hadn't been so hesitant. She wanted him to convince her there was nothing to see. It'd be easier for her to believe I was a lunatic than that he was the head of some crazy conspiracy. Of course it would be. That was why his faction had been able to operate for so long.

"The principle matters," Frankford said. He stood there, managing to look haughty even with his arms still restrained behind his back. "The fact that you'd take this witch's word over mine matters. What kind of justice is this if any maniac can send the Assembly scrambling across the countryside? By the Spark, don't you have better things to do?"

Justin Brimsey shifted his weight from one foot to the other. He didn't want to be here anymore.

"You can't listen to him," Naomi said. "He's trying to cover it up, still. You have no idea how many people he's hurt."

"How?" Miriam Travers said. "With these 'monsters' you're going to claim are lurking around this property? Have you seen them too?"

My cousin hesitated. "No, but I know Rose wouldn't make something like that up."

"*I've* seen them," I said. "So has he." I squeezed Gabriel's shoulder where I was still holding him.

"And me," Damon said grimly. "And believe me, you won't get it until you've seen that thing for yourself. Why the hell do you think we went to all this trouble to get you out here?"

Remington stiffened at his brash tone. A gleam of triumph lit in Frankford's eyes. "You see," he said. "This is what I tried to tell you about. The lengths her little group will go to. The disrespect they have for anyone who's earned their authority. I know you're smart enough not to be manipulated by ploys like that."

They weren't smart enough not to be manipulated by him. The Assembly members exchanged a glance, and I could read their thoughts on their faces. This whole situation was ridiculous. They'd been dragged out here for some sort of petty grudge-match. They might not have any great love for Frankford, but asking them to believe in a conspiracy of this size was a whole different ballpark.

They didn't have any love for me either. He'd already poisoned them against me as well as he could.

I'd faced off against Frankford once and taken a deal to save myself and my consorts. But I hadn't really saved anyone that way. I'd only given him the opportunity to hurt more people. This time I wouldn't make that mistake.

If I had to go down to take him down too, then so be it. I hadn't come this far for nothing. His demonic reign ended now.

I brushed my hand over Gabriel's forehead and kissed him there. "I love you," I murmured, needing to say it one more time so he'd know he hadn't lost me anymore than I'd lost him. His breath stuttered as I stood up. Ky gripped him, helping to keep him steady.

"Sprout," Gabriel croaked. The nickname wrenched at me, but I'd already committed to my final plan.

I'd never cast a spell this finely complex before, and I had to work it fast. But I couldn't say I really cared if I hurt Frankford a little in the process. My fingers interlocked and broke apart. I called up all the energy of my spark, sending it to my hands as they darted and spun to draw the spell I needed.

Ruiz caught the movement. "Lady Hallowell!" she said, starting to move.

Not fast enough. With a tearing sensation in my chest, I threw the illegal spell into Frankford's face.

"You'll tell us the truth," I said. "What's in the cave down the cliff here? All of it!"

The other investigator grabbed me, but Frankford was already under the truth-spell's effect and the compulsion of my question. His mouth twisted as he fought it, but only for a second.

"There's a portal," he said in a strangled voice. "To another plane of existence, where creatures live with powers unheard of here. We call them demons."

His face flushed red. He yanked at his arms, but Ruiz clamped them in place. "Lady Hallowell told us the truth about what she saw?" she demanded. I guessed there was nothing illegal about taking advantage of an unsanctioned truth spell once it'd already been cast.

"She did," Frankford grated out.

Brimsey's face had paled. "What in the world do you do with these 'demons'?" he said.

"We siphon power from them for our own ends," Frankford said. "We—damn it—we let them drink magic from our witches in return."

A chill ran through me. The files I'd read hadn't been that clear about exactly how the witches his faction had used intervened. It wasn't just about controlling the demons. It was about feeding them.

"I've heard enough," Remington said. "I need to see what in the name of the Spark is going on."

She turned on her heel and stalked toward the trees that hid the cliffside. The other two Assembly officials and their assistants hurried after her. Ruiz shoved Frankford toward her car.

"You stay with them," she said to her colleague with a jerk of her head toward the people heading cliff-side. "Lady Hallowell isn't going anywhere, are you?" Her gaze settled on me.

I shook my head. When the enforcer released me, I sank down with Gabriel again. Something in Ruiz's eyes softened. "I'll call for a medic as soon as Frankford is secure," she said.

At those words, a desperation Frankford hadn't quite reached before crossed his face. As if he'd only just realized how fully he'd lost, how far he was about to fall.

"Stop them!" he cried out to the guards he'd brought with him. "Don't let them near that—"

Ruiz cut off his voice with a hand smacked across his mouth, but the guards were already charging after the other Assembly officials. The enforcer with them whipped out a spell, but the nearest guard deflected it and sent her stumbling backward. Frankford's forces were well-trained.

I sprang up and dashed after them, but Thalia was even faster. Her breath rasped as we chased after the guards.

The enforcer tossed out another spell, managing to tangle one guard's legs so she crashed to the ground. Remington whirled around at the sound of pounding feet as we reached the trees. She swept aside the spell another guard cast with a snap of her hand. The third guard hurled herself straight at the International Relations head.

"No!" Thalia cried. Her arms flung out. The magic she sent with them was more an instinctive parry than a consciously constructed spell.

The force of it smacked into the guard, shoving the woman to the side. Toward the edge of the cliff. Her arms wheeled, but she was already tipping. She plummeted over the edge.

Her body hit the rocks below with a sickening thump that made me wince.

The enforcer had just caught up with us. "We need another medic," she muttered to herself, striding up to the cliff. "We…"

She glanced down. Her jaw set. She closed her eyes and turned away. She didn't need to say anything for me to know there was no saving that witch.

"Go back to the house," she ordered me and Thalia. "Keep away from the cliff."

"We were just trying to protect—" I started.

"*Go.*"

Remington hesitated and then walked on toward the cliff's path. I wavered, torn between wanting to confirm that they'd witnessed the horror below and not wanting to witness it again myself. The enforcer glowered at us. Thalia gripped my arm, and I turned back toward the trees.

The rest of my group and Ruiz was clustered around Gabriel, who was lying on the ground now. My heart stopped for a second before I saw him blink. Naomi looked up at me from where she'd crouched by my side.

"I think he'll be all right as long as he's seen to soon," she said.

"The medic should be here in twenty minutes," Ruiz said.

I caught her eye and gave her an apologetic bob of my head. "I'm sorry I couldn't tell you everything earlier."

"It's quite the story," she said with a ragged chuckle. "I think I'm going to have to see it for myself when my partner gets back."

I sat down next to Gabriel, stroking his hair as he rested. He tucked his head closer to my knee. The other guys surrounded me, Seth setting a hand on my shoulder, Damon posing protectively at my other side, Jin rubbing my knee, Ky squeezing my hand.

We sat there for what felt like a long time, but it might have only been a matter of minutes. Then the Assembly officials trudged over to rejoin us, and I realized I hadn't needed to be there to be sure of what they'd seen after all. Gwen Remington's face was nearly green. Justin Brimsey swayed a little on his feet, his eyes blinking fast. A tremor ran through Miriam Travers's shoulders.

Remington stopped by our group and peered down at me. After a moment, she found her voice.

"We'll need to talk further about your behavior here today, Lady Hallowell," she said. "After we've dealt with Charles Frankford and his allies. I understand you have documents we could make use of?"

I nodded, feeling dazed. Ky scrambled up. "I can start transferring them to you right now," he said. "I just need a little information to access your network."

Another car pulled up, and we drew back from Gabriel as the medic knelt to do her work. I stayed close by, my hand still resting on his head. He flinched at one of her spells, but then his bright blue eyes opened and found mine. A pained smile crossed his face that sent an ache through my chest.

I forced myself to smile back. We'd done it, what we'd come here to do. How huge a price we'd be paying for that victory, I didn't know yet.

CHAPTER THIRTY

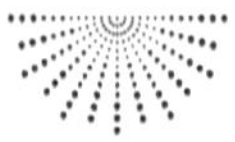

Rose

I might have been happier to see the gate to my home if I hadn't known leaving it again in the next few days would essentially be a crime. "Stay on your estate until you hear from us," Remington had told me sternly as we'd been piling into our two vehicles, and Investigator Ruiz had given her statement additional weight with a firm nod from behind her. I had to assume that applied to all of us, not just me. Not that I would have wanted to let my consorts leave my ring of protection until I knew where we stood with the authorities anyway.

Naomi parked the rented minivan next to Jin's Nissan near the garage. I gave Gabriel's hand a squeeze, and he stirred where he'd been leaning against my shoulder, dozing. The medic's work had patched him up just fine, it seemed, but it'd also left him drowsy.

"Do you need help getting out?" I asked him.

"I'll be all right," he said with a half-smile. His gaze lingered on my face longer than it really needed to, as if he were making up for the time when he hadn't been around to look at me. "I'll just take it slow."

We all gathered on the front drive as we got out. Lesley was holding her phone. She glanced up at me, her mouth twitching as if she wasn't sure whether to grin or not. "I just heard from my cousin," she said. "Enforcers came by my estate and arrested both of my parents."

My heart leapt. The Justice Division was already acting on the files Kyler had transferred to them.

Had they picked up Dad too? While the medic had been treating Gabriel, I'd told Investigator Ruiz more about how his scheme had intersected with the Cliff and what he'd told me in the cave, but she'd been too occupied handling all the new information about the Frankfords to bring me in for a formal interview yet. Dad's name was all over their records, though.

"You could go home then," I said to Lesley. "I mean, after the Assembly has cleared you to leave. I'll tell them you were just doing what I asked."

She frowned. "They can't blame you for what you did. You were trying to protect all of us. I still can't believe—that's really what they meant to do with me—" She shivered. "I don't know. It might be good to stay a little longer, until I know for sure what's happening with the whole conspiracy. If that's okay."

"Of course!" I said quickly. "You can stay as long as you need to. The Spark knows I've got plenty of room around this place."

I'd need to call Imogen when I had the chance. If the enforcers had picked up Lesley's parents, they'd probably come for Imogen's aunt and uncle too, but I could at least tell her why properly now.

But first I had problems right here to deal with. Across from me, Damon folded his arms over his chest and glowered at Gabriel. "Looks like I've got to be the one to say it. Are we really going to pretend that this guy didn't run off on us and leave us in the lurch after tearing you down? He changes his mind at the last minute and all is forgiven and forgotten? I don't think so."

Gabriel tensed beside me. Naomi took in the group of us and motioned to Lesley and Thalia. "I think we'll leave you and your consorts to work this out without an audience," she said.

I grasped Gabriel's hand again as the other witches headed for the house. "He just suffered a near-fatal wound," I said. "A wound he got saving my *life*. It'd be nice to give him more than five hours in a moving car to recover before we're interrogating him. And anyway, it's obvious to me from how things went down by the Cliff that he was always trying to help us."

"I don't care what he was *trying* to do," Damon said. "I was here. I saw how he left you. He ripped your heart in half."

I couldn't say that assessment was inaccurate. I swallowed hard. "Damon..."

"It's okay," Gabriel broke in. "I can talk about it, answer whatever questions any of you have. Explain myself as well as I can. I owe you all that much. Especially you." He looked at me, his mouth twisting.

"Let's at least get inside where you can sit down and rest," I said.

By the time we reached the hall, my guests had already dispersed to their rooms upstairs. My consorts and I ducked into the living room. Gabriel sank into an armchair near the door with an air that suggested he felt he needed to prove he could sit on his own. Damon took a spot beside me on the sofa, braced as if he thought he needed to be on guard for my sake. I nudged him, and he just looped his arm around mine. The twins and Jin settled onto the sofa across from us, their expressions a mix of curiosity and apprehension.

Gabriel bowed his head for a moment. Then he looked up at me. "I was scared for you," he said, his voice rough. "So fucking scared. I believed you could beat the Frankfords—that's not it—but I was afraid of how far you'd have to go to do that, how much of your conscience you might end up sacrificing... I tried to talk you down, but it wasn't as if I had a better strategy to offer you. But I knew I could contribute a hell of a lot more as a sort of double agent."

"You could have told us that's what you were planning," Seth said. "Or at least told *Rose* instead of tearing into her like that."

Gabriel winced. "I wish I'd seen a better way. But I needed Frankford to believe I'd really defected. If you hadn't seemed hurt enough, if anyone had given some sign they weren't as concerned as they should be... He'd have seen through the ploy. I had a hard enough time getting him to use me as it was."

The memory of that moment when he'd left swam up

through my mind with a jab through my gut and a new understanding. "That's why you stopped the car and provoked the argument outside the gate. We knew he was monitoring what was happening there. You wanted to make sure he saw it."

"Yeah." The anguish couldn't have been plainer on Gabriel's face. "I'm sorry, Rose. It's been killing me knowing how much I must have hurt you. If I'd seen some other way to do it... I just hope I've saved you from more hurt than I caused. That's all I could ask for."

"You really can't know, can you?" Damon muttered. "And you all accuse *me* of using stupid tactics."

"Gabriel did get us intel that we hadn't managed to get on our own, and not for lack of trying," Ky pointed out. "It might have taken us weeks and weeks more before we knew how to bring in those Assembly officials."

"Or maybe we'd have figured it out ourselves in another couple days without the whole heartbreaker routine."

"We can't know either way," I said. "And that's all in the past now. All we can do is go forward from here." I let out a ragged breath and met Gabriel's eyes again. "Don't you ever go off like that again without telling me what's going on first. You have no idea... The things you said..."

I was starting to choke up. I blinked hard, struggling for words. Gabriel made a strangled sound and scooted forward on his chair to grasp my knee. "I know. I'm sorry."

"Sorry," Damon repeated in a mocking tone.

Gabriel turned to him and then the rest of the guys.

"I should apologize to all of you too. We're all... We're all family now, right? And I left all of you, in the worst way. I'm sorry for that too. You deserved better from me."

Even Damon's anger wavered a little at those words. Jin cleared his throat. "It's been a long day. I say we all take some down time to process everything, see how we feel after that, and we can always talk more later, as much as we need to."

Damon looked as though he might argue, but he stopped himself with a grimace. Seth and Ky nodded. Before anyone could get up, I held up my hand.

"There's something else we should talk about now, at least briefly," I said. "The way the Assembly officials and the enforcers were talking to me—I used illegal magic on Frankford to get him to admit the truth. They could charge me with a crime just for tricking them into coming out to his property. And I don't know how many people who aren't even part of his faction might have the same prejudices against taking unsparked consorts. I could still be arrested. We could all still be in danger. I just want you to be prepared. If they come for you, I'll fight them with everything I have. You can count on that much."

"Rose," Seth said softly. He stood as I did and tugged me into his arms. "We'll get through whatever comes. We've made it this far."

Jin reached for me next, pressing a kiss to my cheek. "I'll paint our way out if I need to," he said with a wink.

"You painted us out of a lot of trouble already," Ky said, coming over. He kissed me gently and squeezed my shoulder. "We're a good team. We've got this."

Damon had already slung his arm around my waist before Ky let me go. He hugged me to him. "Anything you need, you just ask and I'm there, angel."

Gabriel waited to stand until the other guys had stepped away. He watched me more hesitantly now. "Come out to the garage with me? I'm not sure—I might need a little help on the stairs."

I would have protested that he didn't need to shut himself away from the rest of us in his apartment, but the plea in his eyes suggested he wanted my company more than my physical support. It might be good for us to talk away from the judgment of the other guys.

"Of course," I said, and glanced at my other consorts. "You can crash in my room or any of the unused bedrooms. I'll be back in a bit."

Jin gave us a knowing smile. "No need to rush."

Gabriel walked beside me out to the garage with the same careful steady pace he'd used on his way to the house. I'd have thought he was just taking his time if it hadn't been for the sealed wound beneath the charred side of his shirt. His jaw clenched as he yanked open the door. I grabbed it from him.

"Go on," I said. "You asked me here to help. Let me help."

"I did say that, didn't I?" he said, sounding both regretful and wry.

He took the stairs at about half his usual pace, but it wasn't as if he needed to hold on to me or anything. By the time we made it to the top, a sheen of sweat gleamed on his forehead.

"Sit down," I said as we came into his apartment. "Or lie down. You could get some proper sleep."

Gabriel shook his head. "We should talk. More. I..."

He turned and pulled me into his arms. I clutched at him, burrowing my face in his shirt, breathing in his familiar mossy scent. Wishing I could pretend the last week and a half had never happened, that we were the way we'd always been. But I couldn't. My eyes were already welling up. My chest hitched with a sob I couldn't quite suppress.

"Rose," Gabriel said rawly. He hugged me tighter, bowing his head next to mine. "Oh, God. I'm so sorry. It wasn't true. None of the things I said were true, except that the way I was seeing you fight back was scaring me. I've never, not for one second, stopped loving you. I *know* you. I know that's not you, not really. You were backed into a corner. I couldn't think of anything else I could do to break you out."

"But it is me," I said around the lump in my throat. "I did those things. I hurt Master Courtland to find out what he knew. I wanted to hurt the rest of them."

"Only after they hurt you so badly first. Only knowing how many other lives were at stake. I don't blame you. I just didn't want to give them the chance to push you even farther down that road."

"We could have figured out something together. You didn't have to try to do it all yourself."

He paused for a moment with a bob of his throat. "I guess I felt like if anyone was going to make a move like that, risk what we had, it should be me. I'm the one who dragged you into this to begin with, back when we were kids."

A startled laugh jolted out of me. I eased back to touch his cheek and look him in the eyes. "You can't really be blaming yourself for all of this."

"Your father trusted you before he found out you'd been hanging out with us. If I hadn't drawn you in—"

Oh, my dear consort.

"Gabriel." I traced my thumb over his cheek. "You have to stop beating yourself up for things that weren't your fault. From the way my dad talked, I think he planned to hand me over to those demons pretty much from the moment I was born. And even if he hadn't— do you think *I* didn't know what I was getting myself into when you invited me to join you guys running around the estate? I knew much better than you did how my family felt about unsparked people. I could have said no. But I didn't, because I wanted to be there. You can't make that your responsibility."

He opened his mouth, closed it, and tried again. "Leaving you the way I did was my responsibility. I've got to take all the blame for that. Is there any way I can make it up to you?"

I leaned my head against his chest. My emotions were tangled up inside me, taut and aching. The best I could offer was honesty. "I don't know. It might just take time for those wounds to heal. But I love you. I'm so happy you're here. Don't doubt that for a second."

"That's the most I could really ask for."

He gathered me in his arms again, and for a few minutes we stayed there in silence, simply holding each other and enjoying that we could. Gabriel stroked his hand up and down my back.

"You know," he said softly, "sometimes I can't help trying to imagine what it would have been like if we could have come together without all the schemes and conspiracies going on around us. If you hadn't left; if we could have kept growing up alongside each other and figuring out how we felt about each other like normal people do."

If my father had simply wanted me to find a partner who'd make me happy, regardless of what their bloodline was. If no one in the Assembly had wanted to restrict who witches took as their consorts. What a beautiful thing. The thought of it brought a pang into my chest.

"What do you imagine?" I asked, snuggling closer. "Tell me how it would have been."

He hummed to himself. "We'd have had wonderfully awkward dinners-with-the-parents, me in that grand old dining room of yours and you up here with just me and my dad. He'd probably have had a rule about my bedroom while I was still living here: 'The door stays open if there's a girl in there!'" Gabriel chuckled. "So we'd have gone out lots too. I'd have..." He paused. "Come here. I'll show you. That'll be even better."

His fingers twining with mine, he led me out the apartment door and down the stairs. My pulse thumped with eager curiosity. Why shouldn't we lose ourselves in a bit of fantasy for a little while? But when he came to a stop in the shadowed interior of the garage by my Buick, my legs locked. I hadn't been in that car since the day he'd stopped it at the gate and told me he couldn't stand to be near me one moment longer.

Gabriel's hand tightened around mine. "I don't know if I could ever completely write over that memory," he said, "but we could at least make some new ones to compete?"

I dragged in a breath. My lungs had tightened, but maybe he had the right idea. "Okay," I said. "Let's try."

He opened the passenger door for me and got into the driver's seat, not bothering with his seatbelt since he wasn't starting the engine.

"I had my own car pretty soon after I turned sixteen," he said, gazing through the windshield as if he could see the alternate past he was conjuring in the darkness beyond the glass. "This old clunker I bought for pocket change and then fixed up to something halfway decent. I'd have driven you out to the theater in Hermiston to see movies, or into town for the closest thing I could afford to a fancy dinner out, or just to cruise around the countryside."

I pushed aside all thought of the last time I'd been in this car and focused on the picture he was painting. "We could have gone out to the reservoir. Better swimming than my little pond here. At least, that's what I've heard."

Gabriel glanced over at me. He took my hand again. "We could go out there sometime for real. All six of us. For a bunch of married folks, we sure haven't done much dating."

I had to laugh. "No, we really haven't." The warmth of his hand and the glide of his thumb across my knuckles sent a shiver of a different sort of longing through me.

"Where would we have driven out to if we'd wanted a little privacy?"

The corner of Gabriel's mouth curled up. "Oh, there are a couple of popular spots for that sort of thing. There's a picnic spot in the woods off the highway where no one much goes in the evening unless they're teens looking to make out. And the pond just east of town—too mucky for swimming, but great for bonfires and smuggled beers and pairing off."

All the teenage experiences I'd never had. "Which did you prefer?" I asked.

"Not either of those. I used to imagine where I'd take you, if you came back and I could see you again, even back then. There's a spot along the river where there's not really enough room for people to park for it to get popular, but if you go at the right time you can see the moon shining in the water and the crickets get going... I used to drive out there just to think."

"Always by yourself?" I teased, even though my heart pinched at the thought of him with some other girl.

"I was saving that spot for you," he said, his voice so low it sent a tingle through me.

"And are you going to show me what you imagined we'd have done out there?"

His smile grew. He leaned over and cupped my face, tipping my jaw up to meet his kiss.

It was the first time we'd kissed since he'd come back to me, but it felt as sweet as always. The moment his mouth brushed mine, I didn't know how I'd ever get enough of him. I ran my fingers into his hair and kissed him harder, as if I could mark him with so much love and desire it would hold this happiness with us forever.

A pleased sound reverberated from Gabriel's throat. He met my passion with his own, his lips coaxing mine apart so our tongues could tangle, his hand slipping down over my neck to my chest. He traced the curve of my breast through my clothes, and I arched to chase that contact. Even that muted touch left me shivering with need. To feel him everywhere, to claim him, to remind myself how much he was still mine—and how much I was his.

Gabriel eased back just far enough to say, "Back seat?" in a breathless voice. I nodded and scrambled back there with no further encouragement needed. Gabriel's side bumped the seat as he followed, and he winced, but before I could ask if he was okay, he was there with me, lying me down on the leather seat beneath him as he kissed me again.

Our mouths crashed together hot and hungry, and his thigh slid between my legs with a rush of delicious friction against my core. Like another day, another car, when we'd collided in a haze of longing until Gabriel had wrenched himself away from me.

Maybe we were writing over more than one painful memory today. Remaking every moment he'd pulled back, replacing them with this expression of his desire.

He broke the kiss to tug my shirt up over my head, and I yanked his off in turn. His hand dipped beneath me to unhook my bra as we fell back into each other. His mouth branded mine, and his fingers teased my nipples into peaks. His thigh rocked against my core until I was gasping. He bent over to slick his tongue over my breast, and I moaned, clutching his head.

When he slid lower, my grip tightened. "No," I said. "I want you here with me."

Gabriel looked up at me, understanding gleaming in his eyes in the dim light. He undid my jeans, and I kicked them off at his tug. Then he was leaning over me again, his lips finding mine for another searing kiss.

He caressed one breast and then the other through that kiss and the next and the next, until I was squirming with need, my whole body burning with pleasure. My hands skimmed up and down the hot solid planes of his chest. I rocked up to let my clit brush the bulge in his jeans, and he groaned against my mouth.

I jerked his fly open, and he helped me peel off the jeans between breathless kisses. A shudder ran through his body when I trailed my hand over his erection.

"You've always been the one for me, Rose," he murmured. "You always will be. No matter what happens. No matter what you do. I was meant for you."

"And all I want from you is for you to be here with me," I said, choking up.

Gabriel kissed me with the same heat as before but so tenderly I thought I would melt. His thumb stroked over my clit through my panties, and I whimpered. He kept up that gentle teasing, drawing quiver after quiver out of me. An ache filled my core. I needed *him* filling me.

I wrenched at his boxers, and we wriggled out of our underthings together, almost toppling off the seat in the process. A giddy giggle escaped me before he caught it with a kiss. His lips trailed down my jaw to my neck as he slicked the head of his cock over my clit and down.

He gripped my hip to urge me up to meet him in the cramped space. I clutched his shoulders, and he slid into me with one smooth movement.

A shaky sigh slipped from my lips. I rocked to meet Gabriel's thrusts, urging him deeper, harder. The heady friction radiated through every nerve. I wanted to feel him everywhere, so deeply I could never forget this moment, even if it couldn't completely write over what had come before.

"Rose," Gabriel groaned, plunging far enough that the base of his cock grazed my clit. I arched up, seeking that contact, trembling as the wave of sharper pleasure rolled through me again. He pulled me tight against him, and with his next thrust ecstasy burst through my body. I gasped, my toes curling with it, and Gabriel bucked even faster. His fingers dug into my hip with an enjoyable pain as he spilled himself inside me.

He sagged over me, not quite leaning his weight on my body, and a jolt of concern broke through my joy. "You didn't push yourself too hard, did you? Your injury—"

"I'm fine," Gabriel said gently. He eased himself down beside me at the edge of the seat and kissed me. "Straining that wound a little was worth it to start other ones healing."

Emotion swelled in my chest. "Yeah," I said, and traced my fingers up his jaw to return that kiss. I was pretty sure I'd be able to drive this car again now. Though maybe not without blushing the first few times.

We cuddled there for a little while, until the awkwardness of the cramped space crept in. Then we eased ourselves upright, exchanging fond glances and smiles as we fumbled back into our clothes. The moment I was dressed, Gabriel pulled me onto his lap and kissed me so thoroughly I was tempted to undress all over again. I reined in my desire.

"You should get some real rest now," I said, tapping him on the shoulder.

"You too," he said with a bump of his nose against mine. "It's been a longer day for you than anyone else."

I kissed him one more time before he headed up the stairs to his apartment, and then I crossed the yard to the manor to rejoin my other consorts, wherever they'd ended up in the house.

The hall was quiet when I came in. I could give Imogen that call now. I'd just started for my purse where I'd left it on the hall table when the stillness was split by the jangle of my ringtone.

My heart stuttered as I grabbed my phone. Was it the Justice Division calling me in for questioning already? At least I could hope if they were going to arrest me outright, they'd have simply shown up, right?

The number that came up on the screen had the Portland area code. I braced myself and raised the phone to my ear.

"Hello?"

"Lady Hallowell?" a voice said, so rushed it took me a moment before I recognized it. "This is Gwen Remington. We met earlier today on the Frankfords' property. How much exactly do you know about these demons?"

I blinked, groping for my balance. This wasn't how I'd expected any call from the Assembly to go. "I, um— A little. Not much more than what's in the Frankfords' files. Why?"

"A little is better than nothing," she said. "I think we're going to need your help. The creatures have broken through their portal."

Eva Chase lives in Canada with her family. She loves stories both swoony and supernatural, and strong women and the men who appreciate them. Along with the Witch's Consorts series, she is the author of Their Dark Valkyrie series, the Dragon Shifter's Mates series, Demons of Fame Romance series, the Legends Reborn trilogy, and the Alpha Project Psychic Romance series.

Connect with Eva online:
www.evachase.com
eva@evachase.com

9 781989 096178